THE GOLEM PROJECT

Between the Lines Publishing
1769 Lexington Ave N, Ste 286
Roseville, MN 55113
btwnthelines.com

First Published: May 2025

ISBN: (Paperback) 978-1-965059-48-7

ISBN: (Ebook) 978-1-965059-49-4

THE GOLEM PROJECT

Elijah Bone

The desert wears... a veil of mystery. Motionless and silent, it evokes in us an elusive hint of something unknown, unknowable, about to be revealed. Since the desert does not act it seems to be waiting -- but waiting for what?

Edward Abbey

WORLD OF THE DEAD

A dead world.

A dead world populated by ghosts.

That's what Bruckner saw through his night vision goggles; a barren landscape looking even more dead in the pale image the starved thermal sensors provided.

He'd never gotten used to it, the desert. There were days he almost physically ached for the hills of his native Vermont, covered with greenery so vivid it didn't seem real, like some CGI-created idyll filling one's entire field of vision.

But the desert … pounded flat and lifeless. His minister father, a real Old Testament Bible-beater when he was alive, used to go on and on about how God had destroyed the world once by water. But the next time – and, people, you better get yourself right with God because there *will* be a next time -- it will be by fire.

Out there. The desert. Bruckner thought his old man would've said, "This is what's going to be left! This is what it'll look like after God is done with you!"

It wasn't any better at night. In some ways it was worse. The desert held none of its cruel heat at night, replacing it with a dry, cut-to-the-bone cold which made the empty plains seem even deader than they looked during the day. Adding to the bite of the cold was the sting of sand whipping along, unobstructed across the open flatlands.

But the ghosts…they made Bruckner wish the desert was even deader.

They were beyond the effective range of the goggles, maybe as much as a thousand meters out, and that made what little image the thermal sensors could still grab even more ghostly; vague, shapeless blobs scurrying back and forth.

"What are you doing out there?" He'd asked the question of the ghosts enough times to himself that it reached some sort of critical mass to be spoken out loud. He didn't know the answer, but whatever it was, deep in his gut, he knew it wasn't good.

Then he was on his back, the breath knocked out of him from the fall, a weight pressing down on his chest. He couldn't see the bulky figure standing over him in the dark, looking even hazier through the blowing sand. But what was clear was the rifle muzzle just a few inches from his face.

"Identify yourself." The voice, which Bruckner guessed was muffled by a kerchief to keep the sand out, was calm but cold. This wasn't one of his people; his people weren't this good.

The man's boot holding him in place, he grunted out "Bruckner," against the weight on his chest. "Lieutenant Bruckner."

The muzzle withdrew, the boot lifted, and now a gloved hand was reaching down to help him up.

"Christ, Lieutenant, what're you doing up here?" The hulking man turned to another figure standing a few feet away. The blowing sand slacked off a bit, enough for Bruckner to see, unlike his crew, these two were bulked up in full battle kit. "It's Lieutenant Bruckner, Shep."

"Who the hell is Lieutenant Bruckner?"

"CO for the outer camp, stupid."

"What the hell's he doing up here?"

"That's what I'm asking him. You better call it in, Shep." The first soldier turned back to him. "You heard the question, Lieutenant."

"I, um," which was all Bruckner could muster.

"That's what I figured."

Bruckner could hear the other man on his radio. "Search Six, this is Team Alpha, we've got an intruder in the operations area…No, no sign of the target. Request instructions on disposition, over."

"All respect, Lieutenant," the first man said, "You better come up with something better than 'um' when the colonel calls you out on this. You know the protocol when there's a field op." To his partner: "What do they want us to do with — Shit!"

The other soldier – Shep – wasn't there. Bruckner hadn't seen him leave, but now the first man was pulling at Bruckner, pushing him back toward the rim of the shallow valley at the bottom of which was his command: a cluster of Quonsets surrounded by a chain link fence topped with razor wire, splotches of light from the lamps mounted on the huts flickering in the blowing sand.

"You gotta go!" the soldier said, pushing at Bruckner. "Now! Lieutenant; *run!*"

The fear in the man's voice was unmistakable, clear enough that Bruckner didn't need a second urging. He started scrambling and stumbling down the loose dirt and sand of the valley slope, but the angle of his descent — and his speed — were poor partners, causing him to tumble, getting poked and punched by rocks embedded in the slope.

Once he managed to stop the flailing, he lay there for a second to catch his breath.

The urgency of the soldier's voice still in his ears, Bruckner forced himself painfully to his feet. He made it most of the way down the slope, only a couple hundred yards from the compound below. Limping now, he cast a quick glance over his shoulder but there was no sign along the valley rim of the soldier who'd told him to run, no sign of whatever it was that had made the soldier tell him to run.

Whether he could see it or not, something was out there, because First Lieutenant Amos T. Bruckner — 24, from the lovely little town of Shelburne, Vermont — never made it back to camp.

THE EXILE

"Hey, Major!" the Black Hawk pilot's voice crackled over Pat's headset, "this take you back?" and the pilot waved out the cockpit window. "I could always go higher, give you a better view."

Pat Simons, sitting in the center seat in the cargo cabin, pushed her head harder against the canvas seat back, anchoring it even further so it didn't turn toward the windows on either side of the cabin. She kept her eyes locked on the cabin ceiling.

"Oh, you don't have to do that." She tried to keep her voice even, but it was a little too even. Strained. She tried to keep it conversational: "What do you mean? Does what take me back?"

"Down there. The desert. I heard you deployed."

She cleared her throat, trying to loosen it. "Afghanistan. Not Iraq."

"It's that different?"

"It's that different."

The pilot must've picked up something in her voice. She signaled her co-pilot to take the controls as she twisted around in her seat to look back at Pat. Between her helmet and the large-lensed mirrored shades, there wasn't much of her face to see; just her jaws working a cheekful of bubble gum like a jackhammer. "You ok, Major?"

Even Pat had to smile at the irony: "I don't like to fly."

Those pumping jaws froze, going slack. "You're kidding."

"I wish."

"How long you been in the service?"

"Counting the academy, sixteen years."

"You telling me in all that time, you never got used to heights?"

"Not afraid of heights. *Flying.* They're different."

The pilot grinned, shook her head, started chewing again, blew and popped a pink bubble, then turned toward the front, taking the controls back. "What the hell, Major," she chuckled. "I was going to say, you want to see something impressive, but you got to look down."

"Oh, my."

"Here it comes."

The bird took a slight bank, tilting to the right...and so did Pat's stomach. But curiosity being what it was, she took a quick glance out the window. Sun flared on the plexiglass, then cleared and she saw a massive crater, maybe a hundred yards or so across. From their altitude, it looked perfectly round and smooth-sided, almost like a giant funnel.

"They tell me that's from one of the first underground nukes they set off. Must've made some big bang, huh, Major?"

The pilot made one quick circuit of the crater before resuming course. Pat closed her eyes until her stomach settled.

I've been shot at and shelled, she thought, *been afraid for my life, but flying...* She shuddered.

The pilot's voice was in her headset, again: "Um, hey, Major, mind if I ask you something?"

We've shared brushing with death in the air, why not? "Shoot."

"Well, with all respect, Ma'am, who'd you piss off to get such a shitty assignment?"

Pat had to laugh. "How long have you been in the service?"

"Just signed up for my second hitch."

"Then you should know by now that in the Army, you don't have to piss anybody off to get a shitty job."

It was the pilot's turn to laugh. "True!" Then, "But, still —"

"Let me ask *you* a question: who'd *you* piss off?"

The pilot held up her right hand and crossed her first two fingers. "I guess we're both in the same boat, hey, Major?" A few minutes later. "Coming up on your stop, Ma'am."

Pat risked a look through the cockpit windows but couldn't see anything. She felt the Black Hawk's attitude shift as it slowed into a hover.

"Problem?" she asked.

"They got a pretty tough security protocol. I have to hold for identification."

In her headset, Pat could hear an incoming radio message: "Approaching aircraft, hold and identify, over."

Then the pilot: "This is Taxi Alpha One to El Dorado, carrying one passenger and cargo, do you copy? Over."

"This is El Dorado, we copy. Identify. Over."

"Roger that. Noonan, J. F., Warrant Officer, 1493775025. Carrying one crewman, one passenger, routine cargo. Over."

"Copy that: Noonan, J. F., Warrant Officer, 1493775025. Hold for identification verification. Over."

"Roger that." Warrant Officer Noonan, J. F. turned to Pat. "They have a voice analyzer at the other end. Checks for stress and everything. One time one of the cargo pilots had laryngitis." Noonan laughed, popped another pink bubble. "They almost starved 'cause they didn't have another Jolly Green pilot's voice on record!"

"El Dorado" on the radio again: "Confirming voice identification, Taxi Alpha One. Proceed with identification protocol. First word."

Noonan reached out to her co-pilot who held up a small, sealed envelope. The co-pilot tore open the envelope and handed Noonan a neatly folded sheet of paper. Pat got a quick glimpse of a few words, a series of numbers.

"Peach," Noonan read from the paper.

"Second word."

"Cobbler."

"Copy peach cobbler. You are cleared for assigned approach. Over."

"Roger, wilco. Will be approaching on heading zero-five-zero as assigned. Over."

"Zero-five-zero is confirmed. Proceed. Over."

"What's that mean?" Pat asked. "'Assigned approach'."

"Every flight, just before we head out, I get one of these," and Noonan waved the paper. "New code words, new flight approach."

"Every flight?"

"Each and every."

"What happens if you come in on a wrong heading? Or screw up the protocol?"

"Then an F-35 is scrambled out of Nellis, and I do all my flying after that with wings and a harp."

"Ow."

"Yup."

And that's when Pat stopped worrying about heights and flying and how long it would take for her stomach to settle down after landing. In fact, everything inside her went very still, her thinking became very clear and very focused on a single point: *If the security is this tight, what the hell am I doing here?*

She hadn't been able to see "El Dorado" because the installation sat out of sight at the bottom of a wide valley, the slopes cut here and there by ancient rains.

"Doesn't look like much," Noonan said.

"Not too much," Pat agreed. "Take me around once. Give me the nickel tour."

"I thought you didn't like looking down."

"I don't. But business is business."

Noonan took the Black Hawk in a slow circle around the compound. It was just a handful of structures surrounded by fencing which ambled along with, apparently, no particular care to making any kind of recognizable shape. Pat had enough time in the service she could hazard a pretty good guess as to the purpose of each building. There were two large Quonsets: one was probably the enlisted men's barracks, the other — going by its metal chimney — the mess hall. There was a smaller Quonset that would likely be cut up into smaller compartments for individual bunkrooms for noncoms and junior officers. Another small Quonset: that'd be the admin building. A large windowless Quonset: storage. There were three Humvees in desert paint parked side by side in an open-sided shed -- one of them just pulling out -- and next to that building was an additional Quonset with vehicle-sized doors: motor pool workshop. One Quonset — again, windowless — had heavy cables running to utility poles and connecting to various other buildings: generator hut. There were two storage bladders, partially buried for safety's sake; Pat guessed 50,000-gallon in size, one probably for fuel, the other water. There was a long metal trailer with its own generator parked alongside them. Cables ran from the trailer, along poles, up to the valley rim where one was attached to a tall radio mast, and the others to a variety of antennae and dishes which Pat recognized as sensor and detection equipment. The trailer also boasted a small sky-pointed satellite dish. Then there was a small trailer – or a large camper, depending on your tastes and perspective – set off by itself and mounted on cinderblocks.

She smiled at that one: *Welcome to your new home, Pat.*

Pat wanted the nickel tour, so Noonan's circle of the compound turned into an oblong flight path, extending further up the valley to a much smaller fenced-off circle. There was a paved strip – startlingly black against the glaring desert ground – that ran from the only gate to the enclosure's sole building, a slab-sided, windowless concrete square taking up about half of the fenced off area. The drive led to what Pat thought could be a loading dock. On top of the square, there was a concrete cupola with horizontal windows of smoked glass so dark as to be opaque. Off to one side of the structure was a large grill set in the ground, maybe some kind of vent?

"What's that?" Pat asked the pilot. "Is that the lab?"

"Don't know for sure. You ask and they tell you not to ask, but from what I know, it's where you won't be going."

Parked by the apparent loading dock was a line of six Humvees with rooftop gun turrets. Wrapped to protect against the desert sands were machine guns mounted on the rings: M-240s, Pat guessed by their length.

"You ready, Ma'am?"

"Take me in."

Pat watched the Humvee she'd seen pulling out from the garage shed earlier as it drew up to what she assumed was the camp's helipad; a flat open space in an otherwise empty part of the compound, half circled by white-painted rocks. She saw four men climb out of the

Humvee, one a hulking Black man, his shaved head glistening in the desert sun, who threw a smoke grenade into the LZ to show wind direction for the pilot.

"You're there, Ma'am," Noonan said as she set the bird down neatly in the center of the space. The pilot flicked some switches; the engine died with a gradual whine, and the propeller blades slowed like a lazy pinwheel kicked over by a child.

Noonan's co-pilot slid open one of the cargo cabin doors. Through the great clouds of dust kicked up by the bird's down blast, Pat could see the big guy signal to have one of the other men back the Humvee up to the helicopter while he and the remaining men walked up alongside.

Pat could now get a good look at some of the men in her command. *Oh boy oh boy oh boy…*

The big man was built like a vault door: tall, wide, thick. His bright Hawaiian "aloha" shirt, tight over his chest but loose over his hips, would have been more appropriate as a sail on a catamaran. Almost lost in the brightly dyed swirls of bougainvillea that covered his shirt, were pinned the three chevrons and one rocker of a staff sergeant. He either didn't know — or more likely, didn't care — that such insignia of rank on civilian clothing was not allowed. His cheek bulged with a wad of chewing tobacco.

As for the other three men, their rank was anybody's guess. They were attired in a mishmash of items ranging from "I Hate New York" and Pantera "Cowboys from Hell" T-shirts to a Harley-Davidson ball cap and worn-out sneakers. One was even wearing his fatigue pants cut off to Bermuda shorts length.

There was another soldier not far from the helipad, that she hadn't seen earlier. At least he was probably a soldier, although nothing in his garb of surfer shorts and wifebeater indicated him as such. He was sitting on a milk crate next to a pile of melon-sized stones and a bucket of white paint, carefully painting the stones, which Pat presumed were intended to finish the circle around the LZ.

Now I know why I'm here.

"Hey, Jinks!" the co-pilot called.

"Fuck you," the staff sergeant called back, and spat a long gob of tobacco juice out into the dust.

"Oh, we're in a mellow mood today."

"Fuck your sister."

The co-pilot began tossing the sergeant the loaded duffel bags which had been sharing the cargo cabin with Pat. "I gotcher mail here, some stuff for the docs, new movies —"

The sergeant frowned suspiciously. "What movies?" He started digging through one of the duffels.

The co-pilot reached back into the cockpit and Noonan handed him a clipboard with the bird's manifest. "Lessee, we got us a love story —"

"Fuck me."

"— drama, drama, drama —"

"Fuck me, fuck me, fuck me."

"Oh, hey, there's something here called *Satan's Schoolgirl Slaves*."

"Ahhh!" Jinks pulled out a DVD from the duffel, smiled appreciatively at the no-doubt salacious cover art, and tucked it in his waist band.

"He also brought me," Pat said as she slid past the co-pilot and hopped to the ground. She did enjoy a bit of sadistic pleasure as the sergeant's face went slack. Then he spat a stream of tobacco juice to one side, and his face broke into a Jack-o'-Lantern-wide smile.

"Hey, you must be Simmons!"

"Simons." Pat thumbed the oak leaf insignia on her collar. "*Major* Simons. And what the hell're you?"

"Your Uber driver, Boss. Welcome to Lab 7!"

"Enjoy your stay, Major!" the co-pilot said as he threw the last duffel out of the cabin. He slid the cabin door closed, and the Black Hawk re-started with a whine, even before the bag had stopped rolling in the dust.

Pat and her "Uber driver" stood with heads down against the blast of dust as the Black Hawk's engine pulled the bird into the air, and then headed off down the valley, back the way it had come.

"They don't stick around very long," Pat said.

"Would you?" the sergeant laughed and waved a hand at the spartan compound. "I'm Jinski. Resident badass."

Pat nodded. "Is that so?" She walked past him, past the three men gathered around the Humvee to the probably-a-soldier turning out white-painted rocks. He was a dark-skinned, pleasant-faced youngster. "Who're you?"

"Oh, hey, sir, I mean, Ma'am." He didn't stand and the only salute he managed was a wave of his paintbrush. "Elmonte, Ma'am."

She pointed at the rocks. "This is your assigned job?"

"Assigned job?" Elmonte smiled and continued to happily slap paint on a fresh rock. "No, Ma'am. Somethin' I thought up meself. Why not, right? Somethin' to do. It's harder 'n' it looks."

"Really."

"Oh, yes, Ma'am. You gotta find just the right rocks 'cause you want 'em all kinda the same size so it looks nice. Then you gotta lug 'em in here, clean 'em off —"

"I get it," Pat said, not wanting to hear a full disquisition on the painting of rocks. "Well -- Elmonte, you said? – Well, Elmonte, you keep it up. You're the only person on this base I've seen so far with a purpose." She walked over to where the other men were tossing the offloaded duffels into the back of the Humvee while the sergeant slid behind the wheel.

"Something we can do for you, Ma'am?" the sergeant asked.

Pat nodded. "Yes. You can climb out of there, and all of you can stand at attention."

The four men looked at each other, not quite sure they'd heard correctly.

"Sorry, there, Boss," the sergeant said. "Did you say —"

"I said get your slack-asses to attention!"

She didn't yell; it was a quiet, cold bark, but it set them all blinking like she'd flicked each one across his nose. They all looked to the big sergeant. As the "resident badass," she figured he'd set the pace for them, and she could see he was making some quick mental adjustments as it sank in that his good-natured informality no longer had a home on the helipad.

"You need a special invitation, Corporal?" she snapped at the sergeant.

"Um, it's sergeant, Ma'am."

"One more second in that seat and it won't be."

The big man moved with impressive speed as he flew out of the Humvee, signaling the others to line up alongside him in a pretty good, but not even close to perfect, example of soldiers at attention.

Pat pointed to the sergeant's tobacco-stuffed cheek. "And get rid of that."

The sergeant turned to spit but froze as Pat's head moved slowly side to side. "Mister, you want to keep those stripes, you better think twice about dirtying up my LZ."

It took a few seconds for the sergeant to comprehend what he was being asked – no, what he was being *ordered* to do. His dark face twisted in a horrible grimace, sympathetically echoed on the faces of the other three men, as he forced the tobacco down his throat. Pat gave him credit for not throwing up. *Maybe he is the resident badass!*

"Now," and she held out her hand, "the shirt."

"Huh?"

"It's 'huh, *Ma'am*', or 'huh *Major*'. The shirt. Let's go."

Puzzled, the sergeant peeled off the shirt in question. While he may have been a bit soft in the middle, his broad chest and large biceps appeared rock-hard.

Pat took the shirt, pulled a silver lighter from her breast pocket, and set fire to it, letting it drop to the ground. She looked at the burning rag, looked purposefully at the other three soldiers who were out of uniform, and pointed back to the small blaze. The only one who hesitated was the soldier with the cut-off camo paints, but neither her gaze nor her finger wavered until they finally joined the pile of smoldering material.

As the three of them looked mournfully at their beloved informal wear turning to ash, Pat stepped toe-to-toe with the sergeant. He was easily a foot taller than her and made the mistake of looking down at her face.

"Don't you eyeball me, Mister! Where do your eyes go when being addressed by a superior officer?"

The big man locked his eyes level.

"Better. What's your name, mister?"

"Jinski, Ma'am."

"Where's your acting CO?"

"Admin building, Ma'am. I can show you —"

"I'll find it. Stow the offload and see that my B-4 bag is taken to my quarters."

"Yes, Ma'am."

She stepped back, made a great show of looking disgusted. "Who're the rest of you limp-dicks? Sound off!"

"PFC Sanborn, Ma'am." A young one, his skin burned lobster red showing he didn't have enough sense about protecting himself from the ruthless sun.

"PFC Herrera, Ma'am." A touch of a Spanish accent and a body short and thick bespeaking a fondness for the mess hall and not for PT.

"Private Loomis. Ma'am."

Pat put a mental check by the name. He was older than the other two. That he was a private and not a PFC was one red flag; another was the look he was giving her. She knew that look; every woman in the Army knew that look. He was too busy looking for the curves under her desert fatigues and to ever see the major's oak leaf on her collar.

Pat stood back and raked them with what her father used to call the CO's Stink-eye. She could practically hear his voice in her head: *"It's how you let them know they're already hip-deep in the shit and a warning that they don't want to sink any deeper."*

She let them stand for a few seconds sweating in the desert sun. Then, "Gentlemen — and pass this on to your friends and colleagues — from now on, when I'm walking through my command, it better not look like a casting call for *Gilligan's Island*. As of tomorrow, the next man I see on duty dressed like he's taking a trip to the zoo on the special bus is going to find himself staked to an ant hill covered in honey. If you think that's a joke, try me."

The walk across the compound had the word "campus" coming to Pat's mind because the vibe was more college spring break than military installation. There were two soldiers flinging a Frisbee back and forth. Three others wearing nothing but their boxers were stretched out on beach loungers in a semicircle, gleaming with suntan lotion; one even had eye shields and was holding a sun reflector under his chin. At their feet, a fire bucket filled with ice holding long-necked beer bottles, and a boombox blaring out some ironic 5 Seconds of Summer tune about not having to live a certain way.

The 5 Seconds etc. boys didn't blend well with the loud bumping hip hop coming from the barracks, and the even louder shouts – the kind that went with bored guys doing something they probably shouldn't be doing to break up the boredom.

As for that ruthless sun in a cloudless sky… She could feel her scalp swimming in sweat under her fatigue cap, but it was no great bother for her.

Afghanistan may not have technically qualified as a desert, but when it got hot, it got very hot, and when it got cold, it got very cold. The temperature could rise and fall up to 50 degrees in a day. But Pat had already been primed for those kinds of extremes long before she'd ever put on a uniform.

She'd grown up an Army brat, years spent bouncing from one post to another along with her father. She'd been through the most bitter of Minnesota winters — so cold she could feel the hairs in her nose freeze — and parts of Arizona as sunbaked as this stretch of Nevada. She remembered her father saying, "Watch this, Sweets!" as he cracked an egg on the hood of his jeep, and she marveled as the egg white browned and curled the same way it did in a frying pan.

She smiled to herself. *If the Army's trying to chase me out, they screwed up because, fellas, I can hack this. So, fuck you.*

Even though none of the buildings were marked, the administration building was exactly where she'd assumed from her aerial tour. She did not knock.

After the heat and glare of the compound, it took Pat a moment to adjust to the coolness of the air conditioning and the fluorescent lighting inside the small Quonset. The short, compact man in the front office hadn't heard her come in and he had a phone parked on his shoulder while he shuffled his way through the folders in the top drawer of the sole file cabinet.

"As soon as she comes in, Colonel, I'll bring her right over."

"You can tell him I've arrived," Pat said crisply.

Dropping the phone, as well as the folder in his hand, the startled man turned so abruptly toward her voice that he miscalculated his proximity to the file cabinet and slammed his elbow into it – with obvious and acute pain.

"I didn't hear you come in, Major."

"I got that." She pointed to the phone on the floor.

"Oh, yeah, right." He scooped up the phone and stuffed the scattered papers back into their folder. "Yeah, hey, Colonel, you still there? Yeah, she's right in front of me, Sir, yessir, soon's I can, Sir."

He had a wide, Asian face which was now twisted in pain as he massaged his impacted elbow.

"I bet that hurts," Pat said.

He grunted and nodded.

"Too much for a salute?"

The man's mouth made a silent little "o" as he snapped to attention, providing as much of a salute as his bruised elbow would allow.

Pat returned it. "You are…?"

"Kim Cho, Ma'am."

"It's customary to identify yourself by rank and position, Cho."

"Oh, sorry, Ma'am. Chief Warrant Officer Cho, Ma'am. Your executive officer."

"I would've expected my XO to meet me at the LZ."

"Yes, Ma'am, but we only got the word you were coming last night, and I wanted to try to get the office squared away for you."

Pat let Cho stew a bit, letting him worry if that was a sufficient excuse for her before she gave a slight accepting nod. She ambled over to Cho's desk. Atop a clutter of paperwork was an open book of crossword puzzles and the Merriam-Webster *Official Scrabble Players Dictionary*. "You people seem to have been running a pretty informal shop here."

"I take it you prefer otherwise, Ma'am."

"Very perceptive of you, Mister Cho."

"You're the boss, Ma'am."

"I am the boss. My office?"

"This way, Ma'am."

There was a short corridor off the front office with two small empty offices on one side, a larger office on the other, and a door at the far end of the corridor. Cho opened the door to the larger office and held it open for Pat.

Pat looked at Cho and nodded toward the door at the end of the corridor.

"Armory," Cho said.

Pat glanced back down the hall, then went through the open door. There was the usual gray metal desk, a file cabinet, two spare chairs in front of the desk, and that was it. The top of the desk was bare except for an adjustable lamp. Pat walked around behind it, checked the drawers. Empty.

"A detail from the lab compound came by yesterday, Ma'am, and cleared out Lieutenant Bruckner's effects."

"Lieutenant Bruckner?"

"Um, he was your predecessor, Ma'am."

"What happened to him?" When Cho didn't answer right away, Pat looked up and saw Cho wrestling with how to respond. "Mister Cho?"

"They didn't tell you?"

Pat sat in the uncomfortable desk chair, reached into the shirt pocket of her fatigues and drew out the folded piece of paper she'd read a dozen times since the day before, trying to make sense of it. "I had just arrived in my very comfortable, very air-conditioned office in the Pentagon when I got this." She read: "'*You will report to Army developmental laboratory designated Laboratory Seven with all possible speed to command a Military Police security unit. Previous commander deceased in non-duty casualty. Expedite.*'" She neatly re-folded the paper and slipped it back into her pocket. "'Expedite'; they made it sound urgent. I had just enough time to stuff a B-4 bag and grab a flight from Andrews to Nellis."

"You must be exhausted, Ma'am."

"I caught some sack time on the flight. 'Expedite'." She frowned as she said the word again. "Then I get here and see…this clown show you have. I'm hard put to see the urgency." She looked to Cho for an explanation, but he seemed as puzzled by the circumstances as she was. She moved on to the next point of interest: "What does that mean: 'deceased in non-duty casualty'?"

"The word we were given was suicide."

"Ok, what does *that* mean? 'The word you were given'?"

"The way it looks, Ma'am, is night before last, Lieutenant Bruckner went up to the flat with a pistol and shot himself. That's what they said."

"Who is 'they'?"

"Like I said, Major, a detail from the lab compound. Major, I know it doesn't make much sense, but the colonel can give you a better picture of how everything works here than I can because — Can I be frank, Ma'am?"

She nodded, granting him permission to go ahead.

"Doesn't make any sense to me, either. All I know is yesterday morning we were told Lieutenant Bruckner had been found the night before, dead from an apparent suicide, they cleared out his gear and his desk, and last night we were told a new CO was on the way."

"You never saw the body."

"No, Ma'am."

"Do you know if they notified his next of kin?"

"I know they didn't."

"How do you know."

"Because he didn't have any."

"Come again?"

"Lieutenant Bruckner, he didn't have any living relatives."

"You're sure?"

"I handle the jackets on the personnel, Ma'am."

"I'd like to see Bruckner's jacket."

"Sorry, Ma'am. When they cleared out the lieutenant's stuff, they took his jacket with it."

Pat sat with this for a few seconds. Her Military Occupational Specialty had been Military Police for her entire career, meaning she'd been as much a cop as a soldier, dealing with crime as much as combat. She felt like she was looking at something that was uncomfortably neither. "Were you a friend of his?"

"We were here together for a couple of months. We got along ok. He was a nice guy. Didn't seem the type."

"For a suicide."

"Yes, Ma'am. Colonel McElhone says some guys just don't do well isolated like this."

"The colonel is a very prosaic man."

"You know the colonel, Ma'am?"

Pat gave a vague, non-responsive response of a shrug.

"That was him I was talking to you when you came in," Cho said. "He's waiting for you in your quarters. Shall I bring you over, Ma'am?"

Pat came out from behind the desk, following Cho out, but stopped in the doorway. She looked back at the barren office; desk cleared out, personal effects removed, personnel file taken, no kin to notify.

It was like Lieutenant Bruckner had never existed.

As they neared the trailer that would serve as her quarters, Pat felt the Nevada heat replaced with a different warmth, a slight, welcome wavelet of nostalgia. The trailer reminded her of the campers her dad sometimes rented for them on their vacations. It was a thirty-footer, and she could already see the layout in her mind: a table and bench seats at one end that could collapse into a full-sized bed; along one side would be what passed for a kitchen with a small propane stove, an oven, a tiny sink, a mini-fridge, and a little microwave. Opposite that would be a cramped dining nook, which also could collapse into a narrow bunk. Then, toward the back, a microscopic bathroom would be on one side, and a closet-sized bedroom to the other.

When Cho held the door open, Pat felt a gust of refrigerated air accompanied by a bellowed, "Welcome, welcome, welcome!" and she stepped up into the trailer.

Colonel Ian McElhone's full frame looked comically stuffed into the dining nook. He still had the burly silhouette he'd had playing fullback for Army twenty years ago, along with the squashed pug face his aggressive playing had gotten him. He still kept his hair "high and tight", but Pat could see a dusting of gray in it — in his neatly trimmed mustache — since the last the last time she'd served under him.

Pat and Cho saluted. McElhone returned it and then awkwardly struggled out from behind the table. "Ok, ritual completed." He smiled broadly as he held out his hand to shake Pat's. "Thank you, Mister Cho. You can go."

Pat set a hand on Cho's shoulder to stop him. "Actually, Colonel, I was going to ask Mister Cho for the guided tour as soon as I stowed my gear."

"It'll sit for a day, Pat." The colonel chuckled. "Trust me, you're not going to have anything but time on your hands."

"In that case," she said, turning to Cho, "tomorrow morning, right after breakfast."

Cho winced. "Um."

"What's 'um'?"

"Well, Ma'am, as we don't have a cook, the men have been fixing their own meals. You know — kind of whenever."

Pat looked to McElhone, who seemed amused by the exchange.

Pat didn't say anything, but the look she gave Cho seemed to convey all that needed to be said.

"I presume that's going to change, Ma'am."

"I do like that you and I are in tune, Mister Cho. I want a list of the MOS, past and present, for all my personnel. I want that today."

"Yes, Ma'am".

"For tomorrow, I want to see the men assembled at 0700. Inform them the kitchen will be closed to them after 0700."

"Do you want the engineers there, too, Ma'am?"

"Engineers? What engineers?"

"You have a squad of Army engineers," McElhone said. "The big guy, the sergeant —"

"Jinski?"

"He's their top. They do routine maintenance and repair, small builds, that kind of thing."

"Everybody, Mister Cho."

"Yes, Ma'am."

"And Mister Cho?"

"Yes, Ma'am?"

"That assembly? Warn your people: spit and polish."

"Yes, Ma'am. The expectoration I'm sure they can handle without a problem. I'll have to work with them on the polish."

"You do that," cautioned the colonel. "Your services are now no longer required, Mister Cho. Skedaddle and close the door behind you."

After Cho left, McElhone settled in the larger, more spacious seating area at the front end of the trailer.

"'Expectoration'?"

McElhone laughed. "Maybe he has one of those word-a-day calendars. He's a good man. He may have gone a little slack since he's been here, but this place will do that to you. It's good to see you, Pat. C'mon, sit down."

Pat reached for her B-4 bag Jinski's crew had left by the door. "I'd just as soon get squared away as soon as I could."

"Wet your whistle, then?"

"I can do two things at once."

McElhone drew her attention to what the Army called a musette bag he had tucked behind him in the dining nook, and she smiled, already knowing she would find a bottle of Jameson's Black Barrel inside.

"You can do the honors; I believe you'll find glasses..." and McElhone said as he waved toward the small cabinets above the sink and stove.

Pat cracked the seal on the bottle cap and poured them each a small dose.

"I know alcohol is not recommended in this kind of heat," the colonel said, "but this is a special occasion."

Pat handed him his drink; they touched glasses and held them up in salute. "Congratulations on getting your eagles," she said, indicating McElhone's insignia. "When do you up to a star?"

McElhone hammed up some false modesty. "Well, there has been talk."

"I'll bet," and they clinked glasses again. "To the talk." She took a sip, set her drink down, and turned back to her bag. She opened the zipper to reveal a webbed belt coiled around an old-style black leather flap holster embossed with a large "US" sitting atop her clothes.

"Good God," McElhone said, "what museum did you rob to get that?"

Pat held the belt and holster out to McElhone who opened the flap and drew out a Colt 1911. He laughed as he hefted the pistol. "Old Slabsides! I haven't seen one of these off the range in I don't know how long. Jesus...I forgot how heavy these things are."

"You get used to it."

"Let me guess: your father's?" He re-holstered the pistol and handed the belt back to Pat.

"My grandfather's, actually," she said, hanging the belt and holster on a coat hook by the door. "Dad didn't like the Barettas when they switched out, so Granddad gave him his .45."

"And your father gave it to you. Don't you like the Sigs?"

Pat shrugged. "It's not about the Sigs."

"Ah; sentiment."

Pat grinned a bit self-consciously. "I suppose so." She took another sip of her drink, then grabbed the bag and headed to the back bedroom to unpack.

"I'm glad you're here, Pat." The trailer was small enough; he didn't have to raise his voice to be heard down its length. "They give you much of a briefing?"

"If you call, 'Get packed; you're leaving,' a briefing." She began laying out her clothes in neat piles: underwear here, balled socks over there... "I'm sure you've seen my orders."

"Sorry about that. We were in a rush to fill the slot."

She stopped laying her clothes out on the bunk to stick her head out the door and give McElhone a sharp look. "'So much so no one bothered to tell me it opened up because my predecessor suffered a 'non-duty casualty'?"

"Yeah, well," and McElhone took another sip of his drink, nodded apologetically. "Not that it was relevant, but you probably should've been told about that up front. Bruckner was a good kid. But that was his problem; he was a kid; he'd just gotten his first lieutenant's bars a couple of months ago. This was his first command, and this sandbox can get to you if you're not used to it. You saw some of that with the young ones when you were deployed. That's why I requested you. It's not a hard pull, not like The Alamo or Oak Ridge, certainly not like what you dealt with in Afghanistan, and there's barely enough of a crew to even rate young Cho. Still, I thought maybe somebody who was seasoned..."

"Colonel..." It was a prod.

"We've known each other a while, Pat. Go ahead."

She came and sat across from him and toyed with her glass. "I'm looking around at this place, the personnel..."

"Yes?"

"I can't tell if I'm being promoted or punished."

He gave her a brief, 'I understand' nod. "I guess you could look at it as a little bit of both. After what happened in Afghanistan, the Army was ready to stick you in that Pentagon cubicle pushing paper for the rest of your career…what there was going to be of it."

Pat felt her face redden and it had nothing to do with the whiskey or the Nevada heat.

"If you didn't get fed up and quit, well, they've already passed you over for promotion once. They pass you over again and you know what happens."

"Up or out."

"To — as the civilians say — 'seek opportunities elsewhere'. But you do a good job here, Pat, maybe you can kiss the cubicle goodbye, get back on the track."

"I was grateful for the call, Colonel. I hope you know that." She tried to slide into all-business mode. "So…what is it I'm babysitting?"

"Officially, Lab 7 is one of a series of small labs working on some kind of agricultural project. Something about growing veggies without dirt."

"Hydroponics."

McElhone was impressed. "Didn't you once tell me the only things you ever read were the Army manual and *Cosmo?*"

"I must've seen something about it in *Cosmo*. 'The Hydroponic Weight Loss Program'. That was it."

McElhone laughed lightly. "Back at The Point, they never taught us to prepare for the day when we'd have officers who read *Cosmo*."

"You should do the quizzes." She smiled, then got serious. "Colonel… Voice print ID, that blockhouse I'm told is the lab… You're saying all that's to babysit a Pentagon herb garden?"

"That's the official story. "

"Can you tell me what's underneath?"

McElhone looked down into his glass, sliding it slightly back and forth like that would cause some truth to emerge, like a Magic 8 Ball made from whisky. He finished off his drink, then seemed to take a moment to consider before pouring himself a second one. "You understand this is classified."

She gave him a look that informed him she was not stupid.

"Ok…Tests on low-level radiation exposure. Nothing too heavyweight, but the Pentagon would prefer not to deal with a Greenpeace protest every time the Geiger counter goes up a few ticks. This neighborhood is nice, isolated, and quiet."

"Isolated is a bit of an understatement. What am I supposed to be guarding against? Sand fleas?"

"You'd be surprised. Prospectors, junk scavengers, hippies who think the desert is a great place to drop acid and see God. Google Earth people who've found the place and think we've got UFOs stashed here."

She raised her eyebrows.

"We don't."

They shared a small laugh at that, but then Pat went serious. "Colonel, I've only seen a few of my people, but if they're all like what I've seen, I'm not sure they're fit to be crossing guards for a pre-school."

McElhone nodded. "Pat, you know enlistment has been down the last few years, commands don't want to give up their good people."

"So, I'm like the manager of an expansion team getting everybody's castoffs?"

"I know you, Pat. You'll turn them around."

And then the thought that had been nagging at her ever since she'd stepped foot onto the helipad. "So…" *Go ahead, sister, you know you want to know.* "Does that mean I'm considered a castoff, too?"

McElhone looked her straight in the eye, no smile, no cheekiness to it. "I'll be honest. It's why the Pentagon didn't have a problem releasing you to me. But you're not a castoff to me, Pat. I consider myself lucky to have you." Then he sat back, drained the last of his drink, and got to his feet. "Look, some of the lab staff are having a reception kind of thing tonight for you. Nothing big; Cheez Whiz and punch. But it breaks the monotony. You'll come to appreciate that. I know you've been travelling since yesterday, so if you want to take a pass on this…"

Pat stood. "I'll be fine. Always good to mix with the natives."

"Good deal. Iron your Class A's and I'll see you there. About 1900 at the mess hut." McElhone turned for the door.

"Colonel, I'm responsible for security but I heard I won't have anything to do with the lab itself?"

"They have their own security unit."

"That's a bit odd, isn't it?"

"That's how it's set up, Pat. Problem?" McElhone had a tic at times like this; she'd seen it often enough in their previous service together. It was the slightest tip of his head, eyebrows raised, all of it meaning, *You can go ahead and ask but you're not getting an answer so why bother?* One of the first things he had taught her when she was just a butter bar second lieutenant serving under him on the security detail at the Los Alamos weapons lab, was "Always remember before you open your mouth; the Army is not a democracy."

"If that's how it's set up," she said, "then that's how it's set up."

McElhone smiled approvingly. He nodded at the Jameson's bottle on the table. "That's my housewarming gift to you but take small sips. The next supply bird isn't due for three weeks." He stood but stopped at the door. "I was sorry to hear about your father. I only knew him by reputation, but from what I heard, well, I was sorry I never had a chance to meet him. It wasn't that long ago. Are you going to be alright?"

She nodded. "He used to say that Patton thing, that the only way for a soldier to die was — "

"From the last bullet in the last battle of the last war!" They blurted it out together like a grand declaration.

They laughed.

"I think," she said, "if we séanced him we'd find him pretty ticked off he went quietly in his sleep from a heart attack. Frankly, I'm not sad he passed at home."

"Well, Pat, you know in this job we don't get to pick when or where or how." He sighed. "I'll see you tonight."

As he reached for the door, she said, "Colonel, I want you to know I'm grateful for —"

McElhone cut her off with a grin. "Sit on those thanks, Pat. After a week here, you might not be so grateful," he chuckled as he left.

As soon as the door had closed behind him, the sense of fellowship and camaraderie she'd felt instantly evaporated. She watched McElhone head for the Humvee he'd parked outside. Through the thin curtains, louvered windows, and screens of the trailer, he was more of a vague, bearish shape — like a shadow — than something distinct, something real.

She had served under McElhone at Los Alamos. When he'd transferred to the security detachment at the nuke labs at Oak Ridge, he'd brought Pat with him and pushed for her captaincy. He'd been the kind of mentoring commanding officer her father had taught her to respect.

As she watched him drive off, she couldn't help but wonder, *why are you telling me so many lies?*

His barracks mates had early on dubbed Robert Ray Loomis "Gloomis" after soon finding him a sour-faced, foul-mouthed, work-shirking, gutter-minded pain in the ass. But Gloomis Loomis didn't care. He felt entitled to give the Army as much grief as it gave him, which he estimated to be considerable.

He'd been 19 when he'd been hauled up in front of some smart-ass spic judge after wrapping a stolen car around a utility pole and been given a choice: "It's your call, son; jail or the Army."

"Son." Boy, that really rode him raw, that greaser sitting up on his fucking throne like he was a fucking king talking to one of his fucking peons. "Son." Fuck you, your honor.

It ate at him even more when he found out this wasn't the judge trying to be merciful. Turned out his royal assness had a brother-in-law who was the sergeant in charge of the local Army recruiting center. Fucker was probably getting commissions for every luckless sonofabitch he sent his in-law's way.

But that was life in the "Billyland" section of South Baltimore; every race and nationality that wrote you off as some kind of white trash was lined up waiting for their chance to fuck you over.

Take that big nigger with the Polack name – Jinski – dragging his ass out in the heat this morning to offload the bird, and Loomis not even part of that fucker's mop-and-bucket detail. *Engineers my ass! Those lumps couldn't unclog a toilet with dynamite.*

This new CO was a real bitch on wheels. He could tell the type, and she had caught him eyeballing her out on the helipad this morning — but fuck her. Getting stuck out here at the ass-end of nowhere, if it wasn't for Pornhub and Xhamster, he'd go out of his mind. Then this twat shows up? Sweetheart, you're gonna get the eye; live with it.

He was laying in his bunk, scrolling on his cell phone, trying to find out where these legal Nevada whorehouses were supposed to be. He wanted to know in case he was ever granted leave from this cesspool. He could hear some of the guys talking about the new CO, trying to figure out what to make of her. *She's a bitch, guys, that answer your question?* Two others who were driving him nuts, had been driving him nuts for days. One was trying to teach the other how to play guitar. All that spastic *plink-plink-plink* that wasn't getting any better made him want to break into the armory so he could shoot the player, the teacher, and the fucking guitar. Then there was that other pair; he'd bet they were faggots since one, the colored guy, Willis, was trying to teach his buddy, that Boston mick Delaney, how to dance to that *thump-thump* nigger shit *thump-thump*ing out of his boom box.

"I don't know why I can't get this," Delaney was saying, tripping over his fucking big, fat feet for the umpteenth time.

"Well, one problem," Willis said, "is you're white. I don't know how, but it makes a difference."

Morons. All fucking morons.

Once he asked the colored kid, as nicely he sould, if just for one fucking time, they could put some honest-to-God real music on that thing. Maybe a little Eric Church or that new Kenny Chesney hit. However, looking back, he admitted that starting the conversation with "Hey, Black Jesus!" might not have been the best opener.

"Fool. Nobody wants to hear that *twangety-twang* shit-kicker crap," Willis had replied, and cranked up volume of the *thump-thumping*.

Pricks and morons They were all pricks and morons.

So, it was partly fed-uppedness with all the barracks horseshit, partly boredom, and partly a lot of other anger-stoking issues which had Gloomis Loomis heading out the door once the sun had gone down. Nobody asked him where he was going; he figured they were probably as glad to see him leave as he was.

Except for the barracks, the compound was quiet. There was some buzzing coming from the mess hut; he'd heard they were having some

bullshit party or something for the new CO. Whoop-dee-fucking-doo.
Then it occurred to him she'd be getting ready for that.

Yeah.

The sun was gone but it wasn't quite dark yet. There was a crimson
glow somewhere off to the west behind the rim of the valley, and
overhead the sky was going from purple to black. Gloomis Loomis
didn't like the desert nights. He was a city kid, felt like he owned the
streets he ran. But out here? He didn't like how small the desert made
him feel, how all those millions of stars which had been hidden by the
city lights reminded him of just what a miserable speck he was, not
worth much more than any one grain of sand among the millions then
under his feet.

He looked around to make sure he was alone — knowing he would
be because none of the guys liked being out in that cold desert at night
— and started making his way quietly toward the CO's trailer. As he
got closer, he could hear her shower running.

It's about time God gimme a break!

And a generous break, too. The curtains over the trailer's narrow
windows hadn't been pulled, and the louvred windows had been
cranked open. He got up close to one of the windows, saw he was
looking into a small bunkroom, a set of Class A's laid out on the
mattress. Through the open door of the bunkroom, he could see across
into the cramped bathroom where the shower was running. He'd get a
nice tits-on view when she stepped out –

A hand clamped him on the shoulder, pulled him backward, then
he was in the air somehow, spinning, before he landed flat on his back,
hard enough to punch the air out of him. He was still gasping when the
same hand flipped him on his belly, he felt a weight – surprisingly light
but it came down hard – fall on his back, then one of his arms was pulled
up behind his back – painfully far – and something cold and hard

pressed against the back of his neck and he knew without seeing it, it was a gun muzzle.

"You even breathe, and I'll make your forehead look like a fucking Cheerio."

It was that broad, that bitch of a new CO.

She pushed herself off his back, stepped away. "On your feet."

He still didn't have his breath, and the fall she'd given him had left him wobbly, but he managed to pull himself up to stand on jelly legs. She was standing in the shadows, but the moon picked up her blonde hair, and he could see she was wearing nothing but a GI undershirt and BVDs. But for once, Loomis managed not to pay attention to the attraction of long legs and loose breasts because he was totally focused on the muzzle of the heavy pistol she was holding in both hands aimed at the center of his face.

"You want to look at me? Fair is fair. Drop your drawers."

"Wha'd you say?" Then he heard the clicks of her thumbing back the hammer on the pistol.

"I'm not going to say it twice, lover. Pants and BVDs...*now!*"

He started to reach for his belt buckle, but then... *She's just fucking with me.* He dropped his hands to his side, hoped in the dark she could see the smirk on his –

"*Oof!*"

And the air went out of him again as she speared him in the middle with the pistol, and he dropped to his knees. He looked up and saw she had the pistol aimed at his crotch. "What're you gonna do?"

"I can make the report say whatever I want it to say, lover. Whatever I do, it's going to be legal."

She moved the pistol closer to his crotch.

"Oh, Christ, no..."

"Wasn't getting much use anyway, right lover?" And she pulled the trigger.

Before everything went black for him, Loomis gave up something like a panicked squeak as he felt himself falling forward. He never heard the hammer come down on an empty chamber.

"You need a hand, Major?" Jinski stepped out of the shadows. Like Pat, he was wearing just BVDs and a GI t-shirt. Somehow, the lack of covering made him look bigger.

He stood with Pat over the passed-out Loomis. *This must make quite a picture*, she thought; the two of them in their underwear, the .45 in her hand, and Loomis who'd managed to fall on his face but still on his knees, his butt pointed to the night sky.

"What're you doing here?" Pat asked.

"I was startin' to get dressed for the party; I heard somebody gettin' his ass whupped."

"There's the ass," and she pointed at the unconscious Loomis. "I'd appreciate if you'd dispose of it somewhere for me, please."

"Can do, Ma'am," and Jinski tossed Loomis over his shoulder with no more effort than if he was a bag of laundry. "How'd you get 'im?"

"Oh, he wasn't that hard to read this morning. I had a feeling. Doesn't anybody stand a night watch?

"Never had anything to watch for."

Pat nodded, unsurprised. "Tell Mister Cho that as soon as Stud Muffin here comes to, he's pulling the first one, and it's an all-nighter. And if I catch him napping — or anything else —" she pointed her pistol at Loomis' buttocks draped over Jinski's shoulder "— I'll remember to load this next time. See you at the party."

She watched as Jinski slapped Loomis across his bottom — that bearpaw hand of his landing with a crack loud enough to make Pat wince — and headed back toward the barracks. "If it wasn't under the legal limit," she heard him say to the unconscious Loomis, "I'd shoot it off meself."

Pat used to sit in a hunter's blind with her father, sometimes for hours waiting for something – a deer, an antelope, it varied with where he was stationed – to come down to a pond or creek they had staked out. "Eventually, they come, Sweets," her dad had taught her. "Everything gets thirsty sooner or later."

As she stood in the trailer's cramped shower, it was hard not to laugh at how that long ago counsel had come into play; a thirsty animal had, indeed, come to the sound of water. But when she'd been on the hunt with her dad, there was that day – she wasn't a kid, anymore, home from The Point on the winter break -- sighting in on a doe and her fawns had given her pause, even frozen her trigger finger. And if that had disappointed her father, well, God bless him, he'd never shown it, just nodded like he understood, even stood up in the blind and gave a shout to scare the game off.

They left the blind and sat by that same creek, looking to where the doe and her family had disappeared into the underbrush.

"I'm sorry," she'd said.

He had smiled. "No need."

"We're soldiers, Dad; shouldn't I be able to bag a deer?"

"We are soldiers, Sweets," he'd said. "Doesn't make us killers."

She would still go out with him, although they were more camping than hunting trips after that. And if he ever somehow held that day and the change against her, he never said, and never showed it.

But when she'd caught Loomis, had him kneeling in front of her staring up into the muzzle of her granddad's cannon of a .45… *Buddy-*

boy, you are not a deer. Even though the pistol hadn't been loaded, she was still surprised – afterward – at how easily she'd pulled the trigger.

She stepped out of the shower. The trailer's only mirror was a small one over the bathroom's mixing bowl-sized sink. She'd lied to Cho about having slept on the flight west. High-flying Air Force transports were a bit easier for her to handle than a low altitude zip across the desert in a Black Hawk, but flying was flying. Professional necessity had taught her how to fake a kind of calm, feigning sleep so she couldn't see the clouds slipping by the patchwork countryside rolling along 30,000 feet below, and she'd gotten so good at the performance that she'd even overheard some of her troops marvel at how untroubled she looked considering a war zone was waiting at the end of the flight. But an act it was, one she dropped after mustering a calm walk to the transport's one toilet after most of the troops in the cargo bay had dozed off so they wouldn't hear her throw up.

Her eyes were puffy from lack of sleep, and her time in Afghanistan had put some lines around her eyes and across her forehead – as much from stress as the tough weather – but she was holding up rather well although that came with caveats. She'd always regretted she had her mother's face; not that it was unattractive, but she'd inherited her mother's chipmunk cheeks even into her early 30s. With her large blue eyes, and despite the crow's feet nipping at their corners, it was a little girl's face stuck on a woman's body

But as for the rest of her, she'd been blessed with her father's lean, streamlined physique, and she kept it so with another lesson from him. He used to rail against what he called the "steak and beer brigade" – the brass hats who, no longer having to serve in the field, parked themselves behind a desk and let themselves get fat on lush rear echelon cooking.

Even when her father had gotten his colonel's eagles, he'd been a lead-from-the-front kind of officer, and not just in action: "They do PT,

I do PT; they eat in the mess, I'm eating the same Army slop with them." He'd been reprimanded for it; colonels weren't supposed to be foot soldiers he was told. It was an attitude that cost him a kidney in Desert Storm, and the Purple Heart that earned him came with a reprimand – and a warning. "They told me they make movies about officers like me," her father told her, "but officers like me don't make general." And he never did.

She ran her fingers through her short, dirty blonde hair because – one blessing she'd inherited from her mother – that's all it took to put it in place. There were a few stray grays in there; they'd unsurprisingly started popping up after Afghanistan and seemed to be slowly multiplying since. She'd heard stories that some of her superiors – especially those who showed up for the press briefings -- indulged in touch-ups which she'd thought funny until her own grays began showing. But she'd quickly dismissed the question of *Should I?* with *Screw it. It is what it is.*

She began pulling on her Class A's. The bunk they'd been laying on looked appetizing, and the come-down after nabbing Loomis followed by the warm shower was teasing her like a street corner pusher: *Go ahead, just sit down for a second... Just for a little bit...* But from there she knew it would be laying her head down – just for a minute – and then...

She shook off the feeling, finished dressing, and went to give herself one last look in the little mirror. The image in the mirror, even with modesty, should have had her feeling *Not too shoddy, sister.* Instead, with a look at the major's oak leaves on her shoulder boards, a long, resigned sigh -- and some gratitude that her father wasn't alive for this – that feeling escaped her. Instead: *This is the last stop, sister.*

"This is bullshit, Mister Cho," Loomis fumed.

They were in the barracks, Cho in his Class A's holding out a walkie-talkie and holstered sidearm. "Be that as it may…"

Listen to this fucker, and Loomis didn't even bother to hide his eyeroll. *"Be that as it may" – what is he, the fucking emperor of China now? The fucking head muckety-muck? Fucking Grand Poobah? "Be that as it may" – give me a fucking break.* "Total bullshit, Mister Cho. *Total* bullshit."

Cho stood patiently, unsurprised by the invective or the attitude. "Are you done?" he said quietly.

The rest of the men were gathered at the far end of the barracks, pretending to do their usual horsing around, but paying attention and quite enjoying the little show between Loomis and Cho. *I know; I don't have a single fucking fan in the room, but even you guys know this is total bullshit.*

"She manhandled me, Mister Cho!"

Grins at the other end of the room turned to snickers.

"The gender reference may be misapplied," Cho said.

"She can't lay her hands on me! You know that's against —"

"Write your congressman," Cho said tiredly, cutting him off. "Write the Inspector General. Until then, get your butt into full uniform." Again, he pushed the walkie and belt and holster at Loomis.

Loomis snatched them and started strapping the belt around his waist. "Incredible total bullshit," he grumbled.

Cho pointed to the pistol: "Try not to hurt yourself with that." He brushed past Loomis to the soldier's locker, popped the locker door open and — looking in the pocket mirror affixed to the inside — adjusted his beret a few degrees. "You walk the perimeter. Regular radio checks." He glanced at his watch. "It's almost 1900 now, so make your first call-in at 2000 hours, and then every hour, on the hour after that."

"Until when? When do I get relieved?"

Cho straightened his tie and closed the locker.

Jesus, this little gook fucker acts like he thinks his Class A's add two inches to his dick.

"I imagine," Cho said, "you get relieved when the major feels you deserve to be relieved. I'd wager there's always the possibility that might be never if you continue to be an irritant."

"*Outrageous* total bullshit."

The warrant officer's attitude changed, showing something Loomis had never seen in him: a cold anger. He stepped up to Loomis, and even though Loomis was a good head taller, the hard icy look from Cho had Loomis flinching as Cho punctuated what he had to say with finger pokes to the chest: "Listen, *dumbass* (poke), you're getting off *lucky* (poke)! If it was up to *me* (poke), I would've hung you from the radio mast (poke) by your *testiculars* (poke) *A* (poke) *S* (poke) *A* (poke) *P* (poke) and never have to deal (poke) with you (poke) again (poke)." Cho took a deep breath, regaining his usual blithe composure as he stepped back. "So, you might consider trying to be less of an irritant. Now go and do." And with that, he left the barracks.

Loomis looked toward the group at the far end of the barracks who weren't even bothering to hide their amusement now.

I have a weapon, assholes!

But he kept that to himself, headed for the door, and when some of them started whistling the "Colonel Bogey March" from *The Bridge on the River Kwai*, he flashed them a middle finger without turning around.

He calmed himself with the idea, *Fuck it, it's ok; I have a plan…*

*****

The mess hall had been designed to accommodate a full 200-head company rather than Pat's more squad-sized detail. With even fewer than that attending the reception, it seemed positively cavernous.

Some of that extra space had been put to alternate use. At the opposite end from the kitchen and serving counters, a recreation area had been set up. There were billiards, ping-pong, shuffle puck, and foosball tables, as well as a large screen TV in front of some sofas patched with duct and electrical tape. Gauging by the battered conditions of everything, they were as much Army castoffs as some of the personnel Pat had seen that day.

The party, if it could be called that, was clustered around the serving counters where two enlisted men had been drafted to work as a server and a bartender — although there wasn't much to serve or tend. McElhone hadn't been exaggerating by much, saying it would be a Cheez Whiz and punch affair. There were cheese and crackers (thankfully, real cheese), a tray of microwaved pizza bagels and another of microwaved pigs-in-a-blanket. The bartender's sole role seemed to be twisting the caps off Budweiser long-necks sitting in a fire bucket of ice.

Jinski and Cho were standing together, each with a beer, Jinski managing to hold his with the same hand juggling a paper plate piled high with eatables. They made a comical pair: Cho barely came up to Jinski's chest, and the staff sergeant, who, in his Class A's, reminded Pat of a battleship dressed out in all its flags for Fleet Week, looked almost twice as wide as the warrant officer. She noted that Jinski, unlike Cho — and probably most, if not all of her men — wore a ribbon bar on his left chest. She recognized campaign ribbons for Iraq and Afghanistan.

"Jinski." Pat said, raising an eyebrow in approval, "I barely recognized you cleaned and pressed! Maybe you'll get to keep your stripes after all."

"Took three hours to find an iron, Ma'am," the sergeant said through a mouthful of pizza bagel. "Search party didn't even know what one looked like till I Googled up a picture." He gestured with his beer at her own ribbon bar. "I see we're in the same band of brothers."

"Nothing special, it's a big club." She hoped it sounded dismissive enough to derail a possible comparing of notes, something she dearly wanted to avoid.

"Can I get you a beer?" Cho offered. Before she could beg off — not that she couldn't use one, but didn't want to be left alone with Jinski and those matching campaign ribbons — Cho headed for the beer bucket.

"So where were you?" Jinski said, pointing at her ribbons again.

Just then, McElhone — who had been engaged in conversation with a small group of civilians — spied Pat and headed her way, dragging one of the civilians with him. At first, she was thankful for the excuse not to get into comparing war stories with Jinski until she saw who was with McElhone.

He was in civilian clothes, looking like a small college's cool professor: jacket and a loose tie-up top, jeans and sneakers below, mop of dark hair she knew for a fact he'd practiced letting fall across his forehead, just so he could give it a suave pushback with his hand.

"Pat!" called McElhone. "I know you remember this guy. I didn't want to tell you beforehand; I wanted to surprise you." It was obvious from the colonel's ruddy face that the beer in his hand was not his first. That also explained why he didn't remember that such good fellowship was misplaced just then.

"I am surprised," Pat said with a cool politeness. "Hello, Dr. Cordell."

David Cordell made an equally good show with a mechanical smile. "Nice to see you, again, Pat."

He held out his hand, but Cho showed up just then with Pat's beer and she managed to swing her hand by Cordell's without shaking it to take the offered beer.

"It was 'David' at The Alamo," Cordell said.

"Long time ago, Doctor."

"'The Alamo'?" Jinski asked. "As in Daniel Boone?"

"Actually, that was Davy Crockett," Pat said.

"The Alamo is what we used to call Los Alamos," McElhone said.

"The major was just a lieutenant then, on the security detail," Cordell said. "A newbie, but very…diligent." Pat expected the bite behind the smile, but it didn't sting; she'd been waiting for it.

"And now here we are, again," Pat said. "Small world."

"Actually, when we needed a replacement, it was David here who brought up your name," McElhone said.

"Is that a fact?"

"I couldn't think of anybody better," Cordell said.

"I'm sure if you'd thought about it longer…"

She could see Jinski and Cho exchanging looks, as they picked up on the fact that despite the smiles and polite nattering, all was not well.

"Say, Mister Cho, how 'bout bouncin' the billiard balls around a bit," Jinski offered.

Cho seemed to welcome the excuse to leave and followed Jinski toward the rec area.

"I don't see Dr. Ostrow," McElhone said, looking around, not that there was any place in the big open space to hide.

"He said he'd put in an appearance," Cordell said. "Have you warned the good major about him?"

"Ostrow? Should I know him?"

"Aaron Ostrow," McElhone said, and leaned in for a theatrical whisper. "One of the DoD's better kept secrets."

"This project is pretty much his baby," Cordell said although there was something about the way he said it...

Why am I hearing alarm bells going off in my head?

"What is it about him I should be warned about?" trying to keep the tone light.

Cordell and McElhone shared a laugh. "The good doctor is not exactly a people person," Cordell said.

McElhone polished off the remains of his beer and beckoned to the bartender to bring him another. Pat remembered what the colonel had said about the monotony of the place. Eyeing the colonel's fresh bottle, remembering he'd tossed back two doses of Jameson's to her one earlier, she worried this was how her commander was dealing with it.

"David's being a little unfair, although he's not wrong," McElhone said. "It's kind of a sad story, really. Ostrow had a son in the service. He was with the advance units of the 3rd Infantry when they went across the border on Iraqi Freedom."

"I assume he didn't come home," Pat said.

"Sadder than that, he wasn't lost in combat. Heat stroke."

"Jesus."

"I don't think the doctor's ever quite gotten it back together since then, at least as far as the social graces go," Cordell said.

"Can you blame him?" Pat said. "Parents are not supposed to outlive the child."

Cordell's face changed, musing. "I suppose. I never looked at it that way."

"The Pentagon has a lot of faith in this project and in him," McElhone said. "They've pretty much given him — And here he is!"

Aaron Ostrow appeared in the mess hall doorway and looked around at the gathering, taking a moment. Pat thought he might be considering turning immediately around and leaving. He was a small, unassuming figure, dressed haphazardly in mismatched jacket and tie and slacks, thinning powdery hair barely combed, goggle-sized eyeglasses that appeared to keep sliding down his nose. Ostrow spied the trio, shored himself up and walked over.

"Sorry, sorry, sorry I'm late," he muttered as he came up to them. "In fact, in fact, as it is I can only stay a few minutes." A sharp look toward McElhone and Cordell. "You understand."

"Something cooking at the lab," McElhone said, nodding.

"Yes," Ostrow said. "Well, always. But I thought I should at least come by and get acquainted. You must be this Major Simons the colonel had been telling me about." Ostrow stuck out his hand as if he suddenly remembered that was something he was supposed to do.

Pat took it, noticing as she did a small medallion hanging around Ostrow's neck. "Are you a physicist?"

"No," Ostrow said, appearing surprised. *And perhaps a little alarmed?* "What makes you think that?"

"Well, you're working with David here, and he's a physicist. Plus," and she pointed to the medallion, "That's the symbol for *pi*, isn't it? I figured anybody at this lab, that in love with numbers…"

Ostrow smiled, but there was sadness to it. "I know it looks like *pi*, but it isn't. It's a Hebrew symbol: *Chai.* It means 'life'. It was passed down and there's an irony to that. Yes, ironic; 'Life.'"

"I'm not sure I follow, Doctor."

Ostrow seemed lost in a thought, pushing his glasses back up his nose, then came back realizing he'd been taking a line others couldn't see. "My grandparents, on my father's side. This belonged to them. They were lost. In the camps."

"The Nazis?"

Ostrow nodded. "But they sent my father, he was still a child, to relatives who'd already gotten out. England. They gave this to him. You see? The irony? 'Life'? And they lost theirs."

"A parents wish for their child," Pat said. "I get it."

"Yes, yes. My father passed it to me. I gave it to my son. He was in the service, you know."

"The colonel told me. I'm sorry for your loss."

Ostrow nodded an acknowledgement. "Irony, again. Mm, yes, ironic. They returned it to me. Personal effects, you know. Personal…effects." His hand absently floated to the medallion, touching it lightly. His face clouded, softened. "You have children?"

Pat shook her head. "But I have been someone's child."

Ostrow smiled at that, nodding, again pushing his glasses back into place. Then his face changed again: studious. "I see from your ribbons; you served in Afghanistan."

Pat could feel McElhone and David Cordell shifting uncomfortably.

"Harsh?" Ostrow asked. "I mean, not the circumstances, of course, of course that would be, yes, harsh, the war and such, but I mean hot? Cold? My son, you know, was in Iraq. Desert."

Pat felt herself unwind inside, seeing as this wouldn't be about her service. "It wasn't comfy."

"Yes, yes," Ostrow nodded although he seemed to be mentally connecting it to something else. "This," and he gestured at his body, "the human vessel, it's a fragile thing. Evolution has not prepared it adequately for where it often finds itself."

"I'm not sure evolution counted on global military operations," McElhone said.

"Maybe a better way to put it," Pat said, "is evolution hasn't prepared the body for its assigned tasks rather than its natural ones."

Ostrow brightened, smiled. "Ah, yes! Very good! 'Assigned tasks,' yes, yes, well put, yes." He grew serious again. "The Nazis, you know, at some of the camps, they did experiments. Not just the ones everyone hears about; sterilization and such. But human tolerances: heat, cold, pressure, so on."

"I've read that," Pat said.

"Things we would never do to a human subject," Ostrow said. "But when the Allies discovered those records, they realized how critical they would be to our own programs, like the space program. We would never treat a human subject the way the Nazis did, but – and I guess this is, again, ironic – we did learn from what they did. And you know what the most critical thing we learned, Major? The most important fact? Something we already knew, always knew, but now we had science to back it up."

"What's that, Doctor?"

"What I told you; this – "and he pointed to Pat, his finger – was this coincidence? – seeming to target her ribbon bar " – human vessel is inadequate – too fragile – for, as you put it, its assigned tasks."

And with that, Ostrow again lapsed into some unspoken thought, some unshared tangent. He shook himself out of it, adjusted his glasses again, forced a smile. "Regrets, Major, regrets. This is a party, yes? In your honor? I mean, a welcome, yes? I've never been much for parties, and I apologize if I've dampened the mood."

"No apologies necessary, Doctor. I understand." She could feel it go between them: *you lost your son, and as someone who has been responsible for the sons and daughters of others, I will not judge how heavily you carry your grief…or for how long.* "I don't have any more heart for socializing than you do."

"Pat's always given more attention to duty than frivolity, Doctor. Something you have in common." She saw it in Cordell's eyes: it may not have sounded like it to the others, but Pat knew it was a dig.

The thought stopped Ostrow from leaving. "Ah, yes, yes! A valuable trait in some occupations. Would you say, Major, would you describe this as a singleness of purpose?"

"I don't know, Doctor, I just try to do my job."

"Of course, yes, you have the responsibility." Ostrow's face grew more intent.

This isn't a conversation anymore; this is an examination.

"Tell me, Major, in your estimation, was this, oh, what would you call it? This focus, ability to focus, as Dr. Cordell says, was this something you learned at the Academy? You were West Point, yes? Or do you think you've always had this innate sense of duty? I suppose I'm asking, what I'd like to know is if this is an, um, 'natural' trait?"

"I honestly don't know, Doctor. I've never really thought about it."

"Hm, yes, well, of course." He looked to McElhone and Cordell with what Pat took almost to be a kind of approval. "You're an interesting woman, Major. Welcome aboard and so on. Maybe we can talk again."

Then Ostrow made his farewells, passed a few words with some of the other civilians — lab technicians, Cordell explained to Pat — and then several of them followed the doctor out.

"I don't know about you two," McElhone said after Ostrow had left, "but after that, I could use another beer," and headed for the beer bucket.

"Is he ok?" Pat asked Cordell, nodding at McElhone. "I've never seen him bang 'em back like that, not in public."

"Lot of pressure on him back at the lab," Cordell said.

"David, I worked with him at Los Alamos and Oak Ridge. Those weren't daycare centers."

"I know." Pat felt a "but" hanging in the air.

"Well, I've had about as much of this fun as I can take," she said.

"Can I walk you back to your quarters?"

"David —"

"It's dark, the werewolves are out. Just some harmless company for an escort."

"Harmless my ass."

As she turned for the door with David, a hand lightly touched her shoulder: "You were going to leave without saying hello?"

The voice was instantly familiar. Pat turned, smiling, and before she even got a good look at the person behind her, was in a close hug with Mariska Woltz. She'd barely caught her breath before her husband, Oskar, gave her another rib-crushing hug.

The joke at Oak Ridge was the two of them together looked like the couple from the famous Grant Wood painting, *American Gothic* …only what made the joke funnier was that Oskar looked like the woman in the painting, and Mariska the man. It said something about their good-natured selves that even they saw the joke, and at a Halloween party had made quite the splash coming dressed accordingly.

"You were going to leave without saying hello?" Mariska said, again, as soon as Oskar let Pat breathe. She still had a touch – just ever so lightly – of a German accent.

"I didn't even know you two were here!"

"How long ago was it?" Oskar had a thick, throaty voice hardly matching his spare frame.

"Prehistory, it seems like." She pointed to David. "I presume you all know each other."

"Yes," David said, "but we didn't know we all knew you."

"I knew David from Los Alamos," Pat said. "I know the Woltz's from Oak Ridge."

"Small world," David said.

"Our world tends to be," Oskar said with a certain heaviness.

"I was happy to hear we were getting you," Mariska said. "Not so happy for you to be posted here, but a friendly face, yes? How's your pinochle these days?"

"Rusty. Haven't had a good partner since."

"Maybe this young man," Mariska said with a matchmaking smile.

"I love that they call me 'young man'," David said, although Pat was sure he was reveling in it, taking the opportunity to do his aren't-I-dashing hair sweep.

Pat felt a yawn coming on, tried to politely – and unsuccessfully – stifle it.

Mariska's face turned motherly concerned. "Oh, Pat, dear, you're tired? Of course you are, yes? You just arrived today."

"She's been traveling since yesterday," David said.

"Then we shouldn't keep her," Mariska said, aiming it at Oskar as if he was somehow at fault. That was something Mariska always did, and Oskar had grown so used to it, he often reacted by putting his fist to his heart and muttering, *"Mea culpa, mea culpa,"* only to draw the addendum of an, "Oh, *you!*" from Mariska along with a playful shove.

"You have been commanded by Her Majesty," Oskar said. "You are to take yourself to bed, sleep, and are ordered to dream pleasantly."

"We can always catch up another time," Mariska said.

"That is whenever we can get away from the lab," Oskar said.

His wife nodded grimly. "They do keep us busy. Don't they, David?"

"Very. Ostrow just ran off, said he has something going at the lab he couldn't leave for too long."

The faces of the Woltz's…changed. The smiles were still there, the welcoming air, only now it seemed forced, an act. It felt, to Pat, like there was some special frequency between the three of them, one where an innocuous statement carried an invisible – and unpleasant — meaning with it, privy to no outsider.

They all turned at a raucous, unrestrained laugh from over where the lab techs were gathered. It was coming from McElhone.

"How is he?" Pat asked, nodding at the colonel.

"It's hard for us all," Oskar said gravely, "but I think what happened to the young man who had your job…"

Pat nodded but… McElhone was a twenty-year professional, she knew he'd done tours in Iraq and Afghanistan. She didn't buy it.

"How are *you*?" Mariska asked, setting her hand lightly on Pat's arm. "The colonel told us about your father."

"I'm ok," Pat said. "Right now, I'm just tired."

Mariska's bony fingers gave Pat's arm a squeeze. "We'll talk"

She's not buying, either.

"Maybe over pinochle," Pat said and that seemed enough to bring back earnest smiles all around.

And then Mariska, with that plotting little smile of hers, nodded at David, and sing-songed, "You're going to neeeeed a paaaaartnerrrr…"

Edward "Gloomis" Loomis was 21, two very bumpy years into a three-year Army hitch after nineteen even bumpier years growing up in the Curtis Bay section of South Baltimore, what haughty locals disparagingly referred to as "Billyland" because of the large numbers of Appalachian whites – hillbillies – who'd settled in that part of the city over the years.

Among Loomis' laundry list of unappetizing qualities was an unwarranted high opinion of his mental faculties. Still, stuck with this chickenshit punishment detail that half-pint Cho had dumped on him, he had come up with a good-sounding plan.

The spill from the lights mounted on the various compound buildings didn't reach the perimeter fence. Hell, large swathes of the compound were always left dark, and there wasn't much of a moon this night to boot. Beyond the reach of the lights, it was dark as the inside of a cow's ass at midnight, as his daddy used to say. No one would be able to see if he was walking his circuit or not.

So, the plan: walk out into the valley until he found a nice-sized rock, something big enough to easily conceal him and with a smooth face he could use as a backrest, and instead of pounding sand walking the fence line, he could catch himself some Zs. As for the hourly radio check-ins, in spite of the regs that said he couldn't, he had his cell phone with him. Simple: he'd set the alarm app, wake up to make his check-in, reset his alarm and go back to dreamland.

A good-sounding plan.

The night wind had picked up and Pat's dress jacket wasn't doing much to keep her warm. She made the mistake of shuddering, and David Cordell took that as an opportunity to move in — try to put a warming arm around her shoulders. But she saw it coming, subtly sidestepped to take herself out of reach. She heard a small, peeved sigh from him and knew she was supposed to hear it.

"You have to give the desert some credit," David said, as he again tried to close the distance between them. "It does provide romantic nights."

Pat lengthened her stride. "Harmless my ass. I think the werewolf I need to look out for is you."

He reached out, took her by the elbow, and when she flinched, he immediately let it go — hands held up in a no-foul-intended gesture. "Don't you think we should talk?"

"Ok. Good night, David. That's plenty of talk for me."

"Pat, please. We're stuck out here with each other —"

"Thanks to you."

"No, thanks to your friend McElhone. He was looking for a damned good security officer, he needed one in a hurry, and your name came to mind for no other reason than you are a damned good security officer. He agreed."

She stopped and faced him. "No other reason?"

He flashed a goofy smile, made a grand gesture toward the star-studded sky. "Who knows what influences the subconscious mind might have on our conscious decisions?"

"Get me a shovel. After I clear away the bullshit, I can hit you over the head with it."

"There I was thinking you'd mellowed. There was a point back there, with Ostrow, talking about his son…you sounded almost…maternal. You seemed very feminine then."

"I'll put the sexist subtext to that aside; you never imagined me as feminine?"

"I never imagined you out of uniform."

"David, you've seen me out of uniform."

He smirked and it was hard for her not to do the same.

"Yeah, well, I was speaking metaphorically," he said.

Pat turned and continued her way back to her trailer, David following along.

"Look, Pat, it's been a long time, there's some…unpleasant history. I'm not saying let's pick up where we left off."

She laughed at that. "I wouldn't think you'd want to pick up where we left off. As I recall, that was a bit unpleasant."

"You know what I mean. I'm just saying, can't we reboot? Clean slate, start fresh. Friends."

"Pals?" she teased. "Buddies?"

"How about just not enemies. Pinochle partners."

"I can't afford to screw up here, David."

"I know. But you did seem…different. Back there with Ostrow. From the way you were at The Alamo."

She stopped, again, turned to him, again. He tipped his head down, eyes looking up — puppy eyes — and did that thing with his hair. She had thought it a cute, if silly, affectation back at Los Alamos. Now it just seemed silly. They were near the barracks, the beach loungers were still out there, outside the circle of light from the fixture over the front door. Pat sat, laid back in one of the loungers, David stretched out in one across from her.

She slipped off her beret. It might have been cold, but the wind felt good rifling through her hair. He was right about the desert night sky. There may not have been a moon, but the inky dome was speckled with a heavy dusting of stars. It was, she had to admit — although not wanting to — quite lovely.

But it was also cold. She pulled her jacket close around her. "You know my family has been all Army going back."

"Right. Your grandfather."

"We go back further than that. I had a great-grand-something or other in the First World War. By chance, the family has always had sons, and the sons went into uniform. That's who we were."

David chuckled. "Then you come along and anatomically screw things up."

That was smile-worthy. "It never occurred to me not to go into the service. I grew up thinking that's just what we did; it didn't matter to me that I was a daughter instead of a son. I didn't even think about it.

"My father didn't push me; Dad wasn't like that. Mom, I know she was thinking, 'Hey, at last, a Simons who wears a dress!' Broke her heart when I applied to West Point."

"But I'll bet your dad was proud."

"Of course. So was Granddad; he was still alive then."

"Did your mother ever accept it?"

"What made it easy on her was all my posts were stateside. Safe. Army posts, then Los Alamos, then Oak Ridge."

"She couldn't've taken your deployment well."

"Thankfully she'd already passed by then. If she hadn't, I think it would've killed her — the worry. The thing was my dad…" And as the memory came to her, she felt a kind of heaviness in her chest, like a hand gently but firmly pushing down on her heart.

"I would've thought, you know, that's what the profession is all about, right?" David said. "Hoist the flag and off to war?"

That had been Pat's own thinking when she'd gotten her orders. But then when she told her father… "He was retired by then. I went to see him before I went over. He took me to his favorite restaurant, a farewell kind of thing. Then we went back to his house. I can still see it in my head," and she closed her eyes and could, indeed see the two of them sitting in his parlor. He was living in a small house in Virginia, then. He had a fire going. They sat for the longest time, breaking up the long silences with the most inane comments: how good dinner had been, how each was looking fit and fine; the kind of talk that's about avoiding what's really occupying minds. "The two of us sitting in his living room, very adult, both having a brandy, you know; two professional soldiers. Then he got…" That feeling in her chest, again…heavier this time.

"What?"

It was hard to say it without a catch in her voice. "He said, 'I'm proud of you as a soldier. But right now, I can only think of you as my daughter.' He was scared for me, David.

"I don't pretend to know what it's like to be a parent, and at this point, it's starting to look like I probably never will. I don't know what Ostrow's feeling. But I've seen it up close. My dad almost cried that night; he was that scared for me. I'd never seen him like that, not even when my mother passed."

They lay on the beach loungers quietly for a bit. Pat looked back up at the night sky. It didn't seem lovely or romantic now. Just cold. Lifeless. A perfect counterpart for the lifeless earth below.

"I'm afraid to ask," David said finally, "and maybe I shouldn't, but how did he take it when you came home?"

She remembered showing up on his doorstep, not having the courage to ring the bell or knock. But he must've seen her; the door opened, she bowed her head waiting for some castigation, some condemnation. All she got were those two still-sinewy arms wrapping around her and pulling her to his chest.

"He surprised me," Pat said. "I expected… No, what I *hadn't* expected — him having been in uniform over forty years — was him saying kind of the same thing. 'I can only see you as my daughter and I'm glad you're home.' I told him everything, but he never turned his back on me. I know he must've been embarrassed; *I* was embarrassed. Hell, I was *ashamed!* But he never turned his back on me. 'I can only see you as my daughter'."

They were quiet, again, then David, his voice soft, small: "You have changed."

Pat sighed, shook off the mood, and got to her feet. "Not that much, David," she said firmly. "Security was my job at The Alamo and it's no different here." She started toward her trailer. She laughed as David fumbled his way out of his lounger, almost falling on his ass as he struggled to his feet to follow.

"Security may have been your job," he called after her, "but your *objective* was to make an example of me. Not because of security, but because you wanted to prove you could be just as hard-assed as any other —"

She waved him away. "Ok, end of conversation."

"I damned near lost my security clearance!"

She turned on him. "If it had been up to me, you would have! You have a big mouth, David. The only reason you still have your clearance, if you ask me, is because the Pentagon found a place to let you work where they don't have to worry about you blabbing too much." She gave him a challenging glare. "Tell me I'm wrong."

He said nothing.

"It's cold," Pat said. "Good night."

"And why did they put *you* here?"

"Whatever the reason, it's my last chance. The colonel gave me the cover story, then he gave me what I know was another cover story of low-level radiation exposure. I know that's bullshit. I know the work you were doing at The Alamo; I know the work the Woltz's were doing at Oak Ridge; they didn't put you all out here for Mickey Mouse work. Don't open your mouth, David," which he was starting to do, "because if you think you can get something going with me by telling me any part of the truth, that'd be a violation of security protocol."

"And you'd tag me for it."

"You're damned right. Like I said, I can't afford to screw up here. And that's why whatever line of b.s. the colonel wants me to work with,

I'm just going to keep my mouth shut except to say, 'Yessir, whatever you say, Sir!' And anybody who breaches protocol…"

Then they were at her trailer.

"So, what does this mean for us?" David said as she reached for her door. "I really liked you, Pat. I mean, you know… *Really* liked you. Even with all this time…that didn't completely evaporate."

"I really liked you, David."

"And now?"

The truth of things hit her with a surprising bluntness. David Cordell had not been her last serious relationship, but none since had been as serious. And there'd been no one since Afghanistan. She'd been alone since then; *very* alone. When her father had passed a few months before, he had been the last tie she'd allowed herself with a life outside the Pentagon office where the Army had buried her.

She had been numb to it, but now, seeing David again, being pressed between the cold desert and cold sky, the feeling of loneliness was seeping in.

"Let's just take it a day at a time," she said after mulling it over. "Maybe I'll teach you how to play pinochle."

"So…truce?" He held out his hand.

"Truce." She started to reach out her own hand but then held it up in a pause: "But only as long as you behave."

"Well," he smirked and did that damned thing with his hair. She found herself — and reprimanded herself for it — thinking it was cute that he thought it was cute when it wasn't, "if I don't…you can always spank me."

Instead of shaking his hand, she used her middle finger to draw a line down from her eye…but with a smile. "Harmless my ass."

As soon as her trailer door closed behind her, Pat found herself sagging against it. It was catching up to her all at once; that she'd been running on fumes most of the day. The last sleep she'd had was the final few minutes before her alarm had gone off at 6:00 a.m. the day before when she thought she was looking at just another routine day in her Pentagon cubby. That had been forty-four hours and a transcontinental flight ago. Then there'd been dealing with the obvious fact her new post was some sort of Fort Zinderneuf — maybe as much a dead end as her Pentagon slot — that McElhone was obviously b.s.ing her about what was going on at this installation, and then there was David Cordell...

Physically, mentally, emotionally, the needle was on E. She let her beret drop to the floor, then slid off her jacket, letting it go the same way as the hat. She shuffled on leaden feet toward the bunkroom at the back of the trailer. She didn't bother with lights, or shedding the rest of her uniform, but plopped herself on the edge of the bunk, kicked off her shoes, and let herself fall back on the thin mattress. Even before her head hit her pillow, she was already slipping into blackness.

It seemed like she'd only been asleep for a few minutes before there was someone pounding on the window above her bunk.

"Major! Major Simons!"

She recognized Cho's voice, mumbled something to him about her door being unlocked, and pulled herself into a seated position at the edge of the bunk. Only then did she become conscious enough to worry about being dressed. Groggily looking, she was surprised to see she was still in most of her now-rumpled Class A uniform. She tried to focus on her watch but couldn't get her eyes to work quite that well.

Then Cho was in the bunkroom doorway. She heard him fumbling for the light switch.

"I'd appreciate it if you didn't do that," she said as she got to her feet, pushed past him into the small bathroom, and threw cold water on her face. "Ok, now: give it to me."

"It's Private Loomis, Ma'am."

"What'd he do now?"

"He's missing."

"Shit."

MIA

The night air did more to clear Pat's head than those few handfuls of cold water back in her trailer. Cho was leading her to what he said the troops had nicknamed "The Brain"— the surveillance and communications trailer.

"I'm just curious," Pat said, unhappily aware she still sounded groggy, "did anybody bother to go look for him?"

"Before I came for you, Ma'am. I sent one man one way around the perimeter; I went the other to make sure if he was on the patrol circuit we wouldn't miss him. But, um..."

"Um?"

"Thing is, Ma'am, the opacity of the darkness —"

"I'm sorry, the what? Opacity?"

"Sorry, Ma'am. All those crossword puzzles —"

Pat waved her XO's concerns away. "No, please, it's ok. I'm impressed anybody on this post can speak in more than monosyllables. You were saying about the 'opacity of the darkness'?"

"What I mean, Ma'am, is without a moon, it's so damned dark out there," and Cho pointed into the truly inky blackness just outside – and that sometimes enveloped – the perimeter fence, "we could miss him by a few feet and never know it. If he fell and is unconscious somewhere, or, um…"

"Yes? Um?"

It was clear Cho didn't like where his thinking was going: "If he's hiding…"

"You think he might've gone over the hill?"

Cho shook his head, unsure. "I don't think even Loomis is that cerebrally deficient."

'Cerebrally deficient'; I love this guy!

"But then I reflect and think, well, it's Loomis."

Pat tried looking at her watch. Her eyes still couldn't focus well. "How long's he been gone?"

"We're not quite sure."

"Great. Let's see what this Brain of ours has for us," and Cho held the trailer door for her while she stepped up the one fold-out step and entered the trailer.

It was almost as cold inside the trailer as outside, the space air conditioned to a level low enough to keep an impressive bank of electronic equipment from overheating. As big as the trailer looked on the outside, the interior was quite cramped. Along one side of the trailer, from front to back, was an unbroken bank of control panels and monitor screens. There was a narrow aisle down the other side, and partly blocking it was a single technician in a rolling chair. Pat noticed he wore the specialist first class insignia of two inverted rockers over an eagle.

"Major Simons, this is Electronic Warfare Specialist First Pritchard."

Pritchard started to stand but Pat waved him to keep his seat.

"An honest to God specialist?"

"With all this hardware, they had to send us at least one person who knows what they're doing," Cho said, then winced as he realized how that had sounded. "Ma'am, I mean, I didn't mean that you, Ma'am, I mean --"

Pat put a finger to her lips. "You already put one foot in your mouth, Cho. Don't try to jam the other one in there with it." She turned to Pritchard. He was, she thought, the picture of a typical computer geek: pasty-faced, puffy eyes with bags, hair barely combed, looking as much a part of his chair as the cushions. "You our only EW tech?"

"No, Ma'am, I switch off with Specialist Delaney."

"You two working twelve-hour shifts?"

"No choice, Ma'am."

He doesn't look like this because he's a computer nerd; he's just exhausted. Something else I have to fix.

"Alright, Electronic Warfare Specialist First, what do we have here?" and she nodded at the bank of panels.

"We have a pretty good array, Ma'am. Ground surveillance radar, motion detection, sound detection, seismic, thermal imaging, infrared, radiation detection —"

"Whoa, hold up. Radiation detection?"

"Put a grid map up for the major," Cho said.

There was a repeater screen, which looked like a large screen TV, mounted on the wall over the control panels. After a few seconds of his fingers flying around the keyboard, Pritchard pulled up an aerial view of the area onto the screen. A few more taps on the keys and a map grid was laid over the image. A section of the grid squares north of their location were shaded in red.

Cho pointed to the colored grids. "That red area is what we call Sun City, the eastern edge of the Nevada National Security Site. It's about eleven, twelve clicks northwest of us. That particular area is where they set off some of the first underground nuke tests. Parts of it still have some residual radiation."

"Have you ever had to go in there?"

"No, but if somebody does wander in and we have to get them, we have some hot suits, Geiger counters."

"Dosimeter badges?"

"We have them, but Lieutenant Bruckner never distributed them. Since we never go in there."

"Starting tomorrow, everyone wears one 24/7." Pat was fairly certain McElhone had lied to her about the work going on at the lab, but he had mentioned they were working with low levels of radiation. The best cover stories — she had learned early in her career — were those with a kernel or two of truth in them. McElhone would never have mentioned radiation unless that was one of the kernels.

Cho wasn't sure he'd heard the instruction correctly. "You want them to wear the dosimeters —"

"They can pin them to their jammies; 24/7." She turned back to the EW specialist. "What else do you have? Surveillance drones??

"No, Ma'am." Pritchard seemed as unhappy with his answer as he knew Pat would be. "Lieutenant Bruckner requested them."

"And?"

"And we were told they were redundant and unnecessary."

"That's the damnedest thing I've ever heard."

"Yes, Ma'am."

She looked to Cho to see if there was some explanatory element she was missing but Cho returned her querying look with a helpless one of his own.

"Ok, Pritchard," Pat said, turning back to the bank of monitors, "where does this magic show tell us our missing man is?"

Pritchard's answer was something between a grunt and a groan.

"That doesn't sound promising."

"Our array is set up on the valley rim so we can surveille the flats. But if our man is anywhere *in* the valley, he's literally *under* the radar."

"You're kidding me."

Pritchard shook his head and sighed.

"A couple of million dollars of military grade surveillance equipment and you're telling me —? Christ."

"We could send one patrol up the valley, and another heading south," Cho offered.

Pat weighed that for a moment, then dismissed it. "I'm not crazy about sending anybody out there – especially in this type of darkness – without knowing what happened to him. It's like you said, they're as likely to trip over him as miss him by only a few feet." She studied the grid map. The image, she estimated, covered about a twenty-mile radius from the compound. "If he did decide to go over the hill, where could he go?"

"If he stays in the valley, nowhere," Cho said and had Pritchard pull further back on the aerial image to cover more area. "Closest town is Indian Springs and it's not much. It's eighty, ninety clicks southwest of us across some nasty desert. Maybe if he was some Green Beret survival specialist, possibly…but even under the best circumstances…*Loomis?* He didn't even have a canteen; just a sidearm, a flashlight, and a walkie-talkie."

Shitshitshit…

"Mister Cho tells me we don't know how long he's been missing," Pat said.

Pritchard handed her a bound register. "Here's the communications log, Ma'am. You can see he made his 2000 check-in, 2100, and 2200."

"What's this notation at 2245: 'possible accidental transmission'? What's that?"

"Almost felt like the equivalent of a butt dial, like he'd accidentally thumbed his mic. The line went live, a few crackles, then nothing. I didn't think much of it; it happens." The look Pat gave him was enough for him to understand this wasn't a particularly good response, and he shrank a little in his seat. "Sorry, Ma'am."

"He didn't make his 2300 check-in but says here you didn't notify Mister Cho until 2400."

"I'm sorry about that, Ma'am. I thought, well, Ma'am, it was Loomis. I thought he was goofing off, maybe just forgot to check-in. But when he didn't radio in at 2400, I tried to raise him and —"

"'And' nothing. If someone ever misses a check-in again —"

"Yes, Ma'am, soon as."

"You're supposed to be one of the smart ones," she said, handing back the ledger.

Pritchard turned red-faced: "Yes, Ma'am."

Changing her tone to let him know his misstep was a closed chapter, she pointed to what she recognized as communications equipment. "What's your comms set-up?"

Pritchard scooted his chair down to the communications section, seeming to be happy to move on. "We're too far out for any of the usual line-of-sight platforms, but we do have a standard land mobile radio UHF set-up."

"Our main support is Nellis?"

"Yes, Ma'am."

"Do we do regular radio checks with them?"

"No, Ma'am."

"When does your shift change?"

"Del — I mean Specialist Delaney — comes on at 0800."

"Ok, when he comes on, notify Nellis that from here on out we will be making hourly radio checks."

"Yes, Ma'am. We also have an uplink to connect with DSCS. If you need it, Ma'am, I can get you a satlink to the Chief of Staff's office at the Pentagon."

"Good to know," she said, nodding with approval, and Pritchard seemed relieved to be saying the right things for a change. "What do we have on the post?"

"We have an intercom network; all the buildings are linked. We also have a squawk box line to the lab; that comes here, to your quarters, and to your office. But that's only ever been used for field ops alerts."

"What field ops?" She turned to Cho. "Who's doing field ops?"

"Every so often, we get squawked an alert that the lab's security detail is carrying out some kind of operation out on the flats."

"What the hell kind of field op could a security detail be doing?"

Cho shook his head. "I don't know, Ma'am, but when they squawk an alert, it's always at night, and the protocol is that we shut down the surveillance array and all personnel are restricted to the post until notified. Whatever they're doing, we hear gunfire. Sometimes something heavier." Cho flicked his eyes toward the trailer door, and she knew he had something more to say but it was for outside.

"That's the second damnedest thing I've ever heard."

"Lieutenant Bruckner asked the colonel about it."

"And?"

"I don't remember the verbatim language, but to paraphrase, it was something along the lines that it was some kind of live fire exercise, and it was none of our damned business."

She was still digesting this when Cho asked, "So what do we do about Loomis?"

She tapped Pritchard on the shoulder. "When I'm done here, I want you to contact Nellis. Tell them we have a missing man and request an aerial search by thermal imaging drone; search area, a radius of 25 clicks out from our position. I doubt he could've gotten any further than that. Even if he did fall down and conk his head, as cold as it is out there, they shouldn't have any trouble picking up a heat signature. Then squawk the lab. Whoever you get, have them inform Colonel McElhone about Loomis, and have the lab keep an eye out for him. Tell them we've got a request in to Nellis for an aerial search. If you hear anything from anybody —"

"I'll inform you immediately, Ma'am."

Pritchard knew he'd burned himself, and Pat could see he'd felt stung by his errors. But, she also sensed he wasn't going to let it happen again. "Outstanding. If we don't hear anything from Nellis by the time your shift ends, contact Army Personnel about sending an MIA notification to Loomis' next of kin."

"Um…"

She turned to Cho. "I'm finding these 'um's' of yours never signify anything good, Mister Cho."

"I'll have to check his jacket to make sure, but as I recall, Loomis didn't have a next of kin contact."

"No family?"

"Like I said, I'll check but not that I remember."

"Army Personnel will still have to be notified, Pritchard."

"Yes, Ma'am."

She nodded at Cho to follow her outside.

Pat led Cho away from the trailer until she was sure there was no danger of Pritchard overhearing. "There's something you wanted to tell me back there."

"The night they told us Lieutenant Bruckner killed himself, they were doing one of their field ops."

"Ok."

"The lieutenant actually went up top that night with night goggles for a look."

"In violation of the security protocol."

"Do you think they might've, you know…" Cho made a pained face. "I mean, since he wasn't supposed to be there…"

"Shot him? Unless they were trigger happy or bad at their job, I wouldn't think so. Normally, they would've just detained him."

"Which they would've told us."

Pat turned, and looked out into the night, the desert valley hidden in darkness, contemplating the situation regarding Bruckner and how it might apply to Loomis. *What reason would they have not to tell us? This issue with Bruckner…maybe…but Loomis? It's likely the stupid sonofabitch is still out there somewhere.*

She remembered something her father had told her – taught her, actually – when she was on leave from her first posting, complaining about some of the foul-ups in her detail.

"Jump on them, crack the whip on them, do whatever you have to to get them in line, but always remember, Sweets; they're yours. Whether it's some FNG you think is one of God's mistakes, or a twenty-year man whose head is home with his wife and kids instead of on his job, they belong to you; you're responsible for them. Like it or not."

"They weren't running an op tonight," Pat said, "but you think what happened to Bruckner and Loomis are connected, don't you?".

Cho shifted on his feet knowing it was going to sound thin: "It's just a feeling, Ma'am."

She gave him a reassuring – if grim – smile. "I have the same feeling. I'm going to have to have a conversation with the colonel about all this."

"Do you still want to have the assembly tomorrow? Well, technically, I should say this morning."

A yawn she couldn't hold back reminded Pat of how late it was. "We're still proceeding with the program, Mister Cho. There's nothing we can do about Loomis until we hear something from Nellis."

They said their goodnights, but as Pat turned for her trailer, she was struck by a thought. "Cho…"

"Yes, Ma'am?"

"Who's *your* next of kin contact?"

"Hm, funny, it didn't occur to me, but I don't have one, either."

"No family?"

"We lived in Hawaii, Ma'am. As far as I know, the only one who might still be living is an aunt. I haven't seen her since I was a kid; she lived on one of the outer islands. If she's still alive, I'd have no idea how to get in touch with her. I hope there's not a specific reason you're asking, Ma'am."

"Just curious. Tomorrow, when you get a chance, pull the 201s on all post personnel."

"The engineers' files, too?"

"Everybody."

Pat did not sleep well. Things kept nagging at her. What was this insane business about these mysterious nighttime shoot-'em-ups the lab security troops were holding? Shutting down the surveillance array while they were romping around out on the flats with no drones made no sense. If the job was to keep wayward civilians and deliberate snoops from stumbling into the lab, weren't surveillance drones the better tool?

Then there was Loomis. Maybe he was wandering around out there in the dark. Maybe he fell down and knocked himself out. Maybe…

And that a heavy layer of bullshit that had been laid over what the real purpose of Lab 7 was…

But what bothered her more…

One man with no emergency contacts — *Bruckner* — even in a detail as small as hers, that was a reasonable possibility.

Two? That would be *Loomis* -- ok, two was a bit flukey.

But Three? *Cho…*

And then there's me…

"Respect comes with time," her dad had told her, "and loyalty even longer. But in the short term, sometimes you have to give your people the shock treatment to get them to jump when you say 'Jump!'. In that case, a little showmanship is often required."

To that end, Pat had awakened at five a.m. That gave her time for a light breakfast of coffee and toast, and then to make sure she looked immaculate: showered, uniform ironed, hair severely pulled back into a small bun, cap positioned with the bill low over her eyes. For her finishing touches, she strapped on granddad's .45 and slipped on a pair of gold-mirrored sunglasses. Checking out her image in the small bathroom mirror, she couldn't help but smile.

"Showtime."

Cho was standing in front of the men he had assembled in a line in front of the barracks; only ten of them as Pritchard was still on duty in the EW trailer. In line alongside them, standing a few feet away, were another three enlisted men with Jinski in front of them: the engineering detail. She presumed they had been told to stand at ease although they looked more like a motley bunch of slouchers waiting for a bus. As Pat took her place facing them, Cho and Jinski both called out, "Ten-HUT!"

A ripple went through the rank as they changed position although it didn't look much better than their at-ease stance.

"Security Detail!" Cho called out, "One man missing, all others present or accounted for...and..." with a pained look signaling this was more hope than expectation, "...and ready for inspection, Ma'am."

Then Jinski, belting it out loud enough for it to echo off the valley walls: "Engineering Detail all present or accounted for, Ma'am!"

Pat walked slowly along the line of men. It was about what she'd expected: uniforms were wrinkled, some stained, a button missing here, torn seam there. Some men had caps, some didn't. A few had gone the shaved-head route, which was fine with her, but others were long overdue for a shearing — or even just a combing. Her father's advice in mind, she always made sure to ramp up her displeasure, occasionally stopping to shake her head, mutter something under her breath: "In-fucking-credible...Jesus..." She poked at crumbs on one man's blouse: "What is *that*? Why is *that* there?"

"Uh —"

"Is that yap of yours so small you can't find it with a fork? *Get rid of that!*"

Before he could brush the crumbs away — "Don't you dare dirty up my parade ground!" she barked. Then she stepped in closer and growled, "*Don't you dare!*"

He picked the crumbs off individually and dropped them in his breast pocket.

Now in front of one of the shaggy heads, tugging — and making sure it hurt — at where the hair hung over the collar: "You don't do something about this weed garden *today*, I'm going at it with a buzz saw and a rake!"

Poking an unshaven face: "What's this? *What in the good Christ is this?*"

"Sorry, Major, I didn't have time —"

"Then, missy, you get up before the birds and *make* time! You show up like this on parade again and I swear to God, I'll cold shave you with a dull butter knife then and there!"

She pinched one soldier's midriff bulge. "Oh, God, I was hoping this was just a baggy uniform! But this is all *you!* How do you waddle around carrying all this?"

When she'd finished walking the line, she returned to her place facing the men. She stood a long moment, giving them time to read the theatrically exaggerated disgust on her face. Then, "Jesus Christ, ladies, I've seen Girl Scout troops look more military and in better shape than you…and they could probably take you, too. One handed! Right now, you're an argument that Darwin was wrong. Army'd do better enlisting baboons! Well, ladies, I've got news for you: the vacation is over. Starting today, you are back in the Army. From now on, orders for the day will be posted in your barracks the night before. I recommend you pay close attention to them because they will not be a wish list, they will not be suggestions. They will be the word of a vengeful Old Testament fire-and-brimstone Jehovah!"

She studied them a moment to see if they were taking her seriously. Cho looked genuinely fearful for the men behind him, but Jinski…was that a smirk sneaking around his lips?

"While assigned duties may change from day to day, there will be a base schedule to be followed every day but Sunday. It will run as follows:

"Oh-five-thirty: reveille."

A chorus of groans, shaking heads, eyerolls.

Pat stormed up to them, moving back and forth along the rank shouting in faces: "You are at attention, ladies! You forget what that is? When you are at attention, you stand like you have some kind of spine — which some of you obviously don't — eyes forward and with your *mouths shut!* If you can't do that on your own, I'll run a ramrod up your ass and staple those yaps of yours closed! You can have your bitch-and-moan pity parties when you are dismissed and not before!"

They shaped up a bit with that. Not as much as Pat would've liked but... *Well, it's a start.*

She went back to her place. "Oh-six-thirty: assembly and accountability, uniformed for PT and/or drill. Yes, *drill!* You remember: that thing you used to do back when you were soldiers?

"Oh-eight-hundred: breakfast. Hereafter, all meals will be at regularly scheduled times: lunch at twelve-hundred, dinner at seventeen-hundred. There will be serving windows of fifteen minutes. You miss the window, you starve."

A hand went up. "Uh, hey, I don't know you knew this, Major, but we've all been doin' —"

"Hey, asshat, did I give you permission to speak?"

"Uh —"

"When any of you bug-fucking pencil dicks have a question, you address me properly," she said in a sharply clipped tone. "Identify yourself by rank and name, and request permission to speak. You, asshat! Try again."

"Uh, well, Sir —" a prompt from one of his neighbors "— I mean, Ma'am, PFC Drivas, Ma'am. Permission to ask a question, Ma'am?"

"What's your question?"

"Well, Sir, I mean, Ma'am, like I was sayin', I don't know you knew, but we all been kinda doin' our own —"

"Which stops to-*day!*" Pat pulled a folded piece of paper from her breast pocket, made a show of unfolding it. It was a list Cho had drawn up for her of every man on the security detail and their MOS. "PFC Ormond, front and center."

Ormond was a short, squat kid, who apparently didn't know what "front and center" meant until one of his neighbors whispered clarifying instructions in his ear.

"Ormond, my information is that you flunked out of cook's school which I didn't think was possible. Well, chubs, the Army's going to give you another shot at it. As of now, you are the camp cook," which not only puzzled Ormond but was not news greeted warmly by the rest of the men.

Ormond blinked a few times, trying to make sense of what he'd heard. "Sir? I mean, Ma'am? I don't get it. You said it; I flunked out of —"

"Take that half a brain cell you have and start looking up Rachel Ray videos, because when it comes to the kitchen, you are *The Man* as of today. Each day, you will pick from otherwise unassigned personnel one person to be your cook's assistant, somebody to peel the potatoes and boil the water for you. Try not to poison us. Back in line.

"Only exceptions to the meal schedule will be night duty personnel. You will all be restricted to two beers per day except on Sunday, one snack per day —" this time it only took a pause and a cold look to stifle the groans "— and it'll stay that way until those asses and flapping guts get flat! And from what I can see, that may take some time."

"Oh-eight-thirty: barracks inspection.

"Oh-nine-hundred: duties as assigned.

"Delaney, front and center!"

Pritchard's EW partner could've been his twin: same washed-out pallor, puffy eyes, and a general attitude of exhaustion. "I want you and your EW colleague and —when he has time — Mister Cho, to go over the roster, see which two of these boneheads you think is less dense than the others, and train them to be honorary EW specialists. I want to get you men down to eight-hour shifts and a rotation of three shifts one on and two off. Can do?"

Delaney may have been the only man that morning from whom she got a smile: "Yes, Ma'am!"

"Back in line. Willis!"

He was a wiry, good-looking Black kid, didn't look old enough to drive let alone be in the Army. And, seeing at how things had been going thus far that morning, he was also properly terrified of her. "Y-yes, Ma-Ma'am."

Poor kid's practically shaking, and she tried not to smile.

"My information is that you were on your way to being a Weapons Specialist until you shot the toe off a range instructor. I'd like to think that was an accident."

Willis gulped. "Yes, Ma'am, it was. An accident, I mean."

"We're going to make you a brevet Weapons Specialist."

"A what, Ma'am?"

"Look it up. After parade, take all otherwise unassigned personnel. You and your team will field strip all weapons on the post, clean them, and after they've been re-assembled, take them where you can safely — and I'm emphasizing *safely* — test fire them. You will provide Mister Cho with a weapons status report by end of day. Back in line.

"Elmonte!"

The LZ stone-painter shuffled forward after one of his mates prompted him that that's why his name was called.

"I was so impressed with the job you did sprucing up my LZ that it'd be a shame to let your artistic ability go to waste. You are to create signage for each structure on this post indicating its function."

Elmonte frowned; apparently the vocabulary was going over his head.

Pat tried again: "I want a sign on every building saying what it is."

"Oh, yeah, ok, I can do that. Ma'am." He actually seemed quite happy with the assignment.

"Sergeant Jinski's men can help you with materials. I want that task completed within the week. And Elmonte: spell check those signs before you mount them."

"I can spell pretty good, Major.

Pat leaned forward a bit for emphasis: "Elmonte, if there's one letter out of place, one missing period, you will get such an ass-reaming you'll be able to shit boxcars."

Elmonte out-gulped Willis. "I'll make sure they're checked out, Ma'am."

"From now on, you limp-dicks are going to look and act like the soldiers you're supposed to be and perform your security duties in the way God and the Pentagon intended! Honors will be rendered properly to all superiors. If you've forgotten when, how, and to whom you're supposed to salute, Google it.

"You will begin your workday properly groomed; that means hair regulation length and clean-shaven. You will be uniformed in your BDUs. Those uniforms will start the day clean, pressed, *intact*, and complete, meaning cap and Military Police brassard." She saw a few confused faces over the word "brassard." "Your MP armbands, morons!

"You will wear your radiation dosimeter badges at all times, and 'at all times' means *at all times*. In bed, on the crapper, in the shower; you wear your hot badges at all times!

"All duty personnel will wear sidearms.

"When you are off duty, you will confine your recreational activities to the mess hall, the barracks, and the area around the LZ. The days of this post looking like Weekend at Party Beach are over!

"You are a security detail, so starting tomorrow, you will be securing. There will, at all times, be two armed sentries walking the perimeter. There will be a two-man Humvee patrol during daylight hours on a circuit one click out."

Pat moved over to Jinski and his men. "Engineers. Sergeant Jinski is in charge of your detail. When it comes to all operations relevant to your detail — the administration, planning, oversight and execution of said operations — you report to him. But on all policies and circumstances affecting this post as a whole, Sergeant Jinski is subordinate to me. Do you understand?"

"Yes, Ma'am," Jinski boomed. When he realized his was the only responding voice, he whipped around to his men: "The major wants to know if you deadheads understand!" which finally brought a chorus of cowed, "Yes, Ma'ams".

And now Pat could see it hadn't been a smirk. It had been a smile. Pat moved close to Jinski; spoke low so only he could hear: "Outstanding." She now knew that, along with Cho, she had a partner in what she had to do.

She stepped back. "Sergeant, I have two tasks for your team. I presume that to be our supply hut," and she pointed to the large, windowless Quonset. "By its size and our small number, I'm assuming there's a fair bit of empty space therein. I'm going to requisition some

PT equipment. When it arrives, you are to create something like a gym area. Can do?"

Which brought an enthusiastic, "Can do, Ma'am!"

"More immediately: I also want you to use some of that space to construct a stockade."

"Excuse me, Ma'am, a stockade?"

"In common parlance, a *jail*," and now she made sure when she spoke, it wasn't just to Jinski but to the entire rank. "Two cells, eight by ten, nothing in them but a cot and a bucket. And I want them up within a week."

She began to walk along the line of men, fixing them with her gold-shielded eyes: "I sense some skepticism in you dickless wonders, that some of you think I'm up here blowing off because I'm just that much in love with the sound of my own voice, that I'm all show! Well, ladies, if that's what you think: *try me!* Challenge me, test me, see how far you can bend the law of God. If you think life on this post has been a grind to date, get on my shit list and see how much worse it can be. You'll be christening our new stockade by staring at four blank walls for ten days with nothing to eat but MREs and nothing to do but count your toes. Fuck with me a second time and I'll FedEx your ass to Leavenworth. You can finish your hitch there with some bonus years thrown on before you're busted out on a Dishonorable.

"Ladies, for your sakes, I do hope we understand each other." She allowed a dramatic pause to let it all sink in, then, "Questions."

One tentative hand came up. "PFC Herrera, Ma'am. What about Loomis?"

She'd been waiting for that one. Cho had given her the impression there was no love lost between Loomis and any other human being on the planet, but it didn't mean his unexplained disappearance so soon after Bruckner's badly explained death wasn't unsettling. "Nellis has been informed and is carrying out an aerial drone search. We should hear something today. When I get the news, you'll get the news. Anything else?" *One, two, three.* "In that case…

"People, you are Military Police in the United States Army assigned to provide security for a Defense Department installation. By God, I'll see you look and act like it or you're going to wind up with my boot so far up your ass it'll knock your cover off! Mister Cho, Sergeant Jinski, dismiss your men."

As Cho and Jinski did so, Pat could overhear – and expected she was supposed to – the predictable grumbles: "What the fuck is this?...Oh, man, we are *so* screwed!...I didn't sign up for this kinda Mickey Mouse bullshit...Who's she think she is? Patton?...Who's Patton?"

"Major, with your permission?" It was Jinski, presenting himself at textbook attention with an equally textbook salute.

Pat returned the salute. "You have something to say, Sergeant, shoot."

"Ma'am, I joined the Army because I wanted to be in the Army. Thanks for bringing the Army back to me."

Then he saluted, again, and went after his men: "Ok, you limp-dicks, yer gonna have to 'member what you been gettin' paid for!"

As she watched Jinski lumber away, Pat turned to Cho: "What's the story on that guy, Cho? He seems to be a few more steps up the evolutionary ladder over the rest of these blobs. Present company excluded."

"Thank you, Ma'am. Well, the story I heard, his second deployment was to Iraq. He had a second rocker back then. He was heading up some kind of work detail, digging gun emplacements, I think. You heard what The Sandbox was like; as bad as this if not worse. He kept giving his men breaks because of the heat. His CO caught them more than once, started giving the sergeant grief: 'We're behind schedule, why is it every time I look over here your people are goofing off'…you know."

"I get it."

"Jinski tells him he's not going to send a man to the hospital with heat stroke because they're running a little behind digging holes."

"And his CO didn't take that well."

"The CO tells him – and this is how I heard it, Ma'am, so pardon the language – 'I know how *you people* are' —"

Pat winced. "'You people'?"

"It gets worse, Ma'am. 'I know how you people are, but you get your lazy Black ass back to work."

"Oh my."

"Well, Jinski being Jinski…"

"And being the self-appointed resident badass he is…"

"I don't think he actually hit the officer, but the end result was they knocked him down a rank, sent him home, and had him in charge of details building latrines until this duty came up."

She looked over to where Jinski was already haranguing his men: "You pinheads embarrass me on parade like that again, you're gonna be sorry your mommas ever met your poppas!"

"I'll be sure to watch my language around the man."

"I'd do that, Ma'am."

Pat had Cho tour her around the compound, dictating notes to the XO for littered areas to be policed, building repairs Jinski's group would need to tend to, and the like.

As they ticked off each building — the motor pool workshop, storage hut, and down the list — Pat had a thought. "Mister Cho, I notice there's nothing like an infirmary, we have no doctor, not even a medic, no medical facilities of any kind."

"Yes, Ma'am. That was a concern of Lieutenant Bruckner's as well. He put in a request to the colonel."

"And yet we still don't have a medic or anything else."

"Lieutenant Bruckner said the colonel told him —"

"It was redundant and unnecessary?"

"Something like that. The colonel expressed the view that in an emergency, the lab had facilities, and in a worse-case scenario, Nellis could always medevac someone out."

The list of things she would have to discuss with McElhone, Pat noted, was growing longer and longer.

"Um…"

"Oh, God, Cho, another one of those ums?"

"Am I entitled to an opinion, Ma'am?"

"You're my XO. I always want to hear your opinions even while I reserve the right to completely dismiss them."

"Fair enough, Ma'am," Cho said with a smile. Then, seriously: "I agree with everything you're trying to do, it's long overdue, and with all due respect to the man, Lieutenant Bruckner should've taken a firmer hand early on. That said, it seems to me like you're serving up a lot for these guys to digest all at once. You know; after the way things have been. Like going cold turkey."

Pat nodded; she didn't disagree. "I don't have time to get these men to love me, Cho. Fear of pissing me off is the only shortcut I have."

Cho looked puzzled. "You don't have time? Ma'am, again, with all due respect, out here you're going to have copious amounts of time."

"Mister Cho, this command has lost two men in three days and no good explanation for either of them. I am not going to lose a third." She heard her name called and they both turned to see Pritchard running toward them, waving a piece of paper. "Maybe now at least we find out about one of them." Then Pritchard was in front of them. The morning was already hot enough that the short run from the EW trailer had the specialist sheathed in sweat. "Word from Nellis?" Pat asked. "Good or bad?"

Pritchard shook his head, at a loss. "Just weird. When Del – Delaney – came in for the handoff, I did as you ordered: I contacted Nellis, told them we'd be making hourly radio check-ins. I thought as long as we were in contact, I'd ask if there was any update on the search for Loomis. This is what I got," and he handed the piece of paper – a message form – to Pat.

Pritchard had obviously written it in haste, but had managed to keep it legible if barely:

AERIAL SEARCH REQUEST CANCELLED 0147 HOURS
BY ORDER MILITARY COMMANDER YOUR POST
RECOMMEND YOU CONFER END MESSAGE

Pat handed the message to Cho as she turned back to Pritchard. "This cancellation order, it didn't go through you?"

"No, Ma'am. The lab detail must have their own direct pipeline."

"'Recommend you confer,'" Cho read. "They know we weren't informed."

"Who knows about this?" Pat asked Pritchard.

"Just Delaney and me."

"Keep it to yourselves. Not word one to anyone, understand?"

It was clear Pritchard didn't, but he gave Pat a "Yes, Ma'am," and she dismissed him.

"See the time on that cancellation?" she said to Cho. "The colonel must've cancelled our search request almost as soon as he heard about it."

"Why would he do that? Unless he knows what happened to Loomis."

Pat looked up the valley in the direction of the lab compound, which was obscured from view by her own camp's buildings. "The cancellation order didn't go through us, they didn't CC us on it which means we weren't supposed to know about this. If Pritchard hadn't checked in, God knows when we would've found out."

"Ma'am, I know the colonel is a friend of yours…"

"But?"

"But none of this makes any sense!"

"No, although it's all got a consistent uncomfortable vibe to it. Cho, pull out one of the Humvees. I'll meet you at the gate."

Cho didn't ask where they were going. He already knew. "It's not going to do any good, Ma'am."

SPOOR

It was only a short ride up the valley to the lab compound, but there was nothing resembling a road connecting the two posts. Between rocks, ancient water cuts, and soft spots of deep sand, it was like riding a roller coaster on a bucking bronco. Even with the Humvee's AC unit at full, behind the armor and bullet-resistant glass Pat and Cho were sweating by the time Cho pulled them up to the front gate.

"No sentries," Pat noted.

"They don't need them," Cho said and pointed to a CCTV camera mounted on a fifteen-foot mast inside the perimeter fence. All along the fence were warning signs:

DANGER HIGH VOLTAGE

AUTHORIZED PERSONNEL ONLY

LETHAL FORCE IN EFFECT

"How does this work?" Pat asked.

Cho pointed to a speaker box mounted on one of the gate posts. "If you don't mind, Major, I'd prefer to stay here. I find this place...discomposing."

As Pat climbed out of the Humvee, she understood Cho's feeling — provided she was guessing correctly at the crossword's meaning. Nothing moved inside the perimeter except for the camera on its gimbal mount tracking Pat. There wasn't much to look at, just the blockhouse and its cupola, each featureless except for a single heavy metal door, and the blockhouse loading dock. The warning signs were mounted on ten-foot-high, electrified chain link. Along the top of the fence were twin spirals of concertina wire, and noting the insulators along the fence poles, she could see those twists were also running hot.

They must be running a hell of a lot of juice through that thing; she could hear a hum radiating from the fence from five yards away.

Wait a second…

One coil of razor wire was hung on arms extending over the interior of the compound, the other coil extending outward. *That's what you do to keep people out…but also to keep people* in.

And nothing was going to move around that compound without getting seen. There were a dozen tall poles in a rough circle around the blockhouse carrying floodlights which looked capable of covering the grounds between the building and the fence. *But nothing aimed at the area outside the fence.*

All of it, to Pat, seemed designed less out of a concern for intruders than for… than for what?

As she walked up to the gate, something tickled her eye, at the corner of her vision… A movement far off.

Several hundred yards up the valley, on the far bank: large-winged birds floating in lazy circles over a spot up near the valley rim. Even as far off as they were, Pat didn't need a close look to know what they were: turkey vultures.

Christ, don't let it be…

The CCTV camera, controlled from inside the lab, angled down, fixed on Pat as the speaker box crackled to life: "Halt and identify yourself and your purpose."

"Major Patricia Simons, commanding officer of the security post. I would like to speak with your CO to coordinate our activities regarding a missing man."

Silence.

They're checking my bona fides.

Then, "You are not authorized for entry to this installation. Please return to your vehicle and exit the area."

She looked back at Cho, who gave her a see-what-I-mean look. Turning back to the speaker, she said, "I'm here to speak with Colonel McElhone."

"You are not authorized for entry. Return to your vehicle and exit the area."

Hm, no "please" this time.

"Inform Colonel McElhone that I need to speak with him."

The voice now sounded more emphatic: "Your communication will be relayed. Now return to your vehicle and exit the area immediately or you will be returned to your post under armed escort."

Pat took another look at the grim halo of vultures further up the valley, then went back to the Humvee.

"Inflexible and adamantine, eh, Ma'am?" Cho said. He didn't seem surprised.

"They did not leave much room for discussion," Pat said.

Cho kicked over the engine and started to reverse away from the lab gates.

"Not back to the post," Pat said and pointed to the circling vultures.

"Oh, God, you don't think —"

"I'm trying not to. Can you get us up there?"

"The commercials say this thing can go anywhere."

"Let's see how much truth there is in advertising. Giddyap, Mister Cho."

The shallow slope of the valley wall wasn't much of an uphill challenge to the Humvee, but its rutted, rocky face offered an even rougher teeth-jarring, bone-rattling ride than the one between the two compounds. Pat could see several vultures in a cluster about ten yards below the valley rim, heads bowed out of sight, looking like black-clad priests huddled in prayer. As the Humvee drew close, the noise of its growling engine in low gear working to haul the vehicle to the crest was enough to chase them back into the air. As the Humvee bounced past, Pat caught a glimpse of some kind of carcass at the center of an ugly corona of blood and body matter.

"I don't think it's him," Pat said.

"That's good, isn't it?"

Pat shook her head, unsure since that still left open the question of what had happened to Loomis. She directed Cho to park atop the rim above the carcass.

They climbed out of the Humvee, stood at the rim looking down at the carcass, a bloody lump maybe four feet long which, from that distance, didn't look like much of anything. A smell wafted up to them. Not rot, Pat knew, but the gut-wrenching smell of a recent kill, the stink of organs torn open mixed with the coppery taste/smell of blood.

And there was the buzzing sound — a murmured hymn of the vultures' curates. The cloud of feasting flies was less susceptible to being distracted from their ministrations by human presence and machines than their cold-eyed betters.

Pat looked around for Cho, but her XO was by the Humvee, holding himself up, on the verge of retching.

Pat pulled out her handkerchief, tied it around her face to cover her nose and mouth, and carefully slid down the loose sand and earth to the carcass.

"What is it?" Cho called down, weakly.

"I'm not sure." The handkerchief wasn't very effective in straining out the smell, which only grew stronger as Pat got closer. She blinked against the flies throwing themselves at her face, sensing a possible fresh meal.

The carcass was so mangled trying to figure out what it was was like mentally piecing together a puzzle: the head – just a skull clad only in a few strips of flesh, its eyes long since plucked out by the birds – was separated from the torso by a few feet, and two of the four legs were missing.

But the skull was more or less canine. She considered the skull, the size of the other remains: *coyote.*

But the body… *Jeeeesus…*

The body lay on its right side. There was nothing remaining on the left. Skin, flesh, everything was gone, even the left side of the rib cage was gone, and the interior…empty. Not just gutted, but cleaned out, as if scooped clear.

"Did the birds do that?" Cho called down.

Pat backed away from the carcass. "No. I've never seen anything like this. See if you can find some tracks."

"What kind of tracks?"

"Anything. This is recent, last night. There might still be tracks."

Pat turned to her own search on the slope. Not far from the carcass she found a three-inch length of completely denuded bone. By its curve, she guessed it was from the missing part of the coyote's rib cage. She felt the two ends of the fragment: one end was rough, jagged, the other glassy smooth.

"I've got a track, Major!" Cho called. "Bunch of them."

Pat scrambled back up the slope. Cho was standing a few feet from the rim pointing at something at his feet, then at a line extending into the desert where the night winds had half-erased them.

"What is that?" Cho asked. "Like, a bear?"

The configuration was similar to a dog or cat: four toes in an arc with another pad behind. The print was at least ten inches across. And deep.

"I'm not up on desert fauna, Mister Cho, but I'm pretty sure bears don't live in the desert."

"There's those cats, though, right? What do you call them, pumas? Mountain lions? We have mountains; could one of them have maybe come down here?" Cho was pointing to the jagged crests along the western horizon; the tops of the Shoshones easily more than 20 miles away.

"They wouldn't come down this far," Pat said, "not even close. Besides, this is two, possibly three times as big a print as a cat like that would leave. And whatever it was, weighs at least twice as much. Going by the depth of these impressions, I'd guess three hundred, maybe four hundred pounds."

"Then that's a bear, right?"

"You need to watch more Discovery Channel. Again: desert, no bears." Pat walked up and down the line of tracks, reaching back to all those times hunting and camping with her father and grandfather, hiking in woodlands, high country, and grasslands. They had taught her, even when they weren't hunting, how to read sign, giving her a near-encyclopedic data bank of paw prints, hoof prints, and claw marks. But none of those memories helped put together what she was seeing in any way that made sense.

"A wolf? Maybe a wolf?"

"Wolves don't do deserts either."

Pat kept looking up and down the path of the tracks, waiting for some answering epiphany that never came. "Prints like these, these kinds of pads, the tracks belong to a four-footed animal." She continued before Cho could re-nominate his favorite candidate, "Not a bear. Even if we had a desert-loving bear, it would show five toes and claws, and a large pad. This is more like something related to cats or dogs. Except…"

"Except…"

"Except these are too big and too heavy for anything like that that I can think of. The other thing is — and this is where it *really* doesn't make sense —

"I already don't think it was making much sense."

"The only animals I know that could leave anything resembling prints like these are four legged. But these prints track like something running on two legs. Don't ask me what that could possibly be because damned if I know." She held out the piece of rib bone to Cho. "Feel the ends."

Cho made a face. "Is it icky?"

Pat tried not to laugh. "Your crossword puzzles couldn't give you something better than 'icky'? No, it's not icky. It's bone dry. No pun intended."

Cho reluctantly took the bone, relaxing when he found it wasn't "icky." Then he ran a finger over one end — "It's rough."

"That was snapped off from the rib cage."

"This other end, though; it's smooth, like glass."

"Like it'd been cut through with a really sharp blade in one slice." Pat took the bone back and dropped it in her breast pocket. She followed the tracks back to the valley rim and looked down at what was left of the mangled coyote. Some of the vultures had already felt safe enough to re-plant themselves around the corpse and pick at what little there was to pick at.

"Cho, what do we have in the armory?"

"We lost two pistols with Lieutenant Bruckner and Loomis, but we still have Sig .45s for everybody in the security detail. Then there's ten M4s carbines, and four Mossberg shotguns. There's also an M240 mounted on a gun ring on one of the Humvees."

"When we get back, see that one of the M4 and one of the shotguns is placed in the barracks, and another pair in your quarters where you and Jinski can get at them. Post a memo: off-duty personnel should always have at least one weapon in their party. And the sentries on night duty should walk their posts *inside* the perimeter fence. Instead of hourly check-ins, I want them every 15 minutes."

"You're really concerned about this."

"Aren't you?"

"I am now."

"You look like you're ready with another 'um'."

Cho nodded down at the coyote remains. "Do you think this means, well, I'm thinking about Loomis —"

"Private Loomis is alive until I know for a fact otherwise, so let's keep a good thought."

"Yes, Ma'am," although it was clear that Cho – like Pat – thought that was a pointless exercise.

I know, Cho, but this is the kind of thing I'm supposed to say as a commanding officer, even though you're right. If Loomis bumped into whatever tore that coyote apart…

Pat stepped away from the rim and looked out across the desert. It wasn't as featureless as it had looked from the Black Hawk. Dead, yes, but still… Here and there, low jagged ridges, like icebergs poking through a calm sea. The sun-beaten ground was dotted with anemic looking scrub, cholla, barrelhead cactus, prickly pear, and mesquite. Joshua trees, with their outstretched arms, appeared to be begging for water — like everything else out on that hard-baked ground.

"These field operations the lab detail runs; where do they do that?"

Cho made a vague gesture toward the flatlands on either side of the valley. "No one place. Every place. It's always different."

"The night Lieutenant Bruckner died."

Cho's waving arm, still vague, aimed westward. "Somewhere out there. But that's a lot of ground out there, Ma'am."

"You said Bruckner had night vision goggles with him? The effective range on those is maybe 400-500 meters. Anything past that you pick up is luck and circumstance. So, if they were trying to keep a blanket over whatever they were doing..."

"It'd probably be more than 500 meters out. Still, Major..." and Cho again waved his arm at the expanse of desert.

Pat beckoned Cho back toward the Humvee. "Head over toward the lab. My guess is they would've driven straight up the slope from the lab compound. We might be able to pick up tread marks."

"Ma'am, that was two nights ago. The winds —"

Pat rapped on the fender of the Humvee. "Mister Cho, this vehicular marvel weighs two and a half tons empty, and I guarantee you, they didn't drive out there empty. We should find something."

"Giddyap, Ma'am?"

"You called it right, Mister Cho."

They did find a spot along the top of the valley wall above the lab compound where heavy tires had broken through the crust of the rim. There were tracks – of several vehicles it looked like – heading due west. The tread prints were intermittent, erased here and there by the winds over the last two nights, leaving a track like a stone skipping over water.

But they held a straight course west, and Cho, rolling the Humvee at barely ten miles an hour with his eyes out his side window, was able to coast past the gaps and pick them up again.

"What're you doing here, Mister Cho?" It was a question which had been nagging at Pat since Cho had given her the story behind Jinski's exiling to the desert post.

"As ordered, Ma'am, I'm driving my commanding officer around the great American wasteland."

Smartass, but she grinned as she thought it. "You know what I mean."

Cho sighed; it was obviously a recounting he knew he wouldn't enjoy. "You know Fort Jackson? In South Carolina?"

"Sure. Half the Army does their basic there."

"I was with one of the tenant units, the 34th Infantry, on the headquarters staff. I was maybe one, two months away from getting my silver bars."

"Ahh, a butter bar, eh?"

"That was me: Second Lieutenant Kim Cho, counting the days to becoming a grown-up. Ever been to Fort Jackson, Ma'am? It's right up against Columbia, the state capital. Should you be unfortunate enough to raise the topic of the Civil War — Excuse me," and here he affected a cartoonish southern accent, " — the Woah Between the States, they'll be shoah to tell y'all South Car'linah was the fust state to secede from the oppression of the Union." Another sigh. "And they'll say it like it's a bragging right."

"The local Klan would occasionally like to make their presence known with a display at the capitol building. You got the complete soup-to-nuts presentment: robes, hoods, Confederate flags, chants about keeping the country white, keeping it Christian, and so on and so forth, right there on the steps of the state capitol.

"I was in town on a pass, the boys in white were putting on one of their productions. For someone from Hawaii with little experience with this particular sociological phenomenon, I was curious and went for a look. I must say it was quite a show." Cho was quiet for a bit, shaking his head over the memory, looking as if he still couldn't believe how it had played out.

"Did you know," he went on, "even with a hood on, there are some people you can still recognize? Their voice is distinctive enough, or maybe it's the way they walk. What helps is they're too cerebrally challenged to have remembered to change out of their government issue fatigues and boots, and you see that Army gear peeping out from under their robe."

"You recognized somebody from the command."

Cho made a noise, a short "huh" like a laugh but humorless. "Someone from one of our training platoons."

"You reported this."

"To the recruit's training company CO. The captain maintained that what one of his boots did on his own time was his own business."

"You think the CO was a member?"

That mirthless "huh" turned into an equally mirthless grin. "I prefer to give him the benefit of the doubt and think of him as just sympathetic to their socio-political stances. So, I went to his battalion commander."

Oh-oh, I see what's coming.

"When I presented the issue to the battalion CO and it appeared he, too, lacked any enthusiasm for pursuing the matter, I took what I considered to be the reasonable position that if he felt addressing the issue was not within his province of responsibilities, perhaps I should take the issue to the base commander, or possibly the Inspector General."

"Which he took as a threat, particularly that part about the IG. Was it?"

"Actually, no, I just thought those would be the next logical steps and presented them as such."

"But he didn't see it that way."

"Apparently and evidently. So, the captain was, ah, 'motivated' to transfer out, the recruit was flunked out of basic, and suddenly and mysteriously, my evals started to slide."

"What a shock."

"My evaluations, which had been positive up to that point, began to describe me as insubordinate, uncooperative, not a team player, detrimental to the morale of the command, ineffective…"

"I get the picture."

"Farewell silver bars, greetings demotion. And eventually…" Cho gestured at the desert rolling out in front of them.

"For what it's worth, Cho, I think you did the right thing."

Cho sighed yet again. "There are times I'm not so sure."

"Like now."

"Like —. Ma'am, do you see it?" Cho braked the Humvee to a stop.

They climbed out of the Humvee. Pat guessed they were a bit more than a half mile from the valley. It had been over 80 degrees inside the vehicle, even with the AC running full, yet the heat outside was so much greater, stepping into it felt almost like stepping into a semi-solid.

The tread marks had split, multiple vehicles veering left, multiples turning right. Pat followed the rightward treads while Cho followed the others.

The heavy Humvee treads were one thing, but boot prints were another matter, and Pat didn't expect to find any after two nights. She followed the tire tracks for maybe twenty yards before they stopped, the depth indicating this was where they had parked. She looked over at

Cho, saw him halted about the same distance from the turnoff in the other direction.

"What're we looking for?" Cho called over to her.

"Anything." She started moving out from the tracks, eyes on the ground as she slowly zig-zagged, then…

Something glittering up from the sands. Then others. Dozens of them. More. Like bits of gold scattered along the ground.

Only it wasn't gold. It was brass.

She picked one of the shiny bits from the sand: an ejected shell casing. They were all shell casings, several magazines' worth, she guessed. She whistled to Cho and held the casing up where it caught the sun, shining almost painfully bright. "Five-five-six. Our people. A lot of them out here," and she waved her hand at the ground around her.

"Here, too!" Cho called back, and then, "Oh, wow!"

Pat dropped the rifle shell in her breast pocket with the coyote bone and started toward Cho. "What've you got?"

"Somebody was using a 'blooper'." Cho picked something up from the ground about the size of a small soup can. He tossed it to Pat.

It was the casing from a 40 mm rifle grenade.

"I told you sometimes we heard more than small arms fire," Cho said.

They stood together by their Humvee, looking at where the tire tracks in the desert had fanned out, at the shell casings sprinkled along the ground, and then at the 40 mm shell Pat kept turning round in her hand.

"Tell me, Mister Cho, have your crossword puzzles provided you with an appropriate description for all this?"

"Bafflement, mystification, perplexity. I've got others."

Pat nodded. "Well, Cho, I don't do crosswords. What comes to my mind is that in all the years I've been in uniform, I've never seen anything as off-the-rails, fucked-up-nuts as this...and I include time I served in a combat zone."

At the head of Pat's desk, she had set down the .556 shell casing, the .40 mm casing, and the fragment of coyote bone. Fanned out across the center of her desk, where Cho had left them, were the 201 files for all the men in the command: the 12 men in her security detail (less Loomis), the four engineers including Jinski, and Cho. Her eyes kept shifting from the three items at the head of her desk to the closed files and back again.

Through her open office door, she could hear Cho at his desk with Pritchard discussing possible candidates for EW training.

"How about this guy?"

"Sir, he's a nice guy, but he couldn't find his own ass with a map and a compass."

Pat poured herself a glass of ice water from the pitcher on her desk, ran the moisture-sweating glass across her forehead. Looking down at those files, at the artifacts on her desk, somehow the air conditioning in the Admin Quonset wasn't doing its job.

"Unless you want to keep working 12-hour shifts, we have to find *somebody*. What about *this* guy?"

"Hey, nobody wants off this 12-hour merry-go-round more than me and Del, Mister Cho, but this guy here? Christ, I saw him reading comic books the other day. He was reading comic books and asking me what it meant when Wolverine called the bad guy his 'nemesis'. I don't know if that's who the taxpayers want sitting in that trailer."

Pat poked at the folders, moving them around pointlessly with a finger, reluctant to open them because she was fairly sure all she'd find was confirmation of what she already suspected.

She flipped open a file at random.

Sanborn, R. L.

She went right to the form with the box listing "Next of Kin" and felt an unpleasant ripple in her gut when she saw what she knew she'd find: "None."

And then she was flipping through the files quickly, turning to the same page in each file:

Elmonte, C. T. Next of Kin: None.

Pritchard, D. J. Next of Kin: None.

Delaney, M. C. Next of Kin: None.

With each "None," the sound of Cho and Pritchard panning for mental gold among the troop faded. That's also why she didn't hear a Humvee pull up outside.

Willis, T. R. Next of Kin: None.

Gagnon, A. M. Next of Kin: None.

Goldman, E. J. Next of Kin: None.

She skipped to the last files in the fan, trying to keep a tight rein on a sense of desperation:

Drivas, A. K. Next of Kin: None.

Ormond, L. S. Next of Kin: None.

Brandisi, V. D. Next of Kin: None.

What cut through her narrowed focus was Cho barking out, "Ten-HUT!", the sound of Cho and Pritchard scrambling to their feet, then McElhone's, "As you were." Followed a moment later by a gruff, "Go for some air, both of you."

She heard the front door open, then close.

Pat scooped the 201s into a pile, turned them over hiding the name tabs.

Then McElhone was in her office doorway. She started to stand at attention, but he waved her back to her seat. He looked up and down the short corridor to make sure no one else was in the building but stayed in the doorway for a long moment. She saw his eyes settle on the shell casings and bone fragment on her desk, then his shoulders heaved in a silent sigh, as if he was resigning himself to an unpleasant task. He closed the office door behind him and took one of the two chairs in front of her desk.

Whatever this is about, it's not going to be good.

"You wouldn't happen to have a drink in this place?" McElhone asked.

Pat forced a smile and pointed at the pitcher on her desk. "Just water. But it is cold."

McElhone flashed the pitcher a sour look. He was red-faced which Pat presumed was from the short ride down from the lab, but there was also a fatigued sag to the man which had nothing to do with the heat; it dragged at his face, at his shoulders, slumping him slightly in the chair. His eyes were red and puffy.

Looks like I'm not the only one having trouble sleeping nights.

He threw his right foot across his left knee, slipped off his cap and hung it from the toe of his boot. His eyes flicked to the stack of files on Pat's desk, and she knew – not guessed, not assumed, but *knew* – McElhone knew what they were. Then he looked at the shell casings and bone fragment, again, but she couldn't get a read on how they were registering other than as a source of some kind of unhappiness. He ran a hand over his bristly pate and seemed to settle himself into what he had to do. "You left a message at the lab this morning that you wanted to talk to me."

"Yes, Sir, thank you for coming —"

"What did you want to talk to me about?" There was a flat, exhausted tone to his voice.

"It's, um, hard, Colonel, there's so much, well, I'm not sure I even know where to start because there's —"

"Start with your missing man."

"Well, yes, ok. You cancelled the drone search without informing me —"

"What does that have to do with why you were poking around out on the flats?"

How the hell did he —

"Yes, everything your surveillance gear picks up is fed to us."

"I've been trying to find out what happened to my man."

"Is that all? That's it?"

Is that all? Are you kidding me?

"Sir, the men in my detail, I've been going through their jackets, and I feel like I'm the commander of the Island of Misfit Toys. So many of them have been hit with at least one Article 15 you'd think it was standard issue along with their belt buckles and boots."

"We discussed your personnel yesterday."

Now it was pouring out of her: "I know, but, well, we don't have a medic, and that's unusual for a post isolated like this. We're supposed to be on the lookout for intrusions, but we don't have surveillance drones — also unusual for our mission. There's these field operations the lab detail carries out —"

"Enough," he said irritably although she wasn't sure it was directed at her as much as at the situation. "I get it; you have a shopping list."

"Sir, I understand there's things you can't tell me. My security clearance —"

"Was lost in Afghanistan," which he threw at her like a dart.

"I know that, Sir," she said contritely.

McElhone ran a hand over his face, and Pat noticed for the first time the colonel hadn't shaved that morning. He let out a long breath, studied an empty point on the wall behind her, seemed to be debating with himself about how to go forward. Then he sat up in his chair, erect, his face went hard.

"Pat, I threw you a lifeline with this assignment. If I hadn't, you'd still be sitting in your Pentagon dying room waiting for your next pass-over and a shove out the door. And then what? Maybe you get to head up security for an office building? A high school? Maybe sell used cars?"

"Sir, I appreciate what you did —"

"Then show it."

"I'm trying, Colonel, by trying to do the best job I can. I just can't figure out what that job is."

For the briefest second, Pat thought she saw sympathy on the colonel's face, but then, as if a belated reminder came to him, his face went hard, again, as he got to his feet. "Well, Major —"

She winced as "Pat" was replaced with "Major".

"— let me offer you some clarification. Your job is to make sure nobody stumbles into this area. Simple. Simpler: You use the tools and personnel you've been assigned because that's what you've been assigned. Period. Beyond that, you're in the Army long enough to know that *any* assignment is carried out under the guiding principle of the military: that there are times when you are given an order, you snap to attention, say 'Yessir' and salute, shut your mouth, keep your questions to yourself, and *do what you're fucking told!*"

Pat felt her face flush, her eyes lost on the top of her desk.

"Is that clarification enough for you, Major?"

"Yessir," she mumbled.

"And if you're unhappy with those conditions, I can have a bird here tomorrow morning to take you back to Nellis and you'll be in your little Pentagon crypt by tomorrow night to finish what I can guarantee you will be your highly abbreviated career. Do you want me to make that call?" There it was — the tic — the tip of the head, the raised eyebrows.

Another mumble: "No, Sir."

"Good." He took the shell casings and bone fragment, dropped them in his breast pocket, then put his cap back on, and turned for the door. Pat started to get to attention, but McElhone held out a freezing hand: "Don't get up."

"Sir?" After the colonel's chastisement, she didn't want to ask, but had to: "What do I tell the men about Loomis? I have to tell them something."

The anger was gone from him, now, spent, and there was something in its place. Regret? "Then tell them something," he said tiredly as he headed out the door. "Make it good." He hesitated in the doorway, as he had when he'd arrived, as if there was something else he wanted to say, something to take the harsh edges off having read her the riot act. But then – and she was sorry to see this – he persuaded himself to just turn and leave.

Cho must've seen the colonel's exit because a few minutes later he was hanging in Pat's doorway. She didn't look up from her desk, didn't want him to see the humbled look on her face.

"You ok, Major? Can I get you anything?"

Pat barely managed a shake of her head. She pointed to the pile of 201 files. "You can put those away."

"Ma'am, is there anything I should know?"

Pat looked at the empty desk space where the shell casings and bone fragment had sat. "Unless you want another demotion, Mister Cho, forget everything we saw today."

BREACH

At the next day's assembly, Pat told the men Loomis had violated security protocols and was being detained by the lab detail. She could tell by Cho's face that he wasn't buying that story, and Jinski didn't seem sold on it either, but considering how much Loomis had been universally and deeply disliked, it seemed credible enough for the rest of the detail.

"'Security breach' my ass. That jag-off was goin' over the hill."

"Well, yeah, if anybody was gonna be a big enough prick to try it, it was gonna be him."

That first day's PT session, she knew enough not to push them too hard under the desert sun; a couple of jogging laps around the perimeter, but even that seemed too much for some. Even Jinski labored, but kept up, driven more by sheer will than muscle, haranguing his engineers the whole way: "C'mon, you candy-asses, you gonna let these pansy M-fuckin'-Ps show us up?" When one of his men started to falter, Jinski grabbed him by the collar and gym shorts, and frog-walked him until the man got his feet back under him again.

Pat's MPs weren't in any better shape. She shamed them into keeping up, jogging alongside them backwards as they wheezed and grunted: "You ladies gonna let this little *girl* grind you down? *Shag ass!"*

But day by day, their stamina got better, they slimmed down, and it only took a few drill sessions to bring back their basic training parade ground moves.

She was proud of how quickly they were coming along, she told them so, rewarded them by relaxing the beer ration.

Pritchard, Delaney, and Cho finally settled on two EW candidates ("No promises," Cho had told Pat, "but they seem moderately more humanoid than the rest of the crew") and the two EW specialists had begun a training regimen.

Jinski's engineers had the stockade cells up in just a few days: two windowless cubes of corrugated tin in an empty corner of the storage Quonset. Jinski took the men on a quick walk-through tour and one look at the cells seemed all the incentive the men needed to dispel any doubts their new CO wasn't all talk and to toe the lines Pat had set down for them.

With each passing day, the issue of Loomis became less of a topic of conversation, and any chatter that there had been, had been less than sympathetic – "I don't think they caught 'im, I think the dumb-fuck is dead out there on the flats 'n' that's what he gets for bein' a dumb-fuck."

But he hadn't passed from Pat's mind. And even though she'd never met him, she hadn't forgotten Lieutenant Bruckner, either.

Other than what her duties required of her, she kept to herself. She ate in her quarters and declined Cho's invitations to have a beer at the mess hut, as well as Jinski's offer of a pool match. She busied herself in her office and in her quarters with paperwork, working up duty rosters and the like. And late at night, finding herself unable to sleep, she'd climb out of her bunk, pour herself a shot of Jameson's, and even as she sipped at it, wondered if she was going down the same alcohol-lubricated route she suspected of McElhone.

She kept herself to one drink a night even though it in no way numbed her enough. She would run that conversation with McElhone over and again in her head, pained at the memory of how he'd cowed her, and the haunting thought would come to her each night:

I'm doing it _again!_

Cho would already be at his desk in the morning, wordlessly bring her a cup of coffee as she sat at her desk, and retreat back to the outer office. She felt bad about icing her XO out like that, but she was finding it hard to look any of her men in the eye.

It was her tenth morning on the post when Delaney showed up in her doorway with a message form in his hand.

"Please don't let it be bad news," Pat said, then was puzzled at the odd, silly grin on Delaney's face.

"Depends," the specialist said.

Pat nodded at him to go ahead.

Delaney made a show of standing erect, holding the message form out in front of him with two hands as if he was reading a royal declaration: "From Dr. Cordell, Lab 7, to Major Simons, security detail commander. The doctor requests permission to join the major for dinner some evening at the major's convenience. The doctor offers that he will do the cooking. The doctor has added an RSVP."

For the first time since McElhone had given her that painful reaming, Pat found herself laughing. "Take a message, Delaney. The major grants permission and expects her guest at 1800 hours tonight. Actually, you better make that 6:00 p.m.; Doctor Cordell has never mastered military time."

Delaney disappeared and Cho's head appeared in her doorway wearing the same silly grin Delaney had had.

Pat felt herself thawing. "Mister Cho!"

"Yes, Ma'am!"

"Fuck off!"

"Yes, *Ma'am!*" and he laughed his way back to his desk.

Pat answered the knock at her trailer door and found David Cordell standing at the foot of the fold-out stairs. In one hand, "flowers" composed of pieces of wire hangers for stems, and drooping toilet tissue petals blotchily colored by Magic Markers. In his other hand, a small Styrofoam picnic cooler.

"I'm assuming that was supposed to be some kind of bouquet?" Pat said.

David gave his "flowers" an I-know-they're-pathetic look. "Mariska Woltz made them for me. They looked fine until we tried coloring them in. The tissue paper didn't handle the Magic Marker ink too well. But it was a good thought?" This last asked hopefully.

She stood out of the doorway to let him in. "A good thought."

David stepped into the trailer and handed her the "bouquet." "At least you don't have to put them in water."

"I'm trying to figure out what I should put them in."

He solved the problem himself by taking them back and dropping them in the kitchen waste basket. "It's the thought that counts."

"Thankfully."

He looked around the small trailer. "Tidy. Comfy. Snug."

"Accommodations in the lab better?"

"Roomier, but about as homey as the *Führerbunker* during the last days of World War II." David noted that the curtains around the narrow windows had been pulled back. "Are we a show for the riffraff?"

"I'm already not setting a good example having my personal chef show up. I don't want them getting any other bad ideas. I mean, this is just an innocent dinner, right?"

He hung his head in mock dejection. "Well, yeah…*now.*"

They both laughed and the tension over what the night could have been — dissipated. The guidelines were set, policed by being on view to all passersby. Pat was relieved to see that good-natured acceptance seemed to have been mutually, if tacitly, agreed to.

"Cooking implements?" David asked.

Pat parked herself at the table at the end of the trailer. She waved at the small kitchen area. "Help yourself. What's on the menu?"

David started poking through the few cabinets, pulling out cheap dented pans and utensils with prongs and handles missing, frowning at each item. "Jeez, the Pentagon can blow $10,000 on a toilet seat cover, you'd figure they could pop a few more bucks for a little T-Fal cookware." He drew a piece of paper from his breast pocket and set it on the counter as he laid out his ingredients from the cooler. "I'm trying this for the first time. Frittata. I got the recipe from YouTube."

"Isn't that just an omelet?"

"Don't be a buzzkill. I'm making an effort here. Hey, this is as much a treat for me as it is for you. I've been eating out of cans and pouches for the last ten months. Even if this comes out like swill, it'll be an improvement. Mariska has been trying to teach me pinochle. You don't have a whisk?"

"Damn, forgot to pack it."

David cracked a half-dozen eggs into a bowl. "I'm going to have to use a fork."

"Poor you. How's the pinochle going?"

"No measuring cup?"

"Guess."

David poured a little milk in with the eggs, seemed to think that wasn't enough, tried a little more, then added another dose. "Shit." A pained expression appeared on his face. "Oh, the pinochle? Ya know, I rated pretty high at Harvard, I've had papers published in respected science publications, and your Defense Department thinks rather well of me. Consequently, I'm amazed I'm having so much trouble with pinochle. No salt and pepper? I didn't bring any, I figured you'd have salt and pepper."

"When you assume —"

"Right, you make an ass out of 'u' and 'me', very mature, very adult."

"It'll be fine."

David began whipping the eggs and milk mixture with the fork. "I don't think I should've used skim milk."

"I can run out and get us some MREs if you'd like."

"Why'd you let me come over?"

Pat shrugged. "You wanted a chance to re-start. I'm feeling merciful. And maybe I thought it'd be nice to talk to somebody who didn't have to start and end every sentence with 'Ma'am,' or 'Major'."

He laughed, then stopped when he saw the shape of the skillet he'd pulled out of one of the cabinets. "This looks like it was used more as a club than to cook anything." He pulled a can of Pam from the cooler and gave the skillet a heavy spraying. "You're supposed to use olive oil, but I couldn't find any. This should be fine."

"Oh, I'm sure."

He had a mix of vegetables – tomatoes, onion, spinach – and began dicing them up. Or, more accurately, while he set the skillet to heating on the range, he tried sawing through the veggies with a steak knife he found in a drawer. "Jesus, I've seen butter knives with more of an edge."

"Bitch, bitch, bitch."

"I know McElhone came out to see you last week."

Way to kill the mood. "I don't want to talk about it."

"There's a lot going on you don't know about, Pat."

"I don't want *you* to talk about it."

"I'm just saying cut the man some slack."

"Are you here as his emissary, David? Is that what this is about?"

"No. I did think you might be feeling a bit low after his visit. And, well, to be honest… I missed you." He looked up from the stove. "I've been missing you for years."

Pat groaned. "Oh, Christ, are we going to go Hallmark now?"

He laughed. "God, I hope not." He scooped up the ragged sort-of-diced vegetables in his hands, dropped them in the skillet, and stirred them around with the fork. "I was supposed to have some kind of cheese, but all I could find in our mess was something called 'cheese food' which didn't sound promising." He gave the vegetables a quick stir. "Ok, these look done." He poured the egg mix into the skillet. "Now as soon as this sets, I just zip it in the oven to finish — "

"The oven doesn't work. I meant to have one of Jinski's engineering geniuses look at it, but then I figured why bother; I don't do much baking."

"Oh." David frowned at the mix in the skillet. "Then I guess if I can flip this fucker, we're having an omelet." He made a show of spreading his legs apart to get a good stance, flexed his arms before grabbing the skillet handle with both hands, then, "Ok, now: one…two…"

"I can't look."

Which was a good thing, but then she didn't get to see why they wound up having something more like scrambled eggs for dinner.

Carlos Elmonte liked the Army, and most people he'd met in the Army liked Carlos Elmonte. He was that kind of young man. His asset – his only asset, actually – was his likability. Growing up in the South Bronx, despite his best grades being only middling, his teachers had passed him along because he was such a likable kid. In high school gym classes, he was always one of the first kids picked for teams. Not because he played particularly well — he didn't — but people just liked having him on their team. Girls went out with him not because he was good looking — he was only fair, at best — and not because he had money, because he didn't. And it wasn't because he took them to nice places — which, not ever having much money, he couldn't — but simply because "He was a nice guy."

Only possessed of so-so smarts and without an ounce of ambition, the Army had been a lifesaver for him after his parents were killed when the bad wiring in the tenement where his family lived caught fire. Carlos had been lucky, hanging out with friends; unlucky when he came home to find the fire department already rolling up their hoses in front of the gutted and smoking walk-up.

He had grieved, of course, and the neighborhood was happy to help "that nice kid from the block" pay for his parents' funeral, but he was at a loss of what to do with himself after that. He was just out of high school, had no job, no prospects, not even a place to live, and lost everything – including the only family he had – in that fire.

Then he remembered the Army recruiter who would come to his high school every year. So…

In the 20 months he'd been in uniform, wherever he was stationed, he became something of a barracks pet. Nobody could insult him and mean it, nobody could stand to see him meaningfully insulted without rising to his defense: "Leave the kid alone, eh?" Since there was so little he was good at, the teasing may have been relentless, but it was always good-natured and he took it that way — laughing along, shaking his head, "Ah, you guys, c'mon!"

They may have teased him no end when he decided to arrange painted rocks around the LZ – "Hey, Rembrandt, you missed a spot on this one!" "Ah, you guys!" – but his taking on the job seemed like such an Elmonte-esque kind of thing to do, as was the seriousness with which he applied himself to it, it was hard not to take a tongue-in-cheek kind of team pride in his doing it.

He'd been a little frustrated with this "signage" stuff. He wanted to know why the major couldn't just say "signs" like everybody else. "They teach 'em to talk like that in officers' school, El." It had gotten in the way of him finishing his job on the LZ. The LZ job was, as he'd tried to explain to the major that first day, was not just a simple matter of grabbing up a rock and throwing some paint on it. You needed just the right rocks to make the circle look good, and they weren't always easy to find.

He was walking sentry duty, had the 4-12 tour, had just made his 1900 hours radio check-in. The sun was low, the cloudless sky overhead rippling through shades of red to crimson to purple. He was on with "Dribble" Drivas; one of them would walk the perimeter while the other posted the gate, then they'd switch off, back and forth through the tour.

Elmonte had the gate when he saw the Humvee patrol coming in. The week before, Mister Cho had passed on the major's order that the Humvee patrol had to be in before dark, and here it came — vaulting over the rim of the valley, then skidding and fishtailing its way down the valley slope. The windows on the Humvee were open and Elmonte, even at a distance, could hear the men inside hooting and whooping like they were going through the loops on the Coney Island Thunderbolt —

a hooting and whooping experience with which Elmonte was personally acquainted. When the Humvee hit the valley floor, it made a skidding turn toward the compound and Elmonte could now see the two men inside – Willis and Herrera – cackling like madmen as the Humvee bounced its way to the front gate. The Humvee skidded to a halt where Elmonte was standing his post.

"How's it goin', El?" Willis, at the wheel, called out the window once he stopped laughing enough to catch his breath.

"It goes, it goes," Elmonte said as he unhooked the hasp on the gate. "You guys should be careful. You come down the hill like that, you're gonna turn this thing over 'n' get squished."

"Fuck it, *hermano*," Herrera said, "They oughta have rides like this at Disneyworld! Make a fuckin' fortune!"

"A fuckin' for-*choon*," Willis said, still giddy from their rockin'-'n'-rollin' ride. But then he turned sort of serious. "Whatcha doin' outside, El?"

Elmonte took a prim and proper stance, the kind of affectation that made him so likeable, and pronounced: "The order is we walk the perimeter inside *after* dark. See?" He pointed at the still purplish sky. "Not dark yet."

"Well," Willis said, earnestly concerned for the most likeable man in the barracks, "You be careful. I think one more lap 'n' you 'n' Dribble get your asses inside, ok?"

Elmonte gave them a rightey-o wave and they passed through the gate. As Elmonte re-hooked the gate hasp, he looked to where the Humvee had rocketed down the valley wall. It had kicked up a lot of rocks on its way down, and even at this distance, Elmonte could see that some might make a perfect fit for his LZ garnishment. Since he had started the chore, he'd picked up most of the selection-worthy rocks within easy walking distance of the compound and had been wondering if he'd ever find enough good ones to finish the circle. But what the Humvee had kicked up, well, now…

But he was still on sentry duty, and, well, it wasn't quite dark yet, but it was close to it, and nobody was supposed to be outside the perimeter fence after dark. But…hm…it wasn't *quite* dark… Would he still be able to find those good rocks the next day? It was only maybe 20, 30 meters away, he'd be back before Dribble Drivas had completed his circuit and before he had to make his next radio check-in.

Nobody'd even know he was gone.

Pat took a tentative taste of the watery mess in her dish, something that would've been better eaten with a spoon rather than her trying to fish something up with her fork. She did manage to get some of it in her mouth.

"Well?" David asked although he hardly looked hopeful.

Pat tried not to make a face as she swallowed. "This could be taken as less a peace offering than a declaration of war."

"Oh." Disappointed, he tried a taste himself, making a face of complete disgust. "Oh!"

"But I do appreciate the effort." She stirred the eggy glop around a bit, made a show of taking another mouthful as a way of showing that appreciation, the gesture drawing a wry smile from him. "David, I told you why I opened the door to you. Why did you come? I mean, besides in the hopes of getting laid."

He did that thing with his forelock, a kind of childish *oh-you-caught-me* look. "Give me credit; once I saw that wasn't going to happen —" and he pointed at the opened curtains, "— I still stayed."

"Noble, very noble."

"And, ok, dinner didn't come out as well as I would've liked, but still…"

"Still." She went to the kitchen, coming back with two glasses and the bottle of Jameson's. She poured them each a short drink. "Here, this'll help kill the taste."

"It's that bad?"

She uncapped the bottle. "This is better."

They sat quietly for a bit, letting the whisky do what whisky does. They both smiled at seeing each other slide into Jameson's-fueled reflection.

"I know you only met him the one time," said David, "but what did you think of Aaron? I mean, Dr. Ostrow?"

"Oh, Aaron is it? Good buddies are you?"

"Spend ten months cooped up in the lab with the man, things get informal."

"Interesting guy, but, like you said, I only met him the once."

"I don't know if you picked up on it, but he's actually a pretty spiritual guy. You don't see much of that in DoD science geeks."

"I remember the, um…" and she pointed to her chest, meaning the *Chai* medallion she'd seen Ostrow wearing. "He was talking about paradoxes and seems he's one himself."

"How so?"

"Bomb builder carrying around a symbol for life."

"Oh, Aaron isn't a nuke guy. But that's all I'm going to say, and you should be proud of me that that's all I'm going to say."

"You get a gold star."

David took another sip of his drink, stared down into the amber liquid as he swirled it around in his glass. "Like I said, I've been cooped up with the man. You talk; you know how it is, this and that. About his wife — she died years ago — and his son, the one he lost in Iraq. He said he wasn't very religious before his son died, but something about it…" He looked for words, couldn't find them. "You know."

"I know."

"He showed me this book, I forget the name, something in Hebrew, but it's kind of like the rules to be a good Jew. There are seven — I don't know what you'd call them: requirements? Characteristics? Whatever. Wisdom, meekness, loving truth, loving people, having a good name, not caring about money and…being afraid of God. He said, well, the way he sees it, him losing his son was… I feel funny saying it."

"He took it as a message from God to wise up?" she offered.

"Something like that. He says his work here —"

"Which," and she raised a warning finger, "you're not going to tell me about.

"— which I'm not going to talk about is a way of touching those bases." Something occurred to him over what he couldn't share with her: "Maybe he is a paradox."

Introspection was not something Pat was used to seeing in David Cordell, and more so anything touching on the spiritual. "Has he converted you?"

He smiled, self-conscious at his own seriousness. "It's just you have a lot of time to think out here. You wonder about what you're doing."

"How many of those bases have you touched?"

His smile grew broader. "Well, I did intend to love one particular people, but she's not cooperating. And then she tells me I'm not allowed to be truthful otherwise I could wind up in Federal prison, so that one's not my fault either. And God…" The smile turned thoughtful.

"You're not afraid of God?"

"You can't be afraid of something you don't believe in. It was kind of hard doing the work I did at Los Alamos and thinking there could possibly be a God."

"Major Simons!"

Pat kept a walkie-talkie in a charging station on the kitchen counter. The urgency in the voice crackling from the speaker did more than kill the mood in the trailer; she felt a clenching cold across her middle, already anticipating what she was going to hear. She picked up the walkie. "Simons here, go. Over."

"Major, this is Drivas on sentry duty. I was on the circuit with Elmonte, Ma'am. I can't find him, over."

Oh, Christ, not again, please not _again!_ "Drivas, wait for me at the gate, I'm on my way. Out."

She pulled her belt and holster from the hook by the door. There was an intercom box mounted on the wall there, and Pat buzzed The Brain.

"Delaney here."

As she strapped on her holster: "Delaney, have you got anything on any of your scopes? Any word from Elmonte?"

"He made his last check-in ten minutes ago, he was fine. I'm not seeing anything unusual on the screens."

"Notify Mister Cho, tell him to meet me at the gate and come heavy." She reached for the door. "You stay here," she told David, then froze.

David Cordell was sitting slumped at the table, his face sagging as he stared down into his drink.

"No, wait a minute," Pat said. "Anybody else would've asked me what's going on. But you already know, don't you."

David shrunk further into his seat, drained his drink.

"You better come with me."

He looked up at her but didn't move.

"David; I'm not asking."

Elmonte. That goofy kid painting the LZ rocks. And, she thought with a pang, he was, just that — a kid. As Pat jogged toward the gate, she ran all the possible palatable scenarios: he'd fallen asleep somewhere, fell down and broke his leg, something, anything… But her head kept coming back to a mental picture of a mangled coyote carcass. That image…and just a kid.

She saw Cho coming up from his quarters carrying an M4 and right behind him, Jinski with a Mossberg. The shotgun looked like a toy in the big man's hands.

"Where do you think you're going?" Pat called to Jinski.

"If there's gonna be a party, I'd hate to miss it."

Ok, it is now confirmed: he is the resident badass!

She heard more footsteps. Coming up from the barracks were Willis and Herrera carrying the M4 and shotgun that had been kept in their Quonset, and behind them, several more men from the barracks. Pat took a stand in front of them.

"Whoa, whoa, whoa! Hold it right there! All of you; back to your quarters! Now!" There was some disgruntled milling around until Pat repeated the order with a more emphatic *"Now!"*, then they started reluctantly moving back…except for Willis and Herrera. "You two something special?"

Willis stepped forward, his voice choked: "See, Ma'am, we saw him when we came in from patrol. Thing is, I told him to get himself inside, but he said it wasn't time yet. I shoulda made him come in. I feel like I shoulda —"

"Break that off right there!" Pat said sharply. "He made the call; this isn't on you! Neither of you!" *Trust me, I know what a back-breaking load that can be if you go down that road.* Then, in a less hard tone than her thought and previous statement: "Any idea where he might've gone?"

"No, Ma'am."

"We'd still like to, you know…" and Herrera pointed toward the gate.

Pop-pop-pop-pa-pop-pop.

They all broke into a run, found Drivas by the gate, his M4 aimed at some point off in the dark.

"What was it?" Pat asked.

Drivas shook his head. "I'm not sure. I thought I saw somethin' movin' out there by them boulders 'bout 20-30 meters out," and he pointed to a boulder pile at the foot of the valley wall.

"I hope you didn't just take a shot at El," Herrera said.

"No, no! I finished my circuit, ok? I come back around to here and El wasn't here. I looked for him, I called out, but nothin'. 'N' then just now, I saw somethin', looked like it was scootin' up the hill."

"*What* was scooting up the hill?" Pat pushed.

"I tol' ya, Major, I dunno! Just somethin' in the dark."

Pat took Drivas' torch and aimed it up the slope, but the beam dissipated before it reached the rim. "Whose got torches?"

Willis and Herrera did, as well as Drivas. Pat buddied Willis with Jinski and sent them ten yards out to the left. She sent Herrera with Cho out to the right, and Drivas was with her in the center. David, she told to wait by the gate. "Move out slow. Look for any kind of sign. You see anything doesn't look like it belongs, sing out. Fingers *off* the triggers, gentlemen; our man might still be out there."

They moved slowly, the men with the torches sweeping the ground in front of them.

"Boot tracks here, Major," Drivas said, running his torch beam along a trail of boot imprints leading toward the boulder pile he had pointed out earlier.

But Cho and Herrera got there first.

"Oh, Christ…" It was Cho.

The two other groups headed straight for the boulder pile, finding Cho sitting on the ground, shaking his head, and Herrera further off, throwing up.

Pat took Drivas' torch, beckoned the men to stay back while she moved around to the backside of the boulders, to where Cho was pointing.

It was clearly a man's corpse, but beyond that nothing was clear. The uniform was shredded and blood-soaked, the torso ripped open from collar line to groin, the ribs and sternum snapped and pushed out of the way, internal organs – what remained of them – lay in an unidentifiable mangled mass in the body cavity, matter from inside the body was splattered about. The head was missing.

Just a kid. Painting his stupid rocks. *GodGodGod…*

She could hear the moans of the men behind her, another of them taking himself off to vomit.

Jinski: "Jesus, is that Elmonte?"

Pat steeled herself to bend in close, felt around the bloody stump of the neck until she found dog tags. She had to smear the blood away with her thumb to read them in the torch's beam.

It came back to her; two of her boys laying in the Afghanistan dust. Starkey and Lowe; there was no forgetting the names. It came back to her because even their tags had been taken.

"Yeah, it's him."

"What the fuck!" Jinski fumed. "What the *fuck!*"

She could Herrera murmuring something in Spanish. It had the rhythm of a prayer, and the word *Dios* kept coming up.

"Major?" It was Cho again. He'd gotten to his feet, was holding up what was left of Elmonte's M4. It was in two pieces, the adjustable stock separated from the body of the weapon, the barrel gone.

Pat unhooked the small loop of chain holding the lower dog tag, slipped the tag free and dropped it in her breast pocket. Then, thinking there wasn't enough left of Elmonte's neck to hold the other larger loop, carefully slipped it over the stump and tucked it in Elmonte's breast pocket. She stepped away from the body for a better look at the pieces of carbine Cho was showing her. "Feel the edges," Cho said.

Pat ran her fingertips along the breaks on both pieces. They were perfectly smooth.

She couldn't see Cho's face in the dark, but she knew they were both thinking the same thing: *Like that coyote bone.*

Pat swept the ground with the torch. It didn't take long to find the first track; just like the one they'd found by the dead coyote. Her light went from one to the next, could see they ran up the slope beyond the range of the torch beam, up toward the valley rim.

She heard Jinski coming up behind her. "Let's go get this fucker!"

That was enough to rally Herrera. "Fuck, yeah! *Para mi hermano!*"

Pat remembered the heavy spread of spent carbine shells out on the desert, the 40 mm grenade casing. *Christ, if that's what it takes…* "No."

"Jesus, Major, it can't be more 'n' a few minutes ahead —"

"What part of 'no' don't you understand! Use your head, for Christ's sakes! I want whatever did this, too, but go chasing off into the dark after something that does *this*?"

Jinski may have been a hothead, but he wasn't stupid. He looked up to where the valley rim was lost in the curtain of night, ran that thought around in his head a few times, and saw it made a painful bit of sense. He nodded, turned to the other men: "Tonight's not the night, dudes. Not this way."

She turned back toward the compound, saw David Cordell walking their way, slowly, bent, like a man in a funeral procession. Pat grabbed him and pulled him away from the group.

"What the hell's going on here, David? You *know!*" keeping her voice low, not wanting the others to hear.

David just shook his head.

"You picked a hell of a time to obey the rules! I've got one man dead, another missing, and I doubt very much that Bruckner kid committed suicide. I need to know what's going on here!"

"You know I...I *can't*..."

"Goddammit, David —"

"Pat, *you* can't! You know what they'll do to you if you dig into this? Your career's hanging by a thread as it is!"

"David, right now I don't give a shit if they bust me out as —"

"Major Simons, it's Delaney," coming over her walkie stopped her. "I just got something. Major, are you there? Over."

Pat hadn't heard Delaney at first; the heat she felt boiling up in her at David Cordell eclipsed everything else: the cold of the desert night, the men milling around waiting for her next instructions, whatever might be lurking above the valley rim, Delaney's voice. She was glad she couldn't see David's face in the dark. The slightest sign of him looking for sympathy, looking for forgiveness or understanding, or – God forbid – some kind of stoic that's-the-way-it-is, and she would've pulled him over to Elmonte's corpse by the hair and shoved his face into that massive open wound.

"Major Simons, do you read me?"

She turned away from David and reached for her walkie. "What've you got, Delaney, over."

"Target just popped up on the valley rim, right above you. I'm not getting a clear read, but the radiation detector spiked, and I've got some kind of blurry thermal image. It's moving, heading along the rim, north. Over."

Toward the lab. "Keep tracking it. Patch me through to the lab. Tell them I need to talk to Colonel McElhone. *Now!*"

When McElhone came on, "Colonel, I've got a man down. I need you to come see this, over."

For a long beat, nothing but static.

"Colonel? Did you hear what I said? Over."

"Is Dr. Cordell with you? Over."

"Yes, Sir. Over."

"I want you to provide Dr. Cordell an armed escort back to the lab compound. Over."

That heat started to rise in her again. "Sir, did you hear what I said about my man? Over."

"I want any remains brought here to the lab ASAP. Bring them along with Dr. Cordell. Over."

Remains? <u>Remains?</u> This is a dead boy!

"Major Simons, do you copy? Over."

"Colonel, we have a situation here! My command has lost three men in the last week and a half. We're tracking a target —"

"Say again? You have a target? Over."

"EW surveillance has picked up a possible target heading your direction. Colonel, we should radio Nellis —"

"You've been given an order, Major! I want Cordell and any remains brought back to the lab under armed escort, and I want it done now! I also want your surveillance array closed down immediately until instructed otherwise. Do you roger that? Over."

They were clustered together, her men – *her* men – looking toward her, just shapes, shadows really, in the dark, but she knew – felt the burn of unseen eyes -- they were looking to her to see what her next move would be.

McElhone came back, his voice – even over the small walkie speaker – clearly hard: "Major Simons, if you cannot comply, a detail from the lab will be sent out to execute the order. Is that your choice? Acknowledge."

God, I hope these guys can't see my face. "Roger, wilco."

The channel went dead.

"All respect, Major," Willis said, "are we gettin' fucked over or what?"

Pat could just shake her head. She looked to David, but Cordell had moved off, his head hanging. *I should leave the sonofabitch out here for whatever got this poor kid!*

Ok, nothing you can do about that; what're you going to do?

Back on the walkie: "Delaney, are you still tracking that target? Over."

"Yes, Ma'am, still heading north along the valley rim. Over."

"Keep tracking it, keep me posted. Out." She turned to the men. "Willis, you stay here with me and Dr. Cordell. The rest of you; back to the compound. Mister Cho, open the armory, see that everybody is armed, and they stay in the barracks. Jinski, bring up the Humvee with the M240 mount. Do we, um…" *Gut up and ask.* "Do we have body bags?"

"I think so," Cho said. "I'll check. It's not something we thought we'd ever need here."

As they moved off, David moved sheepishly back to her. He forced what she guessed he thought was supposed to be a disarming smile. "I guess a second date is out of —"

Her slap landed hard enough to send him staggering back a few steps. She stepped away from him, afraid that if she didn't, next time she wouldn't stop, and they wouldn't be open-handed slaps. "Don't you fucking *dare!* If the next words out of your mouth aren't an explanation, then you'd be wise to keep your hole shut."

Willis was at the wheel, Jinski up front beside him. Pat sat in the back with David Cordell. What was left of Elmonte was tucked in a body bag in the storage space in the rear. They rode in silence. David leaned far over against his door, his head low, as if he was trying to put as much space between him and Pat as the vehicle would allow. It wasn't a bad idea because even on that short ride, more than once Pat was tempted to lean over and have another go at him.

As they pulled up to the lab perimeter, the compound floodlights flared on, washing the grounds in an almost painfully bright glare. Silhouetted against the lights, standing in front of the compound gate, were a half-dozen figures armed with M4s and kitted out in full battle gear. One of them stepped forward, raised a gloved hand to slow the Humvee then pointed to a halting spot ten yards from the gate.

"I'm not likin' this," Willis muttered.

"Major Simons," the lead figure said, "Please send Dr. Cordell out and we'll send men to remove the remains."

"Screw that," Pat muttered, then to David: "Don't you move, or I swear to Christ I'll put one through your leg so you don't." She climbed out of the Humvee and started forward, then froze when the security detail, without an order issued, snapped into a firing crouch.

"I would advise you to stay where you are, Major" the detail leader said, firm but not excited, almost machine-like.

"I need to see Colonel McElhone."

"The colonel knows you're here."

As if to emphasize the point, Pat saw the CCTV camera swivel and focus on her.

"Now please return to your vehicle, send Dr. Cordell out —"

"Nobody's going anywhere until I speak to the colonel!"

"Problem, Major?" It was Jinski. She turned and saw the sergeant taking the gunner's position behind the M240. "You boys wanna go O.K. Corral, I'm good for it," Jinski said, directing the M240 at the detail leader.

The leader didn't flinch, stepped closer to Pat, still just a shadow with the floodlights behind him. "I don't think that's how you want this to go, do you, Major? It's not like that'll change anything, will it?"

"Major Simons!" McElhone's voice on the gatepost speaker. "Order your man to stand down, send Cordell in, let my people take the remains! In case you're confused, this is not a request!"

Some of the security detail had their weapons trained on Jinski, some on herself. She turned and looked up at Jinski, standing exposed inside the gun ring, then at Willis, his eyes squeezed closed, his head making *no-no-no* movements.

McElhone's voice, again, but it had lost its hard edge: "Pat! Please!"

Once you get passed being pissed off, what do you think you're going to accomplish? Except maybe getting you and two more of your men killed. How much of a body count do you want on your head, Sister?

"Jinski, stand down."

The sergeant looked down at her, angry, his gun hand flexing around the pistol grip of the machine gun.

"Please, Sarge." It was Willis, his voice almost trembling.

Jinski slowly unwound himself from his weapon, nodding, finally seeing the sense of it.

The detail leader beckoned three men forward to the Humvee. One opened David's door and escorted him from the vehicle, while the other two reached in back for Elmonte.

"That ain't luggage," Jinski called down to them, still standing in the gun ring. "You be careful with that boy."

And they were.

David had stopped by Pat on his way to the gate. He watched the two security men pass by carrying Elmonte's body, then looked to Pat.

It was clear to her he wanted to say something, and at the same time knew nothing he could say would cover it.

"I don't know if that's your fault, David," Pat said, pointing to the body bag now being carried through the gate. "But you're not clean. Sooner or later, I'm going to find out what's going on here and God help you if I find you could've told me something that would've kept that kid alive."

Elmonte and David Cordell, with their escorts, disappeared inside the blockhouse. Once they did, the rest of the security detail withdrew behind the gate, the gate was closed and locked, and there was a hum as electricity was returned to the perimeter fence. As the blockhouse door closed behind the last of the security men, the floodlights went out, and the compound disappeared into darkness.

"Man, you'd never know we're on the same side," Willis said.

"I'm not sure we are," Jinski said.

Pat climbed back into the Humvee, up front alongside Willis. Willis started the engine, but she signaled him to cut it off. She got on the Humvee's radio set. "Delaney, are you still tracking that target? Do you have a position on it?"

"I've got the target still on the west side of the valley but moving out onto the flats, due west from the lab."

Pat tapped Willis on the shoulder and pointed up to the valley rim. "Let's go."

Willis hesitated, but then Jinski's deep voice rumbled out from the back seat, sounding more like a command than Pat's had: "You heard the major, bro. Now!"

The Humvee's diesel growled to life and Willis backed away from the gate and wheeled the front around. "I thought this was an all-volunteer Army. I don't 'member volunteerin' for this."

"Got a complaint?" Pat said, "Write your congressman."

The Humvee bounced over the rim and Pat had Willis pull to a stop just a few yards onto the flat.

"I think my kidneys are up around my ears," Jinski groaned from the back seat. "Was there a bump you managed to miss?"

There was nothing in the spread from the headlights that was unexpected: scrub, the occasional Joshua tree, rock outcroppings.

"Do a sweep with the spot," Pat told Willis, meaning the small searchlight on the driver's side.

The beam knifed out into the dark, and Willis moved it slowly across the flatland, but it revealed just more of the same.

Pat got on the Humvee's radio to Delaney. "Where are you reading the target?"

"If you're facing due west, target should be in your eleven o'clock."

Willis swung the light back toward that position. Nothing.

Pat picked up Willis' carbine and climbed out of the vehicle.

"Where you goin'?" Willis asked, unhappy about any development that didn't involve turning around and heading back to the compound.

Jinski climbed back up into the gun ring behind the M240.

"Willis, ask Delaney where he's reading the target now."

"He says still in your eleven o'clock, approximately 300 meters."

Pat's eyes followed the searchlight beam out into the desert. A large rock, some cacti. She turned to Jinski with his higher vantage point. "You see anything?"

"*Nada.*"

Pat clicked the M4's safety off, charged the weapon, switched the fire select to "burst," and put the stock to her shoulder, aiming down the beam of light.

"That somethin' you really gotta do?" Willis asked.

Pat's answer was to squeeze off a three-round burst down the lighted path.

Willis moved the light slightly to the left, slightly to the right to see if Pat's shots had stirred anything up.

Still nothing.

"Del says target is moving north, from your left to right. Now holding at your two o'clock. Still around 300 meters out."

What the hell is it?

The searchlight couldn't turn that far to the right, and the reported position put the target just outside the spread from the headlights. She fired another burst into that dark spot, putting a little spread between the rounds hoping that would give her a better chance of catching something.

"Target is now closing on our position, moving slow!" Willis' voice was rising. "I'm not likin' this!"

"Jinski," she called up to the sergeant. "Give it a burst. Figure 200-300 meters, a little bit of a spread."

Jinski hunkered down behind the gun's sights and squeezed off a 2-second burst, ejected shell casings rattling down the side of the Humvee, tracers arcing out into the dark.

"Target still closing!" Willis called out. "I'm not likin' this a *lot!*

"Ask Delaney if he's sure his equipment is functioning properly."

"He says he just ran diagnostics. He says that's a solid target out there."

Then where the fuck is it? "Hit it again!" Pat told Jinski and the sergeant sent out another burst.

"Still closing, 150 meters!"

That can't be! There's nothing there! She looked to Jinski, saw the sergeant squinting out into the night. He gave Pat a shrug.

"Major, I don't think this is a good idea!" Willis said, pleading.

She climbed back into the Humvee. "You convinced me; let's get the hell outta here!"

Willis wasted no time in whipping the nose of the Humvee around and sending it on a bouncing, rocking course back down the valley slope.

Pat reached for the radio. "Delaney, where do you read the target's position now? Delaney, come in, over. Delaney, are you reading me? Over."

There was only static in reply.

Back at the compound, Pat had Willis head the Humvee straight for The Brain, but as soon as the EW trailer flared up in the headlights, Willis hit the brakes. There was a wooden porch in front of the door now, one of Jinski's make-work projects to re-instill discipline in his engineers. The door to the trailer was missing, the door frame ragged, as if the door had been forcefully ripped off and tossed a few feet away. The inside of the trailer was dark.

"I'm not likin' this," Willis said.

"I wish you'd quit saying that" Pat said and told him to roll up to the trailer slowly, aim the headlights through the open doorway. Pat took Willis' torch, drew her pistol and climbed out. Jinski followed with his shotgun.

"Anybody mind if I wait here?" Willis asked, then without waiting for an answer, "Ok, then."

As soon as Pat reached the doorway, she held up a hand to stop Jinski. "Smell that?"

"Somebody's been bustin' caps."

Pat cautiously went up the stairs, .45 at the ready, peeped around the doorsill. She must've made some kind of noise aloud, not hearing it herself.

"It's Delaney," Jinski said.

Pat nodded.

"Like Elmonte?"

"That's the thing. Not even close."

SUN CITY

Power was dead in the EW trailer: no light. Where the screens and indicators on the control panels should've been glowing…nothing.

Delaney was sitting in his chair, bent forward over a console. His face was turned away from Pat, but the torch beam showed an eruption of bone and tissue on the back of his head: a bullet exit wound. From where she stood in the doorway, she ran the light quickly the length of the trailer to make sure there was no one else there.

Something nearby on the floor glittered in the light: a shell casing. Pat easily identified it as from a .45 pistol round.

She ran the beam along the consoles. Monitors had been smashed; face plates had been removed. The interior electronic guts for all of them — for each surveillance and communications system — were a tangle of broken and yanked wires and circuit boards snapped like crackers. Behind her she heard Jinski groan at the sight.

She told him to stay in the doorway and not touch anything as she holstered her pistol and stepped inside. Delaney's pistol was on the floor just below his hanging hand. There was more blood and tissue on the seat back, but nothing – including the bullet -- on the wall behind him. The spent shell casing was in the wrong place; the Sig Sauer ejected to the right, but if Delaney had been facing the consoles and pointed the pistol at his face, the casing should've ejected to his left, there should've been blood splatter on the wall behind him.

Pat slipped around the man's body and the torch beam found blood splatter on the floor and sprayed horizontally across the consoles, a small bullet hole low in the wall at the far end of the trailer. She turned the light to Delaney's face. There was a small, jagged, beveled hole in his forehead: entrance wound. And there was his face... Eyes frozen wide, mouth agape: terror.

His collar was pulled up oddly high, the tabs turned up to cover his neck. Pat pushed the collar aside. Almost completely circling the lower part of Delaney's neck was a deep purple bruise. She felt the front part of his throat, probing for the hyoid bone, the larynx. It all felt like ground glass.

"Is this supposed to look like another suicide?" Jinski said, and it was clear he didn't think this was any more a suicide than the late Lieutenant Bruckner's.

"I think that's what they were trying for," Pat said, "but it was done in a rush, by somebody in a panic, by somebody who doesn't do this kind of thing for a living. I don't know many suicides-by-gun where they shoot themselves in the forehead. Besides..." and she got in close, examining Delaney's face, "there'd be more gunshot residue than there is if he'd done the shooting." She went back around to the other side, crouched down to examine his gun hand. "And there's nothing on his hand. There'd be back-splatter on the weapon and there isn't. Going by the splatter on the panels and the floor, it looks like he was facing toward the door when he was shot. Bullet had a downward trajectory; you can see where it went into the far wall."

It was a tight fit for Jinski, but he squeezed around. "He saw *somethin'* he didn't like."

Jinski beckoned for the torch, flashed the beam at the tangle inside one of the control consoles. "This wasn't smart," Jinski said. "This was just somebody goin' ape-shit in there, like they just – Oh."

"What?"

Jinski was focusing the light on the screw hole tabs, then he ran his fingers around the rim of the removed face plate for the screws. "This wasn't unscrewed. The holes are stripped. Whoever did this just *yanked* the panel off."

"How hard is that to do?"

"Without a crowbar, I couldn't do it on my best day. And, you know; look at *me*."

Pat took back the torch. "You're wrong; this *was* smart."

"How do you figure?"

"Because now we're deaf, dumb, and blind, and that's what they wanted. See if you can find out what the deal is with the power."

She played the light over the consoles, the dead and smashed monitor screens, looking for...anything. Anything that might help explain what had gone on here. She slipped past Delaney, again, moving toward the communications gear. She tried the squawk box to the lab since it looked intact, but not expecting anything – and not getting anything. Still, she'd felt obligated to try because...

They know. Those bastards <u>know</u>!

Jinski was back. "The cable's been cut from the generator. It's an easy repair, a simple splice."

"What was the cut like?"

"Ma'am?"

Pat pointed to the open consoles. "Was it like this?"

"No, more like —"

"A big sharp knife making a clean cut?"

"Yeah."

She nodded, unsurprised. "Do you think you and your crew could Humpty Dumpty this mess back together? I especially want communications back."

Jinski shrugged. "We have spare parts, but…" He looked at the mess inside the control boards and shook his head. "I dunno. I'm not an expert on this stuff. I couldn't even tell you how bad this is 'ceptin' it looks really fuckin' bad."

"Go tell Willis to bring up your crew. Have him grab Pritchard, too; he's the expert. He could at least tell us what's possible. Have him also grab Mister Cho and tell Cho I need a camera. I want pictures of the scene. At least somebody's phone, I can use that."

"They're not supposed to have phones here."

Pat flashed a *Seriously?* face.

Jinski gave a self-conscious clearing of his throat before mumbling, "You can use mine," and he fished in his breast pocket for his cell phone, handed it over.

Pat flashed her light one last time over Delaney's body.

I'm sorry, fella. If I'd –

Something on the body's chest flared when it picked up the light. "Hold up, Jinski!" Pat leaned in. It was Delaney's dosimeter badge. "Damn…"

"What is it?" Jinski asked from the door.

"He's been exposed. There's a reading on his dosimeter."

Jinski started to back out the door. "This place is hot?"

Pat looked at her own dosimeter. Nothing. "The trailer's not contaminated, but he must've come in contact with something."

"How bad?"

"Not lethal. But not healthy. One hundred millirems looks like. When you talk to Willis, tell him to have Mister Cho also bring up a Geiger counter. And…we're going to need another body bag."

Jinski started to turn but stopped. "Jesus, Major, you got any fuckin' idea what-all's goin' on here?"

She shook her head. "Here's what I do know. Whoever did this — " and she pointed to Delaney, "— is not who pulled that door off its hinges and did this," and she pointed to the mess inside the nearest open console. "I don't know what's going on, but I have a pretty goddamn good idea who does." She nodded him out to give her instructions to Willis, then started taking pictures of everything for an investigation she doubted would ever happen. *But you do it because you hope, right? Even when you know… Even when you fucking <u>know</u>…*

When Pat finished her picture-taking, she stepped out onto the EW trailer's porch, seeing Jinski sitting on the steps. Willis and the Humvee had taken off.

She didn't know how late it was, but it wasn't the hour that dragged at her. Elmonte. Delaney. It wasn't a fatigue of the body. She knew the feeling, had felt it before. In Afghanistan. It was the feeling she'd had seeing men – *her* men – tucked into the squeaking plastic of a body bag. It was the feeling of losing men she knew by their first names, knew how they laughed, how they walked, how they joked with each other, how they talked about girlfriends, wives, kids waiting for them back home.

You're not done, Sister. Wake up and finish the job.

She took a deep draw of the crisp night air trying to shake off that dragging feeling. She came down the stairs, running the torch beam along the ground, and finding the tracks she knew she'd find.

"Just like the ones where we found El." It was Jinski; she hadn't heard him come up alongside her.

There were actually two sets of tracks leading up to the EW trailer from the direction of the compound gate and heading back the same way. One set resembled the ones she and Cho had found near Elmonte.

The other: human sized. Shoes with flat soles and a shallow heel.

"That's not an Army boot," Jinski said.

Pat went back up the porch stairs, flashed the torch beam one last time inside at Delaney's body. *Fuck me.*

She switched off the light and her body felt leaden. She wanted to lay down right there on the porch, close her eyes, and…

With a quiet sigh, she settled for dropping heavily on the top stair. Leaning against the banister, she let out a louder, more exhausted sigh.

Jinski sat on the next step down, but the big man's head was still even with hers. He reached into a shirt pocket and came out with a half-plug of Red Man in its crumpled wrapper. "I know you're no fan, Ma'am, but under the circumstances, you mind?"

"It's not good for you."

"Not my primary concern right now."

"Go ahead."

He took a pen knife from the same pocket and cut off a chaw and tucked it in his mouth. He held the plug up to her, offering.

"No, thanks."

"I didn't think so, but I didn't want to be impolite."

It was a relief to have something to smile about. She pulled out her silver cigarette lighter, flicked the cap open and closed. "You wouldn't happen to have a cigarette, would you?"

"No, sorry. Not my thing. I didn't know you smoked."

"I don't, but this seems like when it might be a good thing to do."

"But you have a lighter."

She dropped the lighter back in her pocket. "My dad's."

"Ah."

They sat quietly for a bit, then Jinski said, "I'm guessin' here — I mean, I didn't go to no academy — but I think I got maybe as much time in as you."

"I think so, probably. And going by that salad I saw you wearing at my welcome party, you've got more deployment time. Maybe *you* should be wearing the oak leaves."

"No thanks."

"Too much responsibility?"

"Too much paperwork."

"You're not wrong."

"You ever been in combat?"

"Not per se."

"I like that: 'per se'."

"I was in command of a transfer point for prisoners. We'd get a call that a field unit was holding some bodies, we'd bring them in and, at some point, transport them to one of the big detention centers like Bagram or Kandahar. But I have been under fire."

"That was like me. Engineers. You go out to dig a hole and next thing you know you hear that 'crack' of a bullet going by your ear. If you don't mind my askin'; ever lose a man?"

"Yeah."

"More than one?"

"Yeah."

"I know what that's like, too. Ya know, Ma'am, sometimes there's nothin' you can do 'bout it. Like I said, you go out just to dig a hole, 'n' pop; you got a man down with a hole in his helmet. Nothin' you could do. Sometimes the shit's gonna come no matter what you do, wind up beatin' yourself up for nothin'. 'Scuse me, Ma'am," and he spat a line of juice out into the sand. "Disgustin' habit, I know. There's people I let call me 'Jinks'."

"Is this you taking me off your naughty list and putting me on your nice list?"

"Oh, you were never on my naughty list, Ma'am. I know it would always be 'Ma'am' 'n' 'Major,' 'n' in public, we'd have to, well, you'd say, 'observe the proprieties'."

"Well, then, as *you'd* say, I'm down for it, Jinks."

He turned to look at her with a mock frown. "So's you know, Ma'am, I wouldn't say that."

She laughed. A small one, but she needed it.

"You done a good job, Major, the way you brought the guys along and not in much time, too."

The laugh, the smile, evaporated. "Yeah, I'm sure Loomis, that kid Elmonte, Delaney…They're all impressed with my command effectiveness." *Three so far…and I know this isn't over.* "My family's all Army."

"I heard."

"I've been around the military since I was in the womb. It's not like I'm not afraid to die, but you get used to the idea that the possibility is always there. It's part of the job. After a while, you don't even think about it much. What I never got used to…"

"Losing a man."

"Yeah."

And now Jinski sounded almost like he was reprimanding: "Ya know, it's not in my nature to make people with brass on their shoulder feel good 'bout their calls, 'specially when they make bad calls. But you didn't make a bad call. I can't see where-all there was anything you coulda done on this."

"I screwed up. I told them to hole up in the barracks. I should've posted sentries."

"Occur to you if you did, poor Del in there woulda had that much more company?"

They could see the headlights of the Humvee heading back their way. They both stood.

"Ma'am, you'd be doin' us all a favor – 'cludin' yourself – you stop thinkin' 'bout what you mighta shoulda done, 'n' figure out what we do next," and he started walking toward the approaching Humvee.

Pat had Cho and Jinski stand at one end of the trailer by the entry door, while she stood by Delaney's body, and walked them through her scenario. "Delaney was sitting here but facing toward you. Going by the minimal amount of powder residue on his face, he was probably shot from somewhere around where you are. The shell casing is right there on the floor, bullet exits, buries itself down low in the wall behind me. Then, he was positioned the way we found him, pistol dropped by his hand. But whatever tore through that door and went to town on the electronics didn't do the shooting."

"Mr. Shoes," Jinski said. "He killed him."

"Oh, he shot him, but he didn't kill him. Come here and look at his neck. Feel around at the front of his throat."

"Do we have to?" asked Cho.

"The bones in his throat, when there's a strangulation, they're usually crushed. But whatever did this had enough muscle to grind them into powder."

Cho took a moment by Delaney's body. Pat could see the grotesque facts of Delaney's death registering on her XO's face; this was, after all, someone he'd served with for a lot longer than Pat had. The warrant officer finally shook it off, walked to the other end of the trailer, putting distance between himself and the body. He kicked at the bullet hole in the wall. "I find myself baffled and bewildered. Something breaks in here, kills Del, then this…" He waved a hand at the mauled electronics. "*Then* he's shot? Why? Doesn't make any sense. Were we supposed to think he did all this, then what? Killed himself out of remorse or something? Or …" But nothing came together for him; nothing that made sense.

"Frankly, I don't think much thought went into this at all. This was panic. A half-assed attempt to make it look like whatever was responsible for the damage wasn't what killed him. It wasn't anybody from the lab security detail. I've seen them at work. They're all-pro, first string. This was amateur hour."

Through the open doorway, they could hear the trailer's generator in a coughing start and then catch, followed closely by the overhead lights flickering to life, providing a bright yet cold fluorescence.

Jinski grinned proudly at that, did a little flourish of his hands: "*Voila*! My people deliver!"

"Now," said Pat, giving a pained look at the open consoles, "comes the hard part."

"Well, yeah," Jinski said, and the grin turned to a frown.

"Something else," Pat said, and picked up the Geiger counter Cho had brought her. "Watch." She held the probe close to Delaney's body and the sporadic clicks from the counter's speaker picked up, but then she moved the probe away, waved it around away from Delaney. "It spikes around him, but otherwise, just normal background. But…" Now she held the probe in one of the torn open consoles, and the flow of clicks spiked again.

"Whatever touched Del and left something behind was the same thing pokin' 'round makin' a mess," Jinski said.

Pat nodded. "Now, watch this." She walked slowly along the length of the trailer, from Delaney's body heading toward the doorway, the probe held close to the floor. Every few feet, another spike, then falloff, then another spike…

She could see both Cho and Jinski were puzzled.

"Footprints," Pat said. "Wherever this thing makes contact, it leaves a trace." She followed the "footprints" toward the doorway, but Cho held up a halting finger.

"Um, Ma'am?"

Of course: another "um".

"What should we do about…well…" He nodded at Delaney's body.

"Body bag. Bag the pistol, too, and that shell casing. Put him in the armory for now. Tomorrow, we'll bury him until we can arrange transport."

The three of them stood for a bit, looking at the body of Electronic Warfare Specialist First Delaney, Michael C., who died two thousand miles from his native Baltimore, not in a war, not in any kind of conflict, and who was going to be buried in the dead sands of Nevada for no reason any of the three could discern.

As she'd done for Elmonte, Pat reached into Delaney's collar to pull out his dog tags, detached the small loop with the lower tag, then threaded Elmonte's tag onto the same chain before dropping them into her breast pocket.

Cho and Jinski may have known Delaney in a way Pat hadn't, but this didn't weigh any less on her. *Because he was mine and I was responsible for him.*

She led them outside.

The Geiger counter told the same story on the EW Trailer's porch and stairs and on the tracks that led to the gate, even as the night winds had begun to kick up and partially erase them. "Wherever it walks, it leaves mild contamination."

"You can track it," Jinski said.

"Like a bloodhound."

Pritchard came around from the other side of the trailer where he'd been poking around through inspection ports.

"I'm not seeing you smiling," Pat said when she saw him.

Pritchard's shoulders heaved in a grim sigh. "Well…"

"Yes, ok; well?"

Pritchard looked at the trailer with a pained look. "My initial, knee-jerk reaction is we're screwed. It's like a thousand-piece jigsaw puzzle and I don't even know if all the pieces are there, or they're too broken —"

"Ok, fine, I get all that. Skip to the bottom line: can you make *any* of it work? Especially the radio?"

Pritchard thought a moment. "Tell you the truth, Major, I won't be sure until I try. I don't know what we can replace, I don't know what we can cobble back together… At the moment, I just don't know. Regardless, we've got another problem." He pointed to the valley rim where the antenna arrays sat. "We saw it on the way over."

"More good news?"

"All the lines to the radio mast and the surveillance array are down. Looks like they were brought down at the far end."

"That's a simple cabling job," Jinski said.

"I don't know how simple with whatever this is on the loose," Cho said.

"What about the satlink?" Pat said, pointing to the satellite dish on the trailer roof. "We don't need the radio mast for that."

"I haven't checked it out, yet, but if it's undamaged, that'd work. That is, providing I can do some miracle healing and get the transmitter back together."

"See what you can do."

"Do my best, Ma'am," Pritchard said, not sounding very hopeful.

She put a hand on his shoulder, knowing – and letting him know – she was probably asking impossible things of him. "I know you will."

Then she walked away to think.

They were out of the circle of light cast by the exterior lamps of the EW trailer: Pat, Cho, and Jinski.

"We need to go to the lab and ask for help," Cho said.

"You don't think they know what's going on?" Pat said. "At this point, I'm not even sure they aren't responsible in some way."

"Do we have another option? We've got no communications with the outside, no —"

The tension in his voice was clear, and she made sure hers was quiet and calming. *Remember: he's never been in a combat situation.* "I know our situation, Mister Cho."

He hung his head, apologetic.

"If we get comms restored," Pat said, "easy call: we yell for help."

"Ok," Jinski said, "Let's say Wish No. 1 doesn't happen. I don't want to sound too chickenshitty, but why don't we just jam everybody in the Humvees and burn ass outta here? We could be in Indian Springs in two, three hours."

"Tempting," Pat admitted. "We were off chasing after something while this happened. Do the math."

It hit Cho and Jinski about the same time.

"Oh, Christ…" Cho sighed.

"There's more than one," Jinski said.

"I'm trying to imagine what it'd be like, fifteen of us packed in the Humvees, and we bump into these things in the dark."

"Oof," Jinski said.

"I'm not crossing it off the list, but it's not my first choice. And then I'm worried about what happens if we do manage to make it out. Think about it, gentlemen: everything about this place is about keeping it a secret, even from those of us who are supposed to guard it."

"Mr. Shoes," Jinski said.

Pat nodded. "I guarantee you: by the time we get anywhere, there'll be MPs waiting to bust us for desertion. And what can we tell anybody? What can we show?"

"Elmonte —" Cho began.

"Is gone. Loomis is gone. They'll make up a good story for them: wandered off, fell down and broke their necks, something. Delaney, like Bruckner, they'll write off as a suicide. They'll look at us, our 201s, all those Article 15s, and they'll call us — I'm sorry, gentlemen — a bunch of screw-ups who deserted. And not one of us has a mom or pop or aunt or uncle or *anybody* to write to their congressman and make a beef. They'll bury us in Leavenworth until they feel like they don't need to keep it a secret anymore."

"Which could be never," Jinski said glumly.

"We're going to have to operate with the idea we're on our own." Pat gave them a few seconds to let that sink in. She heard Cho let out a long, collapsing breath.

"So, what's the plan?" Jinski asked.

"This thing can be tracked," Pat said.

"Because of the radioactive traces."

Pat nodded.

"You're not planning on hunting this thing?" Cho asked.

"Better than waiting for them to pick their time which is what they've been doing. What's out in that direction?" and she pointed to the northwest.

"Sun City," Cho said. "The nuclear test range. Why?"

"I don't know what we're dealing with, I don't pretend to know, but it's not dumb. The way it's been picking us off one at a time, waiting for me to go off on a chase with the rest of you hole up in the enlisted quarters and then hit the EW trailer, taking down the antenna hookups... The one we were chasing didn't go back to the lab; it went out into the desert, same direction as Sun City."

"It knows it leaves traces," Cho said.

"So, it goes some place already hot," Jinski said. "Like some guy running from a posse, runs through water so the bloodhounds can't track it."

"Right," Pat said. "I'll bet you cash money that's where this one's heading. What I'll do is first go up to the lab. Mister Cho, you're right; we should try everything, just don't expect much. Then I'll go up top and try to pick up its trail. Cho, I'll need somebody to pull out one of the other Humvees. I want to leave the 240 with you. I'll take Herrera and Willis."

"You sure?" Jinski asked.

"They're buddies, they've worked together, they know each other's moves."

"I dunno," Jinski said. "Willis seems a little..." and he made quivering motions with his hands.

"Yeah, a bit," Pat agreed, "but with him, I know I'm getting no surprises. And, like I said, he's Herrera's buddy. They'll have each other's backs.

"Mister Cho, I'll need you to break out three hot suits. Do we have another Geiger counter?"

"Yes, Ma'am."

"Good, I'll need it. What about night vision hardware?"

Cho shook his head. "Lieutenant Bruckner had our one NVG set. So…"

"So. Of course. Do we have a flare gun? I'll need a couple of illumination flares, and a red and a green flare. I don't know how far we'll track this thing or what you'll be able to see. If I can't contact you by radio, I'll send up a red flare if…well…if things don't work out the way we want. A green flare means we're coming back clean."

"What if…?" Cho choked on the rest of it.

"You don't see any flares?" Pat smiled wryly. "Then you're automatically promoted to base commander. Congratulations in advance.

"I would advise you to bring everybody down here, provide security for the repair work and concentrate your firepower. Make sure everyone's armed. Have somebody keep an eye on the Geiger; that'll let you know if somebody's coming to visit.

"If I'm not back by morning, go with Plan B: make a run for it. These things seem to prefer to operate at night so you might have better luck with a daylight run."

She looked at each man in turn. "Well, gents, that's the plan."

"Hold on a bit, Major," Jinski said. "Maybe I should go with you."

"No. I appreciate the offer, but I need you working with your crew trying to make a miracle here."

"Ma'am, are you sure this is the right move?" Cho asked.

Pat laughed but not because anything was funny. "Fuck, no! It's just the least stupid thing I can think of to do."

Cho was off making the arrangements, Jinski had his head stuck in the outside inspection ports with his crew while Pat went back into the trailer. Pritchard was sitting at the far end, a binder of wiring diagrams sitting open on the console near him, but his eyes were glued to the terrified face of Delaney. Pat stepped into his line of sight, blocking the view.

"Sitrep," Pat ordered.

Pritchard seemed to re-focus, pulled his eyes away from Delaney toward the binder. "I'm looking at what we have in stores. There's just some things we don't have replacements for. But maybe… Like I keep telling you, Ma'am, I don't know."

"What about that?" She pointed to the squawk box to the lab.

"Oh, that works, that's fine. It has a direct line to the lab. It just needed power to the trailer."

Pat started to reach for the paging signal button.

"Channel's already open," Pritchard said flatly. "I tried it. There's just nobody answering. There's nobody on the other end."

Pat turned up the volume, heard only an occasional static crackle. "You're sure —"

"It's a buried line, Major, it's intact. There's just nobody picking up the phone, so to speak." He shrugged.

"'So to speak.' If you hear anything, let Mister Cho know, tell him to inform me by walkie-talkie." Pat started to leave.

"Major?" Pritchard nodded at Delaney's body.

"They'll be taking him out soon."

"I don't know if you knew him that well, Ma'am, but he was a nice guy."

"Most of them are." *But only most of them.*

"Ya know, Major, I'm flattered all this attention you give me," Willis said, "But I wouldn't be insulted you spread the love around."

The Humvee was bouncing its way up toward the lab compound, Willis at the wheel, Pat in the passenger seat, Herrera in back.

"I thought Elmonte was a friend of yours," Pat said. "I thought you'd want to get a little payback."

"*Oye*, c'mon, bra!" Herrera crowed from the back seat, slapping Willis – sort of but not quite playfully – across the back of his head. "Le's get a little back for El, right? Hoo-ah, right?"

"Yeah," Willis said glumly. "Hoo-ah. Right. Fuck me."

Willis pulled the Humvee up to the lab compound gate.

"Oh-oh," Willis said, and Pat was thinking the same thing.

The floodlights didn't come on.

"Is it me? It don't feel right?" Willis said.

"Stay here," Pat said.

"Not a problem," which got him another slap across the back of the head from Herrera.

Pat had brought an M4 with her and climbed out of the Humvee with the carbine in hand, and walked slowly toward the gate, looking for some kind of response: a voice on the gatepost speaker, the compound lights coming on, one of those do-or-die storm troopers running up from the blockhouse.

Nothing.

She looked up at the TV camera on its mast. It didn't move with her, no attempt to keep her in sight.

Something else. Something else…not right.

It took a second — and it was hard to be sure, now that the night winds were picking up — but there it was.

No hum from the electrified fence.

She picked a rock up from the ground, tossed it at the fence. It clanged off the chain link. She was looking for some kind of spark, even though she knew that was more Hollywood than reality.

She stepped closer to the fence, just a few inches from it. No hum. The TV camera still locked staring off at nothing. She reached out a single finger – *Idiot! I know, but still…* – and gave the fence a quick, light touch.

Nothing.

She laid her hand on the fence.

Cold metal.

She went to the fencepost speaker. "Major Simons for anybody, answer please." She tried twice more.

Again: nothing.

She climbed back into the Humvee. Willis started to open his mouth, "Don't say it," she said although she was thinking the same thing: *I'm not liking this.*

They drove back to their compound where Pat could pick up the radioactive traces at the gate. Lowering the Geiger's probe out the window, she instructed Willis to drive slowly, and they followed the track away from the compound, up the valley wall onto the flats. Where the track from Elmonte's attacker had led back in the direction of the lab before heading toward Sun City, this one headed straight for the atomic test range.

The night winds were picking up, the visible tracks beginning to disappear in the blowing sand, but the Geiger counter was still picking up enough contaminants that they were able to follow a trail heading out into the desert.

Pat kept the probe dangling out the window, but her eyes were locked forward, trying to reach out to the limits of the Humvee's headlights, into the darkness beyond. *You're out there, whatever you are, and I'd give my eye teeth for any kind of night vision eyes.*

"Hold up for a second, Willis." She climbed out of the Humvee with the flare pistol, warned Willis and Herrera not to look directly at it to preserve their night vision as she sent off an illumination flare. The flare hissed its way arcing into the night, then burst into a cold, flickering light under its small parachute.

Pat walked slowly around the Humvee looking in every direction, now worried that while they were following the trail toward Sun City, it was entirely possible for something to loop around and ambush them from the flanks or rear.

Under the harsh, white light of the flare, the desert seemed unearthly, cold, almost lunar. But nothing moved, there was nothing to see that wasn't expected.

She didn't wait for the flare to die out before she climbed back into the Humvee. She thought it might actually be to their 360-degree advantage to drive under its wavering glow. By the time the flare finally flickered out, they were maybe five miles or so from the valley, and now the Geiger was beginning to click steadily instead of just from the trail. Despite the night wind, there were still the barest visible prints, but the trace contaminants were disappearing among a steady rise in the background radiation.

She ordered another halt, got out with the Geiger. While background radiation was generally increasing, she was getting the strongest readings pointing the probe ahead: Sun City.

"Time to get our hot suits on, gentlemen."

They pulled the CBRN suits out of the rear storage space. Pat made a point of keeping her .45 inside her suit; if the Geiger kept climbing, they were going to have to ditch their weapons and maybe even the Humvee on the return — God willing they were able to return — as they'd be too contaminated to keep.

Suited up, they climbed back into the Humvee. The Geiger was now useless as a tracking device; the background radiation count had gotten high enough to swamp whatever residual traces the target had left. And then the physical tracks themselves finally erased as the night winds picked up into a steady flow, whipping up so much dust it was almost like they were driving through a wavering mist.

"Well, that's that!" Willis said hopefully, or at least that's what it sounded like, muffled through his mask and respirator.

Pat gave him a shake of the head and pointed him forward. The tracks had been going in a straight line toward Sun City, it was a reasonable gamble they'd keep up that way.

She hadn't felt like this in years – muscles tightening, a sickening cold ball in her stomach — not since Afghanistan, but the feeling rushed back into her with a frightening freshness. *It's always there. It never leaves, never completely heals.*

Anytime she and her people had to go out in the field, they called it going out into "Indian country"; unfriendlies everywhere, even the faces smiling at you from the roadside could mask a threat. You could only see what was in front of your eyes, and your middle knotted up knowing something bad could come at you from any direction your 180-degree field of vision couldn't cover. She felt her gloved hand tighten around the pistol grip of the M4, although she was careful to keep her finger off the trigger.

You've done this before, Sister. Control. Discipline. Set the tone for your people.

It was getting harder to see; the winds were getting stronger, sending sand in rippling waves through the headlights, heavy enough they almost didn't see the ditch.

"*Brake!*" Pat yelled.

Even if he didn't see the ditch, Pat's yell, despite coming through her mask, would have been enough for Willis to jump on the brakes and send the Humvee into a lurching halt.

She signaled the other two to stay with the vehicle while she climbed out, .M4 in one hand, a torch in the other. The Humvee had stopped just a few feet short of the ditch. It was a jagged scar in the earth running in both directions out of sight. Pat couldn't tell if it had been a man-made cut as a barrier or something from ancient rains, but it was roughly gouged, the width ranging anywhere – from what she could see – from 5-10 feet across, and 6-7 feet or so deep.

A few yards behind the opposite bank of the ditch, what they initially couldn't see through the blowing sand, was a barbed wire fence also running off in both directions, disappearing into the night. There were signs posted along the fence:

RESTRICTED GOVERNMENT AREA

AUTHORIZED PERSONNEL ONLY

PROTECTIVE CLOTHING REQUIRED

This last over the three-pronged symbol for radioactive contamination.

Right across from them, in line with the tracks they'd been following, was a break in the barbed wire fence.

I'm not liking this. Damn, Willis has me saying it now!

Pat went back to the Humvee, beckoning Willis and Herrera to climb out. Willis pointed to the gap in the barbed wire fence, and she could see the do-we-have-to look in his eyes through his face mask above the respirator. She nodded a yes, saw his shoulders go up and down in a sigh, then he grabbed his carbine and climbed out.

She went down into the ditch first, helping Willis and Herrera down, then they helped each other up the other side, going through the gap in the fence. She held up a hand to halt them, and sent up another illumination flare.

About a hundred yards in the distance, the flare picked up two dozen shapes, no more than shadows under the flare but vaguely resembling houses, vehicles.

She waved Willis and Herrera in close so they could hear her through their masks. "We'll move in slow. Stay close because it's hard to hear through these things, no more than 10 meters apart. Weapons free, gentlemen, because there are no friendlies in front of us. Understood?"

She got a thumbs up from Herrera, something between a resigned shrug and a resigned nod from Willis.

Herrera went to her right, racking a shell into the chamber on his Mossberg, while Willis went to her left. Their weapons were up and ready as they slowly moved forward.

As they drew close to the shapes, even with the blowing sand, she began to make them out better.

"What is all that?" Herrera asked, calling to Pat.

"Targets for the nukes."

During the 1950s nuclear tests, the military had wanted to see what the effects of an atomic blast would be on a typical neighborhood on a typical day. They built collections of houses, populated them with mannequins: dads in their easy chairs, moms in poodle skirts in the kitchen, kids in highchairs. They placed cars and school buses and pickup trucks in front of the houses, stuck more mannequins behind the wheels, more kids in the buses heading off to a nonexistent school. Here it was, two rows of houses along a "street," school buses out front, cars parked in driveways. It was a snapshot of American suburbia c. nineteen-fifty-something an instant before it was to disappear in nuclear annihilation.

The night chill wasn't permeating the suit's nylon skin, and Pat felt sweat crawling down her back, stinging her eyes, and her hands were swimming in it inside her gloves. She had never worked in a CBRN suit, and the feeling was claustrophobic, the face mask limiting her field of vision making her feel even more vulnerable, more –

MMMMMM-CRASH!

They all three turned; it had come from behind them, first the moan of stressed metal, then a louder, even familiar sound…like a car accident?

The Humvee?

The sand was blowing too heavily for them to see that far. Herrera started to move back the way they had come but Pat signaled him to stay in place.

She sent up another flare.

Pat couldn't tell if the blowing sand was too thick or the crash was a worst-case scenario, but even under the flare's glow she couldn't see the Humvee.

Then came the gunfire: Willis' M4 sending off a long burst.

Pat turned to see Willis sending rounds at one of the shadowy houses.

She grabbed him by the shoulder, shouting through her mask and the wind: "What the hell're you firing at?"

"You said weapons free! You said no friendlies! I saw somethin' movin' so…"

"What was it?"

He shook his head. "I saw somethin' move is all I know; I wasn't askin' for no ID."

"Watch my back," and Pat, weapon at her shoulder, started moving slowly toward the house, Willis following a few yards behind.

As she neared, the house became clearer: a slapped-together, bare-bones version of a Cape Cod, a shoebox Chevy in the driveway. There was even a white picket fence around a square of sand that would've been a lawn, an old-fashioned flag mailbox on a white post by the front door. She could see where Willis' bullets had torn apart the glassless wooden frames of a picture window. She slipped her finger around the trigger as she came up to the window, her hand so tense around the M4's pistol grip, it hurt.

Then she was at the window and could see inside. She almost laughed, but more out of relief than humor. She nodded Willis to come up alongside. Willis still kept his carbine at the ready, then looked to where Pat was pointing through the window.

It was supposed to be a living room: a cheap sofa, a couple of stuffed chairs, the kind of mock TV department stores used in their displays. And lying on the bare wooden floor were Joe and Jane Everyperson, their plaster heads shattered by Willis' rounds.

"Gotta admit," Willis said, "pretty good shootin'."

Then it seemed to occur to both of them at the same time.

"Where's Ray?" Willis asked.

They swept the area where they'd been with their torches. Herrera's Mossberg lay on the ground, already half-buried in the blowing sand.

Goddammit…

She could hear Willis' muffled voice calling for his buddy, but she knew between the dampening of his mask and the wind, it was pointless. Then again, she knew it would've been pointless in any case.

A few yards behind them, along the route they'd taken from the ditch, was a boulder, five feet high or so…but…

We came that way. I walked right past that spot. I swear that boulder wasn't there. <u>It wasn't there!</u>

Pat hand signaled Willis to step back, around behind her. She raised her weapon, sighted on the boulder…

Christ, I want to be wrong…

…and loosed a three-round burst.

There were no sparks from the metal-jacketed slugs ricocheting off rock, no puffs of dirt and pulverized stone from the impacts.

The boulder seemed to…heave…then…

UNFOLD!

It opened up like a blossoming flower, limbs unbending and extending — a central mass rising on two long, stout limbs. Pat hit it with the beam from her torch, but it didn't cover much, and the blowing sand didn't help. All she could see was a vague image: a hulking figure, humanoid but not human, seven or so feet tall, broad-shouldered, with four long limbs, and a massive head, but she couldn't make out any features. At first she thought the skin was scaly. but then it seemed to ripple with color -- matching the sand and the flickering light and shadows.

Natural camouflage.

That's what allowed it to fold in on itself, tucking in its long limbs and look like just another desert rock outcropping.

It reached out a hand: three fingers and an opposable thumb. But the claws…

She watched them slide out from the fingers; the way she'd seen cats extend their claws. Except, these didn't have the conical shape of a cat's laws; they were narrow, knife-like blades.

She hadn't been afraid. Not at first. She was too focused on trying to figure out what was rising up in front of her. Then it began to seep in: the coyote, Elmonte — and just what this…this…*thing*…was capable of.

And that's when the muscle memory from training kicked in. She didn't lose her fear, but her weapon came up, she flicked the fire selector to "auto" and let loose a long burst. And another. And another. All the while, shouting to Willis: *"Willis! Fire! Fire, goddammit, fire!"*

The two of them were loosing streams of lead at the thing. It recoiled. It flinched. But…it never stepped back. Then…it began to move forward.

"Oh, fuck!" she could hear Willis yelling inside his mask, "Oh fuck! Oh fuck!"

She grabbed him by the back of his CBRN suit, pulling him along with her as she ran toward one of the houses, ducking behind it. She could see Willis' face mask beginning to fog up; he was panting, frightened, and he was starting to sag against the wall, his knees buckling.

She punched him in the shoulder to get his attention, slapped the side of his head to get him to focus, pulled him up and showed him that she was slamming a fresh magazine into her weapon, for him to do the same. She peeped around the corner. They had lost the thing in the blowing sand; she hoped it had lost them.

From inside the house behind them came the groan of timber straining. She felt the wall behind her begin to flex; even through the suit could hear the wood beginning to crack. She pushed Willis aside as the wall split and erupted and the creature burst through. It passed by so close she could see those color-changing scales rippling and flickering right in front of her eyes. She raised her M4 and squeezed off a burst at the thing's head. It had an effect. The thing staggered, seemingly stunned momentarily, long enough for her to skirt around and grab Willis, who had stumbled away and fallen. She grabbed him by the shoulder of his suit, pulled him around the corner of the house, and ran – practically dragging him – across the "street" to tuck in behind one of the other houses.

"Run! Head for home! I'll lead it off!" He hesitated, and Pat didn't bother trying to figure out if it was just paralyzing fear or some sense of obligation. She gave him another punch to his shoulder and shouted, *"Fucking go!"*

As Willis disappeared off into the blowing sand, she started to creep back the way she'd come. She could see the creature now, between two houses across the "street," still shaking off the impact of the high velocity 5.56 rounds she had shot against its massive skull.

Ok, Fucko, it's just me and you, now.

She wasn't unafraid, she could still feel that cold knot in the pit of her stomach, but it was eclipsed by a hot anger: Loomis, Elmonte, Delaney, now Herrera.

"C'mon, you fucking freak!" It didn't matter if the thing wouldn't hear it; her blood was up. She sighted the M4 again and sent another burst against the creature's head. It started to move toward her, those long legs covering the ground faster than she had figured on. She was backpedaling, firing as she went, but the billowy legs of the CBRN suit, and the awkward "booties," made her clumsy. Moving awkwardly, she felt one of her feet see-saw on a rock and knew her balance was going. She knew there was no way she was going to stay upright, even as that *thing* kept coming at her, closing the distance.

She kept her finger on the trigger, kept sending rounds toward the creature even as she felt herself going down. She found herself on her back, the breath knocked out of her, the M4 silent now, empty, and the creature just a few feet away. That big head, like a gun turret, was swiveling down, targeting her, one of its arms reaching out with the blade-like claws extending…

The side of the creature lit up with a stuttering flash and she heard the chatter of an M4 as the creature staggered. Through the blowing sand she could barely make out a silhouette: Willis. He'd come back.

I'll be damned!

But now the creature's attention was on Willis, who turned and ran, the whatever-it-was taking off after him.

Pat swept her arm around on the ground, found her carbine, went to reload it, but when she tried yanking on the charging handle, it jammed. The sand.

Then she remembered…

She scrambled to her feet, racing to the spot where they'd found Herrera's half-buried Mossberg. She grabbed the shotgun and took off after Willis, who looked to have been heading back toward the gap in the barbed wire fence with the creature tailing him.

As she passed through the torn wire, she saw what had happened to the Humvee; pushed nose first into the ditch it had flipped, landing upside down at an angle.

But…

Where the hell are they?

Then she heard more firing to her left. Willis had found a cleft in the side of the ditch, burrowed himself in, and the creature couldn't get at him without getting a face full of bullets which — despite its seeming ability to take the punishment — was more than it appeared to be willing to take. So now it was beginning to claw at the clay-like earth of the side of the ditch, and it wouldn't be long before it had dug its way to Willis.

Pat's mind was scrambling. She remembered all those shell casings out on the desert that she and Cho had found and knew that even between her and Willis they didn't have enough firepower…

The Humvee.

There was a storage bustle on the Humvee's tail: three 5-gallon jerry cans of extra fuel plus a spare tire. The gas cans had fallen out of the bustle. Pat threw them under the inverted vehicle, unscrewed the

Humvee's gas cap, letting the fuel pour out and pool on the hard ditch floor around the jerry cans.

She slid down into the ditch, brought up the Mossberg and squeezed the trigger, the stock punched into her shoulder as the muzzle flared and sent a fistful of double-0 buckshot at the creature. That was enough to draw its attention. Pat racked in a second shell and sent another cloud of buckshot at the creature's head. It seemed to be debating where to turn its attention, but Pat sealed the debate with another shot to the head. Now it was most decidedly coming for her. She pumped out the rest of the magazine, moving backwards at the same time. When racking only produced an empty chamber, the creature seemed to know the Mossberg was empty and charged. Pat threw the Mossberg at the creature — *Catch, Fucko!* — turned and ran for the Humvee, throwing herself to the ground and crawling into the space under the overturned vehicle.

She knew the thing was close and could swear she felt the tips of its fingers sweep by the soles of her boots as she slithered along the fuel-soaked ground, then scrambled clear of the vehicle. Then she was out the other side and, without even looking, knew the creature had followed her under the Humvee.

Pat slammed a fresh illumination shell into the flare pistol as she ran to put a few yards between her and the Humvee, then turned, aimed not at the creature but at the pooling gas — and fired.

The creature had splashed enough gas on itself coming after her that the flare-ignited flames quickly jumped to its body. Writhing in obvious agony it made no sound, struggling to get out from under the Humvee. Just then, the jerry cans exploded in quick succession — both vehicle and creature were swallowed up in an ugly ball of orange and yellow flame with black smoke. She felt the gust of heat even through the CBRN suit as she watched the creature move less and less…then not at all.

Her adrenaline surge ebbing, Pat felt herself sinking against the side of the ditch — panting and drained. Sensing something standing over her, she looked up.

At the top of the ditch, his CBRN suit aglow with the flames from the burning Humvee, stood Willis. He knelt and reached out a hand to help her up.

BESIEGED

Pat and Willis walked silently side by side, heavy-footed, following the Humvee tracks back to the valley. The winds had died down leaving the tire prints a clear path to follow.

Pat felt they were both in the same headspace; trying to make sense of something that made no sense. It was a weird feeling that something still fresh and vivid in their mind's eye managed to yet seem completely unreal. And so, they'd sunk into a certain numbness and a foot-dragging fatigue which was as much mental as physical.

He's asking himself what they always ask themselves: why him and not me? How come we got picked for this job and not someone else? Was this really something that needed doing?

Pat knew Willis was asking these questions because she was asking them, too.

"Those are dangerous questions, Sweets," her father had once told her. It was the year after she'd graduated from the Academy, and she was wondering if she'd be deployed to Afghanistan. Combat had seemed an abstract during her Academy years, but now it was finally sinking in that it might not be too long before she was under fire…along with the people entrusted to her command. "Those questions are especially dangerous in a commander," her father had said, "because they're not just about you. And you're never happy – I repeat, *never* – happy with the answers. But if you're human, I don't know how you don't ask them."

"How do you live with them?"

Her father had smiled in a sort of bitter way. "You focus on the job you have to do, because you'll always still have a job to do. Giving your head over to questions like that only gets in the way."

She and Willis had walked for an hour or so when she waved them to a halt, estimating that they were well clear of the hot zone. She fired off a green flare.

"Think they'll be able to see that?" Willis asked.

"I don't know. Not the best answer a commanding officer can give when asked a question by one of their men, but…right now…that's my answer to any question; I don't know." She let out a sigh. "We can lose the suits."

As they shucked their CBRN suits, Willis saw Pat wincing as she slid her right arm free.

"You get hurt?" Willis asked.

"That damned Mossberg kicked like an angry mule."

"They'll do that."

"Speaking of…I'm afraid you're going to have to lose the weapon, too."

Willis looked decidedly unhappy.

"It's hot, Willis."

"I'm not sure worryin' 'bout gettin' cancer in five years is my priority."

"Lose it."

Willis may have been a defrocked Weapons Specialist and, according to his file, a danger to people around him on the rifle range, but he knew his stuff. He dropped the magazine out of the weapon, cleared the chamber. He popped a round out of the magazine and used the point of the bullet to push out the two pins holding the M4's upper and lower receivers together, separated them and then threw the pins out into the desert night. He gave her a look as if to say, "Happy?"

She put on a tight smile and gave her head a tilted nod in mock-regal approval.

"I feel kinda naked."

"We have this." Her suit off, she patted the holstered .45 on her hip.

Willis was unimpressed. "What you think you're gonna do with that we come across another one a those big ugly bastards?"

She shrugged. "Hit it over the head?"

Willis rolled his eyes and started walking again.

With the winds down to a breeze, the desert sands settled, leaving the night sky clear, cloudless, the heavy sprinkling of stars as sharp as cut glass. The desert wasn't like other places where Pat had been stationed, none of the usual night sounds: no crickets, no hooting owls, no belching frogs…no nothing. She couldn't remember ever seeing any place so dead quiet. So dead.

A perfect home for that thing. This is why they put us here. Nobody even knows this part of the world exists.

Pat debated bringing up the subject but felt obligated: "I'm sorry about Herrera. I know he was a friend of yours."

"I don't want to talk 'bout it"

She nodded, she understood. But there was something else: "You came back. I want to —"

Willis was already shaking his head, waving at her to cut her off. "Major, 'fore you get too gushy, you oughta know, I didn't wanna do it. I don't know why I did it. Even when I was doin' it, I was sayin' this is the stupidest, godamnedest thing I ever done. 'N' when that thing started chasin' my ass, then I was *sure* it was the stupidest, godamnedest thing I ever done. Even now, I'm still thinkin' —"

"It was the stupidest, godamnedest thing you've ever done?"

He nodded. "Somethin' like that".

"What's your first name, Willis?"

"I don't like it."

"C'mon. I could order you to tell me."

"Theodore," he mumbled.

"Theodore," she said, trying it out. His face wrinkled in pain and there might've even been a slight groan to go with it. "Theodore?"

"Yes, Ma'am?"

"Theodore... Thank you."

By the time Pat and Willis reached the rim of the valley, even though the sun was still well below the horizon, the night had lightened by several shades to a grayish twilight; enough visibility that they had a clear view down to the compound below.

"How come there's no lights?" Willis said.

"Nothing good comes to mind."

"Ooooh, I'm not —"

"I know, I'm already ahead of you." Pat was even more troubled to see there was no activity around the EW trailer. "I think they're in there," and Pat pointed to the mess hut. The two remaining camp Humvees were parked to block the doors on either side of the Quonset.

After a bit, she gave up a resigned sigh. "Well..." and started walking. Seeing the reluctance on Willis' face, she added, "You can stay here if you want," and she resumed walking.

He nodded with the same kind of resignation and followed her down the slope as she drew her .45.

"You think that pop gun's gonna do any good we bump into another one a those BUBs?"

"It's my security blanket, ok? And what the hell is a 'BUB'?"

"Big Ugly Bastard."

"You're priceless, Theodore."

"Ma'am, do me a favor? When we get in there, in front a the guys..."

"Yes, *Willis*."

"'Preciate it."

They walked slowly up to the mess hut. A figure moved inside the Humvee blocking the nearest door, a rifle barrel protruded from the driver's window. "Halt and identify!"

"That you, Ormond? Who the hell ya think it is, ya dumbass!" Willis called back.

"I'm not sure that's the proper protocol," Pat said.

"I'm feelin' kinda cranky."

"Willis, that you?" the Humvee voice said.

"I know I don't show up too well in the dark..."

God bless G.I. humor.

The Humvee engine started up, the vehicle moved clear of the door, and Cho, Jinski, and some of the other men came out to greet them. The welcome dampened when they saw Herrera wasn't with them.

Pat went up to Cho and Jinski.

"Bad?" Jinski asked.

"Not good," Pat said. "Let's talk."

The mess hut was dark except for some emergency lanterns scattered about. Pat sat with Cho at a table away from the men who were gathered around Willis, pumping him on what had happened out at Sun City. Jinski came over with a meal tray carrying three cups, setting coffees down for each of them.

"You look beat," Jinski said. "Figured you could use this."

It only occurred to Pat then that she'd been going for twenty hours or so. When she'd dropped into the chair at the table, she'd felt her body sag, and rubbed at scratchy, burning eyes. She took a sip of the coffee. "Good God! How long's this battery acid been in the pot?"

"You're the one made Ormond chief cook," Jinski said. "He's come a long way on the cookin', but he hasn't figured out the coffee tastes better you clean the urn out oncet in a while. But I guarantee it'll wake you up."

"Hell, I may not sleep for a week." Then she went on to give a less colorful account than Willis' of what had happened out at Sun City.

"At least we know it can die," Jinski said.

"Ma'am, any idea what we're dealing with?" Cho asked. "I mean, what are these things?"

"The circumstances didn't exactly allow for a detailed examination, so let's just leave it that they are what they are, they have no interest in peaceful co-existence, and they're damned hard to kill. Now, why don't you catch me up on what's been going on here."

"Maybe two, three hours after you left, all the power went out. I tried reaching you by radio, but we couldn't get you."

By my estimation, that would've been about the time we walked into Sun City.

"We could hear something rooting around in the generator hut," Cho went on. "I guessed it was one of these things, but I didn't want to risk a man to find out."

"You did the right thing. Why here?"

"I thought if we had to fort up, might be best to be close to food and water."

Pat nodded approvingly; she hadn't thought of that. "Weapons status."

"With what you had to leave behind at Sun City, what we lost with Loomis and Elmonte, Delaney… I make the count at seven M4s, three Mossbergs, and we still have a dozen Sigs, so everybody has at least something. Plus, we still have the 240; I had Jinski bring it inside."

"What's the sitrep on the comms repair? I'm guessing nothing good."

Cho called Pritchard over. The EW specialist sat at the table with his own coffee, seeming to drink it without a problem.

"You must have a stomach like cast iron," Pat said.

Pritchard shrugged the comment off. "You get used to it."

"I am assuming the reason you're here instead of tinkering inside The Brain is it's not fixable."

Pritchard shook his head. "The damage to the transmission equipment is total. Even with what we have in stores, there's not enough to stitch something together."

"Even the satlink?"

"Whatever did the damage didn't miss anything. If the goal was to completely cut us off from the outside, mission accomplished."

"But he has an idea," Cho said, nodding at Pritchard to go ahead.

"It's only a possibility," Pritchard said. "I don't know if it'd actually work, there's compatibility issues, power output issues —"

"Do you mind?" Pat said and made an impatient rolling-ahead motion with one finger. "I'm not going to sue you if it doesn't pan out."

"The radio in one of the Humvees. On their own, those sets don't have the range we need. But I think it might be possible to splice into the main radio antenna up top. If — a big if — if we can tie into the antenna, the Humvee's engine might — I emphasize *might* — give enough power, maybe not to reach Nellis but we might possibly maybe be able to reach somebody somewhere."

"'If,' 'might,' 'possibly,' 'maybe'; think you could maybe possibly squeeze more qualifiers in there?"

"I got another one for you," Jinski said. "Bigger problem is goin' up to the antenna."

"Indian country," Pat said.

"Yup."

Pritchard started to stand to leave but Pat waved him back down. She was running through options, possibilities – *anything* usable, workable, helpful – when something bubbled up from the back of her memory. "Remember the night we lost Loomis? And the next day, we received that message from Nellis that the colonel had cancelled the recon drone we'd asked for? Didn't you say this meant the lab had their own comms set-up?"

"I think what I said was they *probably* did. It just made sense."

"They don't have their own antenna so they must be using the same one we do. But there's no overhead wires connecting the lab to the antenna."

"Then it's probably a buried line like they have for the squawk box."

"So, like the squawk line, their connection to the antenna should be intact."

"Stands to reason."

Pat could see a look of alarm seeping into Cho's face, and he looked ready to say something, but she held up a finger signaling him to hold on it. She thanked Pritchard and sent him off.

"You can't be thinking what I think you're thinking," Cho said, keeping his voice low so the soldiers at the other end of the hut couldn't hear.

"What happened to that fancy crossword vocabulary of yours?"

"Major —"

"Major! I've got something!"

It was Sanborn – she remembered him as one of the men slouching around the LZ the day she'd landed. Cho had him monitoring the Geiger counter. Pat, Cho, and Jinski went over for a look. The clicks from the counter's speaker were increasing, and the meter needle was spiking. "It's moving," Sanborn said. The count would ease until Sanborn moved the probe. Whatever was spiking the Geiger was moving around outside the mess hut.

"Douse the lights!" Pat said in a loud whisper. "Weapons ready!"

She heard the murmurs ripple through the men: "Shit...Oh, Christ...Fuck me..."

Willis found a corner, sank down onto the floor, his arms wrapped around his knees, head down. "No more," she heard him mumble, shaking his head, "No more..."

Poor kid. How much could he take?

Sanborn followed the radiation spikes, walking slowly around the mess hut, the weapons of the rest of the men swiveling along with his moves.

"It's lookin' for a way in," Jinski whispered.

"No," Pat said. "It's just picking a spot. Trust me; it doesn't need a door." She remembered the creature that had chased her bursting through the wall of one of the Sun City houses. "Get away from the walls!" Pat said as loudly as she dared. "Away from the walls!"

Pat went over to Willis. "Stand up," she said quietly. "Stay with me." She held out her hand the way Willis had held out his back at Sun City. Somehow Willis found it in himself to reach out, getting pulled to his feet. "You're my man, Theodore," and she pulled him behind her back.

"You promised."

She had to smile: "Ok…*Willis.*"

Sanborn was back-tracking toward one of the Humvee-barricaded doors. He looked to Pat: "It can't get through there, can it?"

"Get away from the wall!"

But Sanborn's attention was on the Geiger's meter. The signal kept rising and falling as if what was outside was walking back and forth. Instead of backing away from the wall, Sanborn got closer, holding the probe near the wall trying to get a better reading. "I can't get a, it's, it's… I dunno…"

"Get away from the goddamned wall!"

"Bobby!" Jinski barked. "Back off the fucking wall!"

"Sarge, this thing is up and down, up and down —"

Jinski started to move toward Sanborn…

He never made it.

The claws, those knife-like claws, came through the thin metal skin of the Quonset as easily as if it was paper, opening a gap, just enough for the thing to force its head and shoulders through, its one arm reaching in, extending…

Sanborn was frozen in shock, surprise, disbelief. His paralysis only lasted a second, not even that long. He was already starting to back away when those four blades pierced him through his chest and midriff, lifted him up on his toes. His shrill pain-fueled scream was almost instantly lost in the blood bubbling up out of his mouth. Then the thing hiked him clear of the floor and easily flicked him away as it bulled its way further into the room.

"Fire!" Pat screamed. *"Fire fire fire!"*

They had all been transfixed as Sanborn had been, seeing but unable to comprehend. Pat was popping away with her .45, knowing it was useless but hoping to spark the men as she ran to them, punching them, slapping them, yelling at them to free their frozen minds, Willis behind her, hanging on to her belt.

One by one, they began to fire their weapons until it became a cacophony. The mess hall, with its metal walls capturing and rebounding the sound, becoming home to a constant roar of overlapping automatic gunfire, occasionally punctuated by the deeper singular blasts of shotguns.

The creature was now fully in the room, twisting under the shower of lead, the metal wall behind it alive with the sparks of bullet strikes.

Then a string of tracers cutting across the room: Jinski, the only man big enough to hold the M240 the way the other men handled their carbines, loosed a steady stream of tracer-laced machine gun fire, screaming, *"Die, you motherfucker! Fuckin' die, die, die!"*

The creature began to stagger further into the room, the constant bombardment of metal-jacketed bullets gradually taking a toll. It made no noise, no sounds of pain, just silent writhing and flinching, lit in a strobing, jerky fashion by the rapid-fire flickering of muzzle flashes.

"Pour it to him!" Pat screamed.

Willis let go of her belt, pushed her aside, went to the nearest man and grabbed his M4 away and opened up on the creature. *"Fuck you! Fuck you!"*

The creature staggered, then dropped to one knee, seemed to gather itself for a last surge and lunged toward one of the men – Ormond, the failed cook – and managed to get its hand around his right ankle. Ormond screamed as the creature started to drag him close, frantically clawing at the floor.

The firing eased, the men scared of hitting Ormond.

Pat heard a heavy metallic *clunk* to one side, and out of the corner of her eye, saw Jinski drop the machine gun, run out of sight, then charge back toward the creature -- something red held over his head.

He'd grabbed a fire ax from its bracket on the wall next to an extinguisher. *"Gaaaaa!"* He brought the ax down where the creature's arm joined its shoulder, and cleaved clear through, freeing Ormond. The creature's head reared back in a silent scream. Jinski took a stance like he'd stepped into a batter's box, brought the ax around sideways in a swing that would've sent a baseball out into the parking lot of any major league ballfield, and neatly severed the creature's head from its neck, sending it bouncing along the length of the mess hut, the torso collapsing forward so heavily the plank floor cracked when it hit.

All was quiet, then, except for the ringing the gunfire had left in Pat's ears, the men coughing from the acrid fumes left by the fusillade, and a groan from Ormond.

"You'd never believe I didn't make the Braves' training camp," Jinski said.

"Get him on one of the tables," Pat told the men gathering around Ormond, prying off the hand still clamped around his ankle. She looked over to where Jinski was kneeling by Sanborn's body. He looked up at her, shaking his head, not that she'd expected anything else.

Ormond couldn't straighten his leg, the one the creature had grabbed. Pat ran her hands lightly up the limb. There was no tear in his pants leg, no blood; she had a suspicion about what had happened. "Where do you feel it, Ormond? Your knee?"

"Yeah – oh, Christ, that hurts – that fucker only grabbed my ankle, but I feel it – oof! – it feels like my knee."

Pat gingerly felt around Ormond's knee and could feel it was misshapen with a lump to the outside of the joint; the patella had slid out of place. "You've got a dislocation. Some of you gentlemen hold him."

"What're you gonna do?"

"I'm going to fix it."

"You know how to do that?"

"Well, kind of. I saw a training video once."

"*Kind of?* Oh, God. Is it going to hurt?"

"Quite a bit. Jinski, get over here. Hold his ankle. When I give you the nod, gently – *gently* – push his leg up, his knee back toward his chest, ok? I'll do the rest. The rest of you hold him still." Pat stood at Ormond's side and put both hands on the lump. "Ok, Ormond, on the count of three."

"Is this where you fuck with me and we count one, two, and then before we get to three – *OWWWJESUSFUCKINGCHRIST!*"

Pat had given the nod to Jinski while Ormond had been babbling, and when Jinski'd pushed the leg up, Pat wrestled the patella back into place with a *pop* which had everybody around the table wincing.

"How's that?" she asked.

"Still hurts like a sonofabitch…Ma'am," Ormond groaned. "But it's better."

"Well, it's going to be sore for a couple of weeks. Gentlemen, if we still have any ice, make an ice pack for your buddy and get it on that knee."

"What the hell is this thing?" Cho asked. Pat was standing with him and Jinski over the creature's body.

"Bring me one of those lanterns," Pat said, "I want to get a good look."

Cho brought one over and handed it to Pat. The lantern revealed dozens of bullet wounds on the body, each in a halo of crusting crimson blood. The color-shifting scales were fading into a pale milkiness.

"Damn," Cho said, "the blood's already drying."

"Not drying," Pat said. "Clotting."

"Ma'am, you wanna hold that light a little closer. What's goin' on here?" Jinski was looking at the stump of the neck.

Pat saw what looked like little slowly spreading blooms dotting the raw, red tissue. "I don't believe it."

"Is that…?"

Pat nodded. "Fresh tissue."

"You tellin' me this thing's growin' another head?" Jinski said.

Pat shook her head. "No, it's just to cover the wound."

"Looks like it's slowing."

"Naturally," Pat said, stepping away from the corpse. "It's dead. But if you hadn't …" Pat shook her head. "Gentlemen, this thing's a killer."

"No shit," Jinski said. "Ma'am."

"This isn't natural, the pieces don't go together. Heavy and tough but light on its feet and fast, that camouflage ability, those claws that look like they can cut through damned near anything. The clotting, the tissue generation… If you don't get a kill, this thing has the ability to go off somewhere and heal. Not natural. If you need proof…" She held the torch where the light came down across where the tops of the creature's legs joined its torso. There were no genitals.

"Fuuuuuuck…" Jinski murmured.

Pat went over to examine the separated head. The face was almost like a child's drawing; that simple. Large eyes with vertical tapered pupils, large earholes but no visible ears, slits for a nose, a wide mouth of jagged shark-like teeth. "Look at those eyes."

"Like a cat," Cho said.

"Perfect for night vision. That's why the attacks have always been at night. This…*thing*…is *designed*, it's a construct, bits put together to make a perfect killer. I don't want to be overly dramatic, gentlemen, but by definition I think this qualifies as a monster."

"A fuckin' Frankenstein," Jinski said.

"Bingo," Pat said. "The only flaw is that radioactive trace it leaves."

"You think this is what they've been doing in the lab?" Cho wondered.

Pat nodded. "David – Dr. Cordell – and the Woltzes, they were working with nukes at Los Alamos but part of what they were researching had to do with the effects of radiation exposure. But none of them are any kind of biologist or anything like that. I'd love to know what Mr. Philosopher – that deep-thinking sonofabitch Ostrow – is into." She shook all that off; there were more immediate concerns to deal with. "Jinski, have some of the men carry this thing out, all the pieces, take it outside, douse it with gasoline, burn this fucker. Have them carry it out on something; I don't want them taking any more mils than they have to. Then have them pile up furniture over that hole in the wall."

"Why?" Cho asked. "I thought you said there were just two of these things. You killed one out at Sun City —"

"What we figured out was there was more than one. That's not the same thing as only two. What we don't know is how many more."

"Oh my God, you mean —"

"Well, keep a good thought, but fact is we don't know."

Cho started walking in little circles, shaking his head.

Pat went to kneel by Sanborn's body. She'd been putting it off; this should've been what she did first. But, as much a nightmare as the creature was, she would rather have poked around that grotesque collection of stalking, hunting, and killing traits than do this. She reached into Sanborn's collar, found his tags, detached the lower tag and added it to the chain with Elmonte's and Delaney's tags. Small blessings: because they hadn't found Loomis or Herrera, she didn't have to look down at a fistful of tags in her hand instead of "just" three.

Jesus, how many more?

She did something she knew she shouldn't do; she held the lantern up where she could see Sanborn's face. Like most of the men, he was young, somebody anybody over thirty would've called a kid. He'd died so quickly his face had frozen in wide-eyed horror, his mouth, stained with the blood which had surged up and out, agape in a silent scream. She reached out and closed his eyes, setting the lamp down on the floor so his face fell into shadow.

She noticed Cho standing behind her. "He was at the LZ when I landed that first day," Pat said. "Other than that, I don't know much about him."

"He's one of Jinski's people," Cho said. "I remember he was from New Jersey. Some little town on the coast. He was always telling us: in New Jersey you don't call it 'the beach' or 'the coast,' he would be lecturing us that you say, 'the shore'. He used to say this place, the desert, felt like a cheat because it was like the beach but without the ocean. He missed the ocean. He missed the water. Um, Ma'am…"

"I know. Put him with Delaney in the armory," Pat said as she walked away, "We'll figure something out later." She left the lantern behind and sat off at a table by herself someplace in the dark.

Her head was throbbing, and as drained as she felt, she could feel her teeth grinding against each other so hard she wouldn't've been surprised if they shattered. Her fists kept balling up so tightly her hands hurt. It went with the pulsing heat she felt in her face which was making her head pound. She wanted to scream, to overturn the table, grab the chair she was on, and smash it against the floor until it exploded in pieces.

But the men… She could hear her father's voice in her head: "*They can't see you lose it, Sweets. They're looking to you. Like it or not, you have to be their rock. That's why you have those oak leaves on your collar.*"

She took deep breaths until her jaws relaxed, her fists slowly opening. She stood, saw two of her soldiers picking up Sanborn's body, and the rage came back.

She thought of David Cordell, her one-time lover. Of Colonel McElhone, her one-time mentor. Mariska and Oskar Woltz, the one-time friends with whom she'd spent many a wine-and-laughs night playing pinochle.

And Aaron Ostrow, musingly toying with his *Chai* medallion.

Whatever else happens in this place, I swear to Christ, I'm going to fucking kill you all.

GAMBITS

Thank God for G.I. humor:

"Ya know, Ormond, there's a bright side to this."

"Oh, yeah? Like what?"

"Like you don't have to cook...and we don't have to eat your cookin'!"

And somehow they found it in themselves to laugh. Even Ormond: "Yeah! Win-win!"

They went there because it helped put distance between them and the thing still smoldering under a gasoline fire outside. It also helped put distance between them and the two bodies lying in the armory; men they'd known well, men they'd lived with and worked alongside since the lab had gone operational ten months ago.

As ordered, the men had piled most of the mess and rec space furniture against the gap in the Quonset wall although Pat knew – and she was sure if any of the men had taken a minute to think about it, they'd know it as well – it was a useless gesture. These things could just punch through the walls somewhere else. But it was something for them to do, to preoccupy them. It was busy work. And, like her .45, it was more a security blanket than an effective response.

Now, while one man monitored the Geiger counter, the rest were gathered around two of the remaining tables, those who had the stomach for it having whipped up something to eat for themselves. They'd been up all night, yet none seemed to be much for sleeping.

Pat was with Cho and Jinski at the pool table, the one piece of furniture in the mess hut too heavy for the men to move. Jinski had a trio of peanut butter and jelly sandwiches piled on a plate for himself. In front of the bulk of the sergeant, the sandwiches didn't look any bigger than petit fours. Pat envied his appetite; she was one of those with no stomach for food just then. So was Cho.

"We've got to make a move," Pat said.

"Why don't we just dig in here and send two men in a Humvee to Indian Springs," Cho said. "They can call for help."

"I did consider that…for about two seconds. What if one of these things catches them out on the flat? Two men —"

"You and Willis took one on and killed it."

"We were lucky, that's all. You have a short memory, Mister Cho; it took World War III and Duke Nukem here —" meaning Jinski "— to bring this one down. But let's say our people get through. What are our ammo stocks like?"

Cho frowned. "We never anticipated this kind of usage."

"Right, so in the hours it takes our mission of mercy to get to Indian Springs, make the call, and a rescue bird to get here, how many more of these attacks do you think we can take?"

Cho's frown grew deeper. "One. Maybe. Maybe two."

"Maybe," Jinski said, sounding less convinced about the possibility of "maybe" than Cho. His opinion almost got lost in a mouthful of bread, peanut butter, and grape jelly. He held up a finger for everyone to take a Time Out until he swallowed. "Somethin' else, Mister Cho. We got no power means we got no A/C. Once that sun's up 'n' starts cookin' these metal walls, it's gonna be like gettin' hit with the hammers a Hell 'n' we're gonna be sweatin' in here like whores in church. Pardon my language, Ma'am."

"It paints a picture," Pat said.

"Point is, how long we gonna last 'till we get help?" Jinski said.

"If our people get through," Pat said.

"Big 'if'," Jinski said, picking up a second sandwich, half of which disappeared in a single bite. "'Amn 'ig 'if'," he got out around his food.

Cho mulled this over unhappily for a moment, then said to Pat, "I know what you were thinking about, what you were talking about with Pritchard."

"He's got ESP now," Pat said to Jinski.

"You can't seriously be thinking about trying to get into the lab," Cho said.

"You're right; I'm not serious. It's part of my stand-up comedy routine; I thought it would perk up the troops' morale. Laugh a minute. How'm I doing?"

Cho stepped away from the pool table with an exasperated sigh, doing his pacing about and head-shaking routine, again. "For the love of God, Major, how you can joke right now —"

"Because if I don't, Cho, I'll crawl under this pool table and close my eyes and curl up in a ball. I don't think that'd be good for any of us, do you?"

"You don't even know if you can get in there! What's your plan; walk up and knock on the door like a Girl Scout selling cookies?"

Pat exchanged a smile with Jinski: *That was pretty good!*

"And let's say you do find a way in. You said when you went up there, the power was out on the fence —"

"That's just the exterior power —"

"It means you don't know what's going on inside! You say there's more than two of these things? What if they're on the loose in there? None of us knows the lab layout, you'd have to find their comms station, hope it's intact, hope you can find a power source for it —"

"Quite the pessimist, isn't he?" Pat said to Jinski.

"He's having a bad day," the sergeant said and popped the last bite of his last sandwich in his mouth.

"You're going to be a wiseass, too?" Cho reprimanded Jinski.

"'Wiseass'?" Pat made a show of contemplating the word. "His vocabulary is really suffering. He used to be so much more loquacious and erudite."

"Oooh, I like that," Jinski said, "'Loquacious'."

"Would you even know how to operate their radio set-up if you found it?" Cho said, playing another hurdle card.

Pat shrugged, trying not to show how concerned she was about this. "I've fiddled with some knobs in my time, I'll figure it out. Wasn't it you, just a few hours ago, saying we had to try everything?"

Cho started doing his little head-shake-and-circle-walk yet again, muttering, "Insane. Insane."

"Now that I'm thinkin' on it," Jinski said, "there might be a way in."

Which froze Cho. "Jesus, it's a virus, you've infected him."

"Mister Cho, you got that little notebook a yours?"

Cho came back to the pool table, fished his notebook and pen out of his breast pocket and handed them over to Jinski.

Jinski found a blank page, drew two parallel lines far apart. "Ok, here's the valley." He drew a circle close to one of the lines. "Here's the lab grounds. When they built this place, they built a kind a tunnel, an outlet, something for drainage, right here," and he drew a line from the side of the circle closest to the valley wall stopping in the middle of the in-between space. "Big enough to walk through. It empties into a ditch," and now Jinski drew another line from the "tunnel's" end running parallel to the valley edge.

"Which runs where?"

"Nowhere. It just goes for a couple hundred yards, enough for whatever drains out of that tunnel to evaporate. There's also some conduit lines run from that tunnel into the valley slope. They might be those buried connections to the antennas on the rim Pritchard was talking about. This tunnel is set down I'm guessin' even with the second underground level of the lab. There's an electrified grill over the entrance, but with the power dead that's no problem long's it's on the same circuit as the fence. There's an electronic lock, nothing special, should be able to pry that thing open without too much trouble."

"How do you know about all this?"

"Couple months ago — Mister Cho, you remember — the concrete around the entrance was cracking, they musta set it wrong when they built it. They asked my detail to do the repairs."

"But you don't know where that tunnel goes," Cho cautioned.

"He's right," Jinski said. "We weren't allowed inside. I can't tell you if it reaches the lab, or even if it does, if there's any access. But if it's possible to get in, my guess is their comms are on one of those two above-ground levels, probably the top one."

"That would be the place for command and control," Pat said, agreeing.

"Great minds, Major. Now, this water that drains out, it's not much but it's contaminated."

"Radioactive?" Pat asked.

"About as hot as what you found on Delaney, between 100-200 mils as I 'member. Since we were gonna be in it for a while, they had us wearing hot suits as a precaution. Was a bitch wearin' those workin' in the heat. Pardon my language, again."

"Forgiven." Now it was Pat's turn to step away from the pool table, pace as she started mentally running over what Jinski had reported. *"You need to have more than one plan, Sweets. Always need a backup."*

She came back to the table. "Ok, so that's Plan A."

"There's a Plan B?" Cho asked warily. "I'm almost afraid to hear it. No, I'm *definitely* afraid to hear it."

"I'll have a walkie-talkie with me, but I don't know if a signal will carry out of the lab. If I pull this off, I'll try to give you some kind of sign, but…" She looked at her watch: it was just turning 0600. She looked to the Quonset windows where the gray pre-dawn had grown still lighter; daybreak couldn't be far off. She did some mental calculations: how long of a walk to the lab, traversing the tunnel if it was accessible, a good amount of time to flounder around inside the lab looking for the communications station. "…if you don't get anything from me by, oh, call it 1100 hours, you try Plan B."

"Which is?" Cho asked the way a dental patient asks the dentist, "How much is this going to hurt?"

"Pritchard's idea; see if he can tap directly into the radio mast up on the flat and using one of the Humvee radios to transmit. But everybody goes with him. If he runs into company, you'll need that kind of firepower. Whether or not he can pull off what he says, soon as he's done doing what he can, you pack everybody up in the Humvees and bug out for Indian Springs."

Cho shook his head. "Ma'am, a dozen men and only two vehicles, they won't all —"

"I don't care how you do it, Cho. Grease them up, use a crowbar, a shoehorn, tie some of them to the roof, but you get them in those vehicles, put the pedal to the metal, and get the hell out! Then, however and whenever you make contact with Nellis, that's when you go to Plan C: you have them bomb this place, bomb the hell out of it, everything from here to Sun City, blow it to fucking atoms."

Cho's face sagged. "Major, if you're still in the lab, I can't give that order."

"Mister Cho," Jinski said with a solemnity seeming even more funereal and grave rumbling up on the big man's deep voice, "what the major is saying is if you don't hear from her by 1100 hours, you're not going to hear from her."

It took Cho a moment to digest this, not so much because he didn't understand as he didn't want to. "Oh…*man*…," he groaned.

Pat came around to Cho's side of the pool table, propped herself against the table close to her XO. "I know, Cho, but understand something: the second I start walking up toward the lab, your sole responsibility is to them," and she tilted her head to indicate the men at their tables at the other end of the mess hut. "Your job when I leave – your *only* job – is to get them the hell out of here. Read me? Let me hear it."

After a moment, Cho nodded. "I read you, Ma'am," he said quietly.

Pat gave him a thank-you squeeze on his arm.

"I'm goin' with you," Jinski said.

"The hell you are."

"Like Mister Cho said, you don't know what's goin' on in there. If it's hairy, you're gonna need somebody watchin' your six while you're messin' with the comms gear. Somethin' happens to you 'fore you get to it, I'm the checkdown man. I've done some knob-fiddlin' in my time, too."

"Jinks, I appreciate it but —"

"Ma'am," and the sergeant grinned broadly, "you can tell me I'm not goin', you can even order me, but unless you put one through my leg, I'm goin'." His grin faded considerably as he nodded toward the men at the mess tables. "They're my boys, too. Sandy Sanborn was one a mine."

It didn't take much studying of the set of Jinski's face for Pat to see that any argument – as the sergeant had said, short of putting a bullet through one of his legs – was pointless. "Mister Cho, we'll need two hot suits. You better make one of them an extra large."

Based on what Jinski had reported about the level of contamination in the lab tunnel and that it seemed to be confined to a trickle of draining water, Pat wasn't worried about weapons contamination the way she'd been concerned out at Sun City. Still, her .45 having survived several wars in the hands of her grandfather and father, she thought better safe than sorry and wore the pistol inside her CBRN suit. She took up an M4, Jinski went with a Mossberg. Suited up but with their hoods still hanging loose on their backs, they looked at each other sighing in a manner that said, "Let's go," and signaled for one of the blocking Humvees to clear a door. The rest of the men were quiet and still as they watched them head for the door.

"They really gonna do this?" she heard one of them whisper.

Outside, the sun had just broken the horizon, but thankfully, the morning air was still cool. The sky was a brilliant, cloudless azure dome, and Pat took some satisfaction in that. At its height, the desert sun had a tendency to burn the richness from the heavens the same way it burned the color out of the land, but now, in these early hours, thinking this might very well be the last sunrise she'd see, the rich blues and soft yellow of the low sun cresting the valley rim felt a bit like a final small gift.

Cho had followed them outside, then the other men, one by one, the limping Ormond helped by one of his buddies, drifted out behind the XO, gathering around the doorway. Willis slipped through them carrying the fire ax and a musette bag.

Willis had scrounged up some rope and fashioned a sling for the ax. He handed it to Jinski. "Seemed to work well for you, so I figured, well, you know…"

Jinski accepted the ax with a smile, slung it crosswise across his back. "Thanks, Willie."

Then Willis handed the musette bag to Pat. She opened the flap and saw a half-dozen long-necked beer bottles with rags stuffed in their open necks. She caught a whiff of gasoline. "Molotovs?"

Willis grinned. "'Memberin' what happened out at Sun City, your weapons specialist figured you needed some special weapons. You got a lighter?"

Pat nodded, patting the shirt pocket where she kept her father's lighter.

"Major, Ma'am?"

"Yes, Willis?"

"Good luck, Ma'am."

"Thank you, Theodore."

"I'm gonna let that go this one time."

Then Willis joined the ten other men who had formed a line by the Quonset door, with Cho standing in front.

Cho straightened up. "Company…ten-*hut!*"

The men snapped to, even Ormond, or at least as well as he could leaning on the man next to him.

"Company…*salute!*"

And the rank snapped out as perfect a set of salutes as Pat remembered ever seeing. Or at least that's how it struck her just then.

"Attention, Jinks," she murmured as she held herself erect, and returned the salute, Jinski following her lead.

"Major Simons," Cho said, in a clear, declarative voice, "on behalf of the entire detail, let me say it has been a privilege to serve, Ma'am."

"Mister Cho, gentlemen," and she felt her throat tighten, her eyes sting, "the privilege has been all mine." Then, out the side of her mouth, to Jinski, "Let's go before I start getting misty."

The men stayed there at the door, Pat could feel their eyes on her and Jinski until they passed through the gate and out of view.

THE PENITENT

They were about halfway to the lab compound when Jinski stopped and sat down on a large rock.

He'd been strangely quiet since they'd left the camp, and Pat could see there was something on his mind. She didn't think it was second thoughts; she'd come to know Jinski well enough to immediately dismiss that possibility. It was something else, and now that he was on his rock, it almost seemed like he was studying her, a scrutiny that made her uncomfortable. He reached inside his hot suit and came out with his bar of Red Man and pen knife.

"Special occasion 'n' all that, ok, Ma'am?"

"By all means."

He cut himself a chaw, tucked it in his cheek, neatly re-wrapped the bar of tobacco and tucked it back inside his suit, wiped the pen knife clean on his suit leg, and put that away, too. There was such a slow, deliberateness to his actions that Pat sensed he was working his way up to something.

"Tired?" she asked.

"Well, I kinda had a rough night."

"Me, too. Something on your mind, Jinks?"

He looked toward the rising sun, his face wrinkled in frowning thought. "See, Ma'am, all respect 'n' all that, I'm findin' I gotta ask you somethin'."

She nodded at him to go ahead although she had a sense of where this was going.

"You know my history with officers doesn't zackly paint them in glowin' colors for me."

"I know your story, Jinks."

"I mean, I don't want to —" His frown grew deeper. "What the hell's that word? *Impugn* your motives —"

She almost laughed. "'Impugn'? You been doing Cho's crossword puzzles?"

"I read books. I'm good at finding Waldo."

"Color me impressed."

"Like I was sayin', I don't want to impugn your motives, but I'm gettin' a feelin' there's somethin' workin' here more'n what's up front. I'm thinkin' 'bout that little talk we had last night… I mean, yeah, I buy that it's-my-job stuff, but there's somethin' else cookin' underneath. Somethin' happened to you, 'n' if I had to bet, I'd say it was in Afghanistan. I mean, Ma'am, let's face it; nobody gets sent here as some kinda ree-ward."

It was not something she wanted to revisit. God knows she saw it all again often enough in her sleep, and then McElhone's slap-down back in her office brought it all back even more vividly. The embarrassment — no, the *humiliation* — of it was bad enough, but there was no way to tell it without reliving it and that was something she definitely did not want to do.

But you owe him. He's decided to follow you into God-knows-what and he knows as well as you do that neither one of you is probably coming out again. You owe it to him to tell him who he's following.

Still… The words hung up in her throat.

Jinski didn't push, sat there on his rock as relaxed and patient as a lizard sunning itself. "Eleven hundred's still a ways off, Ma'am. We got time."

For God's sake, Sister…<u>Do it!</u>

She nodded, not so much in agreement with Jinski as settling it with herself. "We received a message; a recon sweep had picked up two Hajis. I sent two of my people out in a Humvee to bring them in. On the way back, an IED took out the Humvee. My people, the prisoners; killed them all. I went with the recovery detail." Pat looked up and down the valley, up to the rim, trying to find something to fix her eyes on so the pictures wouldn't come back into her head. But they did. "Our people…they'd been stripped…and mutilated. Starkey and Lowe."

"You still remember the names."

"I still remember the names." *And always will.*

Oh, Christ… She could see them. The shredded flesh, the bearded vultures pulling at spilled intestines, the genitals… Running at them, firing to chase the birds away…

She took a deep breath, hoping the chill morning air would clear the pictures away. It didn't. "The boys were pretty hot about that."

"I bet."

"We got back, they got to talking to some of the other boys, somebody had a bottle…"

"Damn," Jinski sighed, "Somebody always has a bottle."

"They got themselves pretty fired up."

"They start thinkin' payback."

She nodded. "We already had two detainees. Zeroes, nothings. That night, they took them out into a field close by, stripped them, chased them around in a Humvee; hollering, firing off their weapons. It was like the way you see cowboys in the movies rustling cattle. Having a grand old time of it. I didn't know they'd taken the prisoners out until I heard the gunfire. I went to see what was going on.

"I had a top kick, career man, full set top and bottom —"

Pat could almost see him standing there in front of her, a wall of a man, his buzz cut exposing a scar across his skull. She'd seen him drilling the men in his sleeveless T: more scars set off against his deeply tanned skin.

"E-8?"

"Master Sergeant Earnest Engstrom. I'm coming down the corridor and Engstrom stands in front of me. Big man, kind of like you. Looks down at me and says, 'Major, this is going to happen, so why don't you just go back to your quarters and go to bed'. It wasn't a statement; it was an order. My sergeant was giving me an order." And here, she almost choked on the words: "And I backed down.

"I don't know why. He'd done two tours in The Sandbox, and this was his second go-around in Afghanistan. I guess he'd seen enough to get hard, know what I mean?"

"I know the type. Stone cold."

"Part of me figured, who am I to buck this guy? As much time outside the wire as he's had, who am I? Maybe he's right; this is what happens. Or maybe I just chickenshitted out.

"So I went back to my quarters, climbed into bed, put in my iPods and turned up the volume. I still remember: Deep Purple. 'Hush.' Cranked up so loud my head hurt. I haven't had a decent night's sleep since."

Pat wished there was another rock to sit on. Her legs felt weak. "One of the prisoners, he was kind of an old guy… Heart gave out, I guess. They literally ran him to death. They must've figured the other prisoner was a witness, so…"

"Shit." Jinski spat out a string of tobacco juice, more an expression of disgust than a chewing necessity.

"I don't know who actually pulled the trigger. Never found out. Not that it mattered. They buried them out in that field. The way things were, it looked like nobody was ever going to know."

"But somebody found out."

"Couple of them asked for leave right after. I was happy to give it to them. Better than having to look them in the eye knowing what they did. They were at a bar, started swapping war stories with soldiers from another unit, got into a can-you-top-this thing."

Jinski shook his head. "I know how that goes."

"There was a journalist in the bar. Nobody important, not from any of the major outfits, but she used to hang around soldier bars hoping to pick up a story."

Jinski saw where this was going: "So she overhears and thinks she hit the lottery. Win herself a fuckin' literary prize, a fuckin' *Poo*-litzer."

"She starts asking questions, making an all-around nuisance of herself, and that finds its way up the chain. Next thing I know, somebody from the Inspector General is in my office."

Jinski…*smiled.* He understood: "You told."

"I couldn't find it in me *not* to tell him, at least tell him as much as I knew. I just couldn't…keep it…"

He nodded, as if he was telling her she didn't have to explain. "I'm surprised you all didn't get busted out right then."

"Thing is, they had nothing. There was a rumor, and they had what I said, but the boys all clammed up once the IG got involved, nobody was ever going to find the graves, not that the Army was going to spend time looking for them. This was after Abu Ghraib; the Army was more worried about additional negative PR than what happened. If they court-martialed us, then it'd come out; there'd be a record of the incident. Even if we managed to skate past a conviction, it'd still be confirmation that it had really happened.

"They were very slick about it. They transferred out all the men they knew were involved, sent them off to the ends of the earth. One guy wound up at a base in Greenland, another guy in Guam… That kind of thing. Then, couple months go by, the story's died out, one by one they dishonorabled them out on some bullshit charge. It's not like any of those guys were going to beef; how could they?"

"What about that sergeant? Egg-whatever?"

"Engstrom. He was persuaded to take early retirement without his pension. And me, they buried in a Pentagon 'A' ring cubicle with a do-nothing job, waiting for me to get passed over."

"Up or out. And they had you on an off-ramp out."

"When McElhone threw me this assignment, I thought he was doing me a favor, a way to get back in the game." She shook her head over how eagerly – hungrily – she'd bought into that hope when the call had come. "It's just because I was an extra set of oak leaves they could afford to lose."

They were quiet for a bit; Jinski musingly chewing his Red Man. Pat, not waiting for his judgment as she — for what felt like the millionth time, already having judged herself — said, "I know your story, Jinks, and Mister Cho's. Neither of you deserved to be sent here."

"Major," he started, trying to cut her off, seeing where she was going.

"But I did. I failed my people, Jinks."

He let another stream of tobacco juice go. "Ma'am, they made their choice. What're you supposed to do? Protect them against doing stupid shit?"

"Yes! That's part of my job! If I'd stood up to Engstrom, those guys'd have clean records, no DDs, Engstrom'd be getting his pension —"

"Ma'am —"

"—those two Afghans would still be alive —"

"Ma'am! Ever occur to you, if you'd faced off with those guys, you mighta wound up buried in that field, too?"

"I've thought of that. Maybe that was even why I backed down. But like I said: that's the job. And I was starting to do it again. *Here!*" Her voice was rising; she was angry with herself. "After we lost Loomis, I was poking around, asking questions, and McElhone came to me and read me the riot act. 'Shut up, behave, do what you're told!' Maybe if I hadn't let him steamroller me —"

"Look, Major, I'm not in the business of givin' out ass-covers, but be real; if you'd beefed, what woulda happened? Colonel'd have you outta here on the next supply bird and we'd get stuck with some dickhead flunky 'n' be in the same deep shit we're in now. Only probably without somebody tryin' to dig us out." Jinski slowly rose from his rock, dusted off the seat of his CBRN suit, and walked over to her, blocking the sun. He pointed his thick index finger at her forehead. "I'm just hopin' you're straight in your own head, Ma'am. You gettin' yourself killed isn't gonna change anything. Ink's long dry on all those pages."

"I know. I'm just trying to do my job right…just once. Look, Jinks, if you're worried I'm on some kind of penance suicide run and you want out, I understand. I'll even radio Cho and tell him I ordered you back. No blame, no bad feelings."

"Like I keep tellin' you, Ma'am," he said, adjusting the ax hanging across his back, "it's my job, too. Let's do it to it."

They started walking toward the lab compound, side by side.

"Impugn," and Pat chuckled over it.

"Like that, did ya?"

"Color me impressed."

KATABASIS

The ditch was narrow and steep-sided making for a clumsy climb down, almost a controlled fall. It was cool and shadowy at the bottom, which was deep enough to be sheltered from the low morning sun. The ditch's floor had been smoothed by its occasional trickle of water and cracked by interstitial bakings from the late day sun — high enough to pound directly into its bottom — sucking every bit of moisture out of the ground. There was no water now, just a dinner plate-sized puddle at the lip of the concrete frame of the tunnel.

The air from the tunnel carried the musty smell of damp concrete. Pat flashed her torch through the grill over the tunnel entrance, picking up the gleam of a skinny snake of still water. She traced the water with her light until it picked up an end to the tunnel twenty yards in. She couldn't see any kind of egress, as details at that end of the tunnel were lost in shadows.

She nodded at Jinski, and he reached out with the metal head of his ax. Counting on the CBRN suit's gloves for insulation, he tentatively touched the grill. No sparks.

"We're good," he pronounced, then jammed the ax blade between the edge of the entrance gate and the jamb near the lock.

Pat stepped away from the racket Jinski was making and raised Cho on her walkie-talkie. "We'll be going in in a few minutes," she reported. "Once we're in the tunnel, I'm switching off my radio. If these things are loose in there, I don't know how sensitive their hearing is, and I don't want to wake up anybody from their morning nap. I'll try to get back in contact when we reach the command center. Over."

"Roger that, Ma'am. Over."

"Remember your orders, Mister Cho. Eleven hundred hours and then it's up to you. Over."

There was a pause; Pat could picture Cho unhappily mulling this over. Then, "I'll do my best, Ma'am. Everybody here wishes you good luck. Over."

"Thank you, Mister Cho." *Good luck to you, too, because if I don't pull this off, you're going to need it.* "Simons out." She switched the walkie-talkie off and hung it on her utility belt.

Jinski was standing by the pried-open gate looking quite proud of himself.

"Ready?" she asked.

"Does it matter?"

"If you don't want to swim in it, you might want to…" She pointed at the bulge in his cheek.

Jinski spat out the wad of tobacco, and the two of them pulled up the hoods on their hot suits and secured them.

Pat took the lead, moving through the gate, her M4 cradled in one hand, torch in the other.

As Jinski had told her, the tunnel was big enough to pass through, but barely: low, narrow, she couldn't imagine how uncomfortable it must be for the bulkier Jinski following behind her. As they neared what she had first thought was the end of the tunnel, it became clear the tunnel didn't so much end as change; the floor sloped up sharply until it tapered into a low-ceilinged ramp leading to a small overhead grate — a drain, Pat guessed — another five yards along.

But this wasn't a dead end either. To her left were ladder rungs embedded in the concrete wall which led up to a small door, something like what Pat had seen on naval ships: heavy, steel, rounded corners, set in a rubber gasket, held airtight closed with dog latches around the frame.

Pat looked questioningly at Jinski who shrugged: why not?

She slung her M4, climbed the rungs and tried the dog latches. There was, thankfully, nothing locking the door, and once the latches had been released, a slight push and the door swung open. Darkness.

She ran her torch beam around the interior of a small room, some kind of utility closet, she assumed. It was lined with shelves stocked with bottles and cans marked with long chemical names she couldn't pronounce. There were what looked like stainless steel surgical instruments gleaming under her light inside their sealed sterile plastic bags, piles of sheets, towels, folded disposable hospital greens in their own plastic bags, and boxes of sterile gloves. She climbed into the room, unslung her weapon and beckoned Jinski to follow.

There was a sign on the wall by the tunnel door:

INSPECTION PERSONNEL MUST HAVE

WRITTEN AUTHORIZATION

BEFORE ENTRY

LEVEL 3 PROTECTIVE CLOTHING ADVISED

There was a regular wooden door and a light switch nearby. Pat tried the light switch. Nothing. She tried the door. Locked. Again, she stood aside to let Jinski do his magic. With a grunt and the pained sound of metal twisting, the door popped free.

Through the doorway was a shadowy room lit only by glaring, battery-powered emergency lights mounted high on the walls.

Ok, Sister, here you go. This is what they pay you for.

She took a deep breath, brought her M4 into ready position and hand signaled Jinski to follow.

Pat's first impression was of some kind of medical facility. It was a large room with tiled walls, vinyl flooring, stainless steel sinks, stainless steel instrument stands — almost everywhere her torch beam touched, it bounced off gleaming steel and hard surfaces. Positioned over an operating table in the center of the room were twin banks of circular lights. Hanging down between them was a recording microphone.

As she stepped closer to the table, though, she realized it wasn't for surgery.

It was extraordinarily large, eight feet in length she estimated. And crisscrossing its surface, an "X" of narrow runnels.

Not an operating table.

Oh my God…

Those were blood gutters. It was an autopsy table but built for larger-than-human dimensions. And that's when she noticed along one wall the steel faces of mortuary cabinets.

She left Jinski to puzzle on the oversized autopsy table while she went to one of the cabinets, grabbed its handle and — not wanting to do this but knowing she needed to — pulled the drawer open.

She almost vomited into her respirator.

Jinski saw her violently back away from the open drawer and came over to see what it was that had hit her so hard.

"What the _fuck_!" he bellowed loud enough she could hear it clearly through his mask and hers.

Laid out in the drawer was one of the creatures, its torso opened in a textbook autopsy "Y" incision, its trunk emptied of organs. The top of its skull had been removed with a neat saw cut and whatever these things had for a brain was gone.

Jinski slammed the cabinet closed. He looked to Pat for answers, but she could only shake her head.

"I don't know," she said, taking deep breaths to calm her stomach.

There was one door leading out of the room, another naval-type door shut with a locking wheel in the middle of it. Weapons at the ready, Pat led Jinski toward the door, spun the wheel open, and gave the heavy door a shove with the muzzle of her carbine.

The doorway opened on a small chamber, some sort of transition space with another wheel-locked door on the other side. There was a warning sign over the door they were exiting through:

CAUTION: LEVEL 3 PROTECTION EQUIPMENT ADVISED

The next door opened on some sort of laboratory: worktables, microscopes, glass doored refrigerators containing what she assumed were tissue and fluid samples. There were no warning signs of any sort, so Pat felt comfortable loosening her hood and flipping it back. She hadn't been aware how badly she'd been sweating inside her hood until the air in the room hit the moisture on her face. But it was not cool air; it was stale, uncirculated, smelling of formaldehyde and disinfectant.

There was a watery, wavering sound coming from somewhere beyond the room, its rises and falls had Pat thinking some kind of music. There was something vaguely familiar to it.

Jinski looked at the sample jars in one of the refrigerators. "Are they building these things here?"

Two more wheel-locked doors led off from the lab in either direction. One was marked NUCLEONICS with warning signs posted alongside, each including the three-pronged alert symbol for radioactive materials:

LEVEL 1 DECONTAMINATION PROTOCOL IN EFFECT

LEVEL 1 RADIATION PROTECTION MEASURES REQUIRED
LEVEL 1 QUALIFIED PERSONNEL ONLY

The other door was marked EMBRYONICS.

"Not building," Pat said and went to that second door. She spun the locking wheel, pushed the door open. "Oh, Christ…"

The room was lined with a dozen wall-to-ceiling transparent tubes filled with a opaque fluid. Inside each, hooked to a variety of tubes and wires, were creatures…sort of. Not fully developed, not grown. Different stages of embryo.

"Not building," Pat repeated. *"Growing."*

"This…this is fuckin'…" Jinski's mouth worked but there were no words.

Pat understood because there simply *were* no words for this.

She pushed the big man back toward the door, closed it and spun the locking wheel, sealing it. Like the sergeant, a paralyzing daze was creeping into her, swamping her with questions and ugly suppositions, none for which she could find a response. Five of her men were dead because of what this lab was — literally — cooking.

Focus on the mission. Focus!

She shook off the daze. "Cmon," and she punched Jinski in the shoulder to do the same for him. "Let's do what we came here for."

There was another door, more like a standard fire door than one of those heavy steel naval affairs. The watery sound of music was coming from the other side.

After what they'd seen, the next room was almost laughably mundane. A collection of desks with desktop computers, a conference table in the middle of the room, a coffee maker, silly decorations on the desks: a long-haired troll doll hanging from an adjustable lamp, someone had hung a poster on the wall over a desk picturing a life-sized window with an airliner ready to crash through, a Garfield coffee mug with the cartoon cat grumping, "I may rise but I refuse to shine."

The music…

A CD player on someone's desk, the music now distorted and wavering with the batteries running down. But Pat could still pick out the lyrics even with Michael Hutchence's voice stretched out and brought down to bass level by the dying player, the watery vocals going on about how everyone has a devil inside.

She switched the player off and opened another fire door, this one leading to a long corridor.

"This can't be good," Jinski said, as they stepped into the corridor.

The emergency lights were feeble enough to just barely pick up splotches on the walls; Pat's and Jinski's torch lights showed them to be dried blood. Blood spill was up and down the corridor, sometimes in blots, sometimes in sprays and smears. It was there on the floor, some of it in streaking drag marks. There were even sprays on the ceiling.

The corridor also was heavily scarred with battle damage: the walls pockmarked with bullet holes and graze scars, the floor heavily littered with 5.56 shell casings and even several 40 mm rifle grenade casings.

Jinski leaned down to her. "Ya know," he whispered, "I never thought this was a great idea, but now I'm thinkin' this was a fuckin' awful idea."

Pat pointed back to the door to the lab suite. "That's the way out, Jinks, and I wouldn't blame you."

"If I ever made it to Heaven, my momma would never forgive me."

"I like that you think you're going to Heaven."

"I did say, 'if'."

They were standing at the midpoint of the corridor. At one end – a direction leading deeper into the lab complex – was a wide set of double metal doors. At the other end…

It was something she'd only seen in movies, the kind of heavy metal door in dungeons or old prisons. While there was a keypad alongside an electronic lock, there was also an old school heavy bar, with a lever, mounted across the back of the door to be used like a giant deadbolt.

The door was open, nothing but blackness on the other side. The bloody drag marks led to that open door.

It wasn't just curiosity prompting Pat. *I have to know what's been going on here. I have to know why I've lost five of my men.*

"Stay here," she told Jinski.

"By myself? Bullshit to that!" and he followed her as she slowly moved down the corridor, both of them with their weapons up and ready.

In the close air of the corridor, she was glad she'd taken off the CBRN suit's hood so she could quickly wipe away the sweat beading heavily on her forehead before it could run into her eyes. She could feel her heart pounding against her chest, her index finger so tense around the carbine's trigger she had to consciously force it not to start squeezing off rounds into the dark on the other side of that open door.

Jinski's right; this is fucking stupid. But I have to know…

At the door she signaled Jinski to position himself to one side of the doorway while she took the other side. She peeped around the rim of the door jamb, swept her torch beam around the chamber on the other side.

It was some kind of detention area. They were facing the bottom of two levels. On either side and across from them were five cells, each fronted by a heavy, windowless steel door which had a keypad lock and a steel crossbar, like the entrance. All the doors were open, with the bloody drag marks leading to some of the cells.

"Cover me," she told Jinski as she slid around the edge of the doorway, staying close to the wall and low.

Drag marks led to the nearest open cell. Steeling herself, already having some idea of the grotesquerie she'd find, she turned into the cell doorway, her torch beam quickly finding a corpse. Or rather, what was left of one.

From the shreds of uniform remaining, Pat assumed he was one of the lab's security detail. He was mutilated worse than Elmonte; more closely resembling the coyote she'd found with Cho. It was completely gutted, decapitated, limbs separated and stripped of flesh down to the bone.

She had a mental flash: Starkey and Lowe, stretched out on an arid strip of Afghanistan, flesh torn by the blast from an IED and worse done by the Taliban blades.

Her knees threatened to buckle, the urge to vomit was back, close now, her midriff tightening on the verge of retching –

"Major!"

She turned away from the cell, Jinski had his torch aimed upward, toward the ceiling. Just detaching itself from the ceiling, its camouflage scales reacting to the beam of light sweeping across its body, was a creature.

Pat froze, mental gears gnashing and grinding as she was stuck between still reeling from what she'd found in the cell, the surprise – and yes, fright – of what was now crawling down one of the walls...

"Major!" and the blast from Jinski's Mossberg, thundering in the amplifying acoustics of the detention chamber jolted her out of her paralysis.

Now, training, habit, and instinct kicked in. The M4 was up, and as Jinski sent blast after blast at the creature, Pat added to it with long bursts aimed at the thing's head as she backpedaled blindly toward the door.

Keeping her sights on the creature, she found herself bumping along the wall as she kept firing —

WHERE THE FUCK IS THE DOOR?

— until Jinski grabbed her by the back of her hot suit, yanking her through the doorway so hard she fell to the floor outside while the big sergeant slammed the metal door closed and shot the heavy bolt, locking it.

If either felt any sense of safety, it immediately evaporated with the loud *thump* of the creature ramming into the other side of the door.

"You think that'll hold it?" Pat asked.

"Let's not stick around to find out," and Jinski pulled her to her feet.

They ran down the corridor, the sound of the creature pounding at the detention area door as regular as a heartbeat. Pat skidded to a stop at the door to the lab suite. For a moment, she considered leading them back the way they'd come. The sight of the creature — flinching yet unstopped in their muzzle flashes still vivid in her mind — told her their mission was pointless. She'd hoped otherwise, but she now truly believed this was a one-way — and impossible — mission.

You have to try everything. You don't just owe it to them. It's your goddamned job, Sister!

Pat pushed Jinski toward the lab suite doors — "Go!" — and continued down the corridor.

He ran after her. "We came in together, we stay together!"

Pat flashed the torch beam down the corridor toward the detention door: it was beginning to bend. There was no time to argue.

She led them to the double doors at the end of the corridor. There was a push-pad on the wall; it was supposed to automatically open the doors, but without power, they would have to muscle through.

"Get 'em open!" Pat yelled to Jinski as she ran back down the corridor.

"Where the hell you goin'?"

The detention door was groaning as the creature had partly peeled it away from the jamb and was now trying to shoulder its way through the gap.

Pat reached into the bag Willis had given her, grabbed one of the beer bottles, fumbled her father's lighter out from inside her hot suit, flamed it and touched it to the rag wick.

The creature had frozen in its effort to get through the door, its eyes fixed on her, head cocked, as if puzzled at what she was doing.

She got within throwing distance of the door and hurled the Molotov cocktail. It didn't hit the creature but smashed against the door, flaming gasoline blossoming out like a firework. Pat felt a gust of heat against her face from the detonation, and the same thermal wave triggered the corridor's fire system: a clanging, deafening alarm, sprinkler heads dropping from the ceiling and opening up. The dried blood on the walls, freshened by the spraying water, now began to run, tendrils crawling toward the floor, the corridor now alive with moving blood.

The explosion of flame had chased the creature back inside the door. Pat hunched over against the raining water to shelter her lighter, lit a second Molotov, ran even closer to the detention door and threw it through the gap. The interior of the detention center flared into flickering light as the second gasoline bomb went off.

Jinski was yelling for her. She turned, saw he had pried open the doors enough for them to slip through. The water in her eyes, and the blood on the floor now made slick, running became a slip-sliding affair. She was practically blind by the time she got to the doors where Jinski grabbed her by her hot suit, yanked her through, and shoved the doors closed behind them. Thankfully, the fire response was confined to the corridor behind them.

On the other side of the doors: what appeared to be a hub aligned with the center of the lab complex. Several doors led off to various branches of the complex, and at one wall, an elevator. The elevator doors were stuck half-open, the lift itself frozen a few feet above the floor.

Behind them, they could hear the detention door groaning as the creature resumed pushing and pounding on it through what was left of the flames.

There were hand grips on the hub side of the double doors. Jinski jammed his shotgun through the grips as a bolt. Pat pointed to the elevator. Jinski effortlessly picked Pat up and almost threw her through the partly opened elevator door before climbing up into the lift after her.

"There should be…" he muttered then found an inspection hatch in the ceiling. He popped the hatch open, boosted Pat through and climbed up after her, then closed it. They stood to either side of the hatch, Pat with her M4 aimed at it, Jinski with his unslung ax in his hands and cocked on his shoulder.

They heard the distant crash of the detention door giving way, then the sound of the fire alarm blared more insistently as the doors to the hub were more easily bulled through.

Again, eye lined up in the sights of the M4, Pat had that pounding feeling in her chest, the tenseness in her trigger finger, but there was – strangely, she noticed – instead of fear, a cold, hard anger.

C'mon, fucker, come on through! C'mon!

They could hear the creature stalking around the hub, even heard it by the elevator.

It's here! That big ugly bastard's got his big ugly head in the elevator car!

And then it was gone, thumping its way off down another corridor.

As Pat released her breath, she found herself panting, realizing she'd been holding her breath the whole time. The adrenaline tide had ebbed, and she sagged against the wall of the elevator shaft. She and Jinks even grinned at each other as she watched him doing the same on the other side of the shaft.

Pat did a quick recon of the shaft with her torch, found a maintenance ladder running up the side of the shaft. "What do you think?" she whispered to Jinski.

"I think we don't have much of a menu."

"I don't think we need these anymore," and they shucked their hot suits before they began their climb, Pat in the lead.

Pat tried to visualize what their position might be in the lab. The drainage tunnel had taken them into the second underground level, the hub was probably in the center of the complex, and that meant the elevator shaft could possibly take them where they needed to go. Her light had picked up the doors to three levels above them. That meant the top set should open into the cupola.

Dodging the elevator winching machinery at the top of the shaft, there was a narrow ledge extending from under the doors that opened onto the floor. Jinski, skirting the winching machinery, managed to get himself braced in a corner near the doors, a position so precarious Pat had to look away. He then leaned over to get the ax blade in the seam between the doors, shimming it enough to open sufficient space for him to get a hand in.

"Ma'am," he grunted, "If you wouldn't mind?"

She got in the opposite corner and placed a hand in below Jinski's pulling on the other door. The two of them managed to grunt the doors open a foot, then two…

The muzzle of an M4 slid through the opening. Then the beam of a torch.

"Oh, thank God!" said Colonel McElhone. He helped them pull the doors further open and then extended a hand to pull Pat and then Jinski through the gap.

As Pat had guessed, the cupola was the command-and-control center for the lab's security. The round room resembled a more expanded version of The Brain: similar consoles, monitors, gauges on either side of the smoked glass observation window looking out on the lab grounds toward the entry gate. But, like the rest of the complex, there was no power, the only light coming from the harsh emergency lights, the air stale, smelling of sweat.

Poor as the light was in the cupola, Pat could see McElhone was beaming. He was balancing on one leg. The other pants leg was torn from hip to knee, and Pat could see a blood-soaked bandage through the tear.

"I can't tell you how glad I am to see you, Pat!"

"Well, Colonel, before you start throwing me a parade, you should know that after you tell me what the hell's been going on here, I'm going to put a 5.56-sized hole in your head. You and anybody else in here."

"Take it easy, Pat." David Cordell arose from where he'd been sitting at one of the dead consoles in the shadows. "You've got every right to be mad."

"Generous of you to say so, David. So, you'll understand why, on second thought, instead of the colonel here, maybe I'll start with *your* head."

ENTOMBED

"How is he?"

Pat was leaning over Mariska Woltz, who was kneeling by her husband, Oskar. He was unconscious, lying on a pillow made from a folded lab coat with, his head wrapped in a blood-splotched bandage, his breathing shallow and labored.

"I can't be sure, but I think he has a fracture of the skull. He will probably not live very much longer." Her voice was flat. Her heart was dying along with the man lying next to her.

But Pat had no pity for Mariska Woltz, not for anybody in the room, not for McElhone with his gashed leg, not for Oskar Woltz dying on the floor by his wife, and certainly not for David Cordell who'd had the bad taste to make it to the command cupola completely unscathed.

"Mariska, how could you be part of this …this…whatever the hell this is?"

Mariska Woltz gave a slightly sad smile. It was not a condescending twist of the lips. It was a reflection of her own amusement at how it had happened. "It's like sinking into quicksand one slow inch at a time. They give you a grant for something they know you're interested in, that's important to you. And they're impressed by the work you do. They say all the right things. They think so highly of your talents they want to bring you into the organization to work on projects of great importance; you feel valued. These are defensive projects, things that protect people, and you feel good about that. And then, at some point…the language…twists. 'Defense' becomes 'deterrence' — the best way to prevent annihilation or so they tell you — is to threaten annihilation. You've been in the culture long enough that this makes a bizarre sort of sense to you…until it doesn't. But by then, you're so deep into the quicksand there's no way back to where you were."

"I understand that," Pat said, "I really do. But *this*…"

"How is this different from what we were doing at Los Alamos, Pat?" Cordell was on his knees in front of a seated McElhone, changing the bandage on the grimacing colonel's leg with gauze from a first aid kit. "We were devising and refining devices that could obliterate an entire city in a flash. You're going to tell me that was the moral high ground?"

"I'm going to tell you you weren't dropping those bombs *on your own fucking people!* And that's a hell of a difference!" Pat rolled one of the console chairs over to where McElhone was sitting while Cordell worked on his leg. "Is it possible there's anybody else alive somewhere in this complex?"

McElhone's face sagged. "From what we could hear before we lost the intercom … they were thorough. I'm pretty sure we're it."

"How come they haven't hit this place yet?"

"I don't think they've figured out how to navigate the elevator shaft. Yet. I've heard them in the stairwell, but the flight to this level — "McElone pointed to a tight alcove off the main room at another naval-styled hatch. "— was intentionally designed to be too small for them. That was the contingency plan -- the fail-safe."

Pat pulled herself out of the chair with a sigh, went to the observation window which looked out over the lab grounds toward the gate. She looked at her watch: almost 0900. She thought about Cho moving out with the men into the open to try Pritchard's plan in two hours. And then she thought of something that, even in the stuffy air of the command cupola, turned her cold. "What are the chances of these things making it to a population center?"

"Not probable." But then McElhone mulled it for a bit. A reluctant nod: "But possible."

"Christ, Colonel, what were you thinking?"

McElhone almost looked amused at the question. "*I* wasn't thinking anything. Lab 7 was built for Project Golem. And Project Golem was *his* idea. Ask him."

McElhone looked over into one of the dark places in the cupola along the consoles; a barely perceptible figure sitting at one of the dead control panels, scribbling notes on a pad under a penlight. The spill from the emergency lights revealed a pair of suede desert boots and twill pants legs. "Ask *him*," McElhone said again, this time sounding damning.

Pat flicked on her torch, aimed the beam into the dark and found Aaron Ostrow, still fixed on his note-making. Pat found herself nodding, understanding. "Golem."

"What's a golem?" Jinski asked.

"Every culture has its Frankenstein, Jinks. Right, Doctor? Just what is it you do for a living?"

Ostrow switched off his penlight, very carefully closed his notebook and returned it and his pen to his breast pocket. He pushed his glasses up on his nose, squinted into the torchlight, the lenses of his glasses flaring, and made a gesture asking Pat to turn off her torch. He pushed his chair out from the shadows into the glare of one of the emergency lights. "I'm a microbiologist."

Everything about Lab 7 came together for Pat in an exhilarating swiftness. She was almost giddy at the way all the unanswered questions lit up brightly with answers. "Oh, I get it now! Recombinant DNA, wading around in the gene pool and doing some slicing and dicing, mix and match, a little of this, a little of that. And then I guess with this bunch —" meaning the Woltzes and Cordell "— you introduce a little radiation-induced mutation, and then you come up with…with what? What's this end-product of yours supposed to be, Doctor?"

Ostrow seemed unperturbed by the burst from Pat. "Are you acquainted with the writings of Thomas Hobbes?"

"Isn't that the little cartoon kid with the toy tiger?" said Jinski.

Ostrow ignored him. "He described primitive life as 'solitary, poor, nasty, brutish, and short'. Don't you think, Major, that could also serve as an apt description of the plight of the frontline soldier?

"Since the close of World War II, we've had to consider the possibility of combat in environments defined by non-conventional weapons. The Nightbreaker tests carried out in this very desert studied the ability of soldiers to effectively operate in a nuclear environment despite certain long-term hazards —"

"Like sterility, cancer, leukemia…"

Ostrow didn't even break stride. "We have vaccines to counter certain biological weapons and protective gear for chemical agents. But vaccines take time to administer and in extreme environments…" Something changed in Ostrow's face, his eyes; this was no longer a purely academic discussion.

"During the first Gulf War, because there was a concern Saddam Hussein might use his chemical weapons, our troops were equipped with protective equipment, something like your CBRN suits. What we learned in that experience was that a soldier in his protective gear, with the stress of trying to operate in a desert environment, could be rendered combat ineffective in as little as fifteen minutes. In desperate enough circumstances — the heat, the stress, the ...' Ostrow touched his chest, where the *Chai* medallion sat inside his shirt, and Pat had the answer to her last question: *why*.

"You're talking about your son," she said.

"Are we gonna kill these guys or what?" Jinski asked impatiently.

Pat held up a hand: *wait*.

Ostrow seemed offended that his thinking could be accused of being so parochial. "I'm talking about *all* sons, Major. And daughters. And fathers and mothers."

He went back into lecture mode: "When we speak of biological weapons, we typically mean things like viruses, bacteria. But what if we could create a full biological system, not just a weapon, but something that could completely replace the soldier? Almost like a living drone, but without the need for a controller. An entirely new kind of weapon system."

Pat laughed bitterly. "That's what you're calling these things? A 'weapon system'?" She turned to Mariska Woltz. "I see what you mean about how the language gets twisted; sugar to help the medicine go down. Take the hard edges off."

This was probably his pitch to the DoD for funding. Pat was sure of it as Ostrow continued, as if on automatic. "Able to absorb great amounts of physical violence, resistant to chemical, biological, and radiological threats, chameleon-like camouflage capability, intelligent enough to operate independently and make tactical decisions and work in concert. And able to operate free of logistical support."

"Logistical support?" Pat asked.

For the first time, Ostrow grew uncomfortable, realizing maybe he'd gone further than he should have. "Well, uh, obviously the system wouldn't need, you know, the typical support. I mean, um, such as munitions, fuel, shelter…" He looked down into his lap, spoke in an almost inaudible mumble: "Um, rations."

"No food?" Jinski asked and Pat could see the same alarm bells were going off in her sergeant that were now going off for her.

"They would, you know," Ostrow cleared his throat, "…live off the combat environment."

Pat found the nearest chair and dropped heavily into it. "They'd feed on their kills."

"Fuck me, they're cannibals?" Jinski said.

Ostrow seemed eager to get back into his lecture voice: "A misnomer, Sergeant. A cannibal eats its own kind."

"Oh, well, I feel so much better now!"

"Not that these systems wouldn't avail themselves of such should the circumstances —"

Jinski stomped around in a small circle. "Are we gonna kill these crazy fuckers or what?"

Pat gave him a look that said *I don't blame you* but waved at him to hold off. She turned back to McElhone. "Those maneuvers out on the flats at night; you were field testing these things. Bruckner got curious about what was going on and that's what got him killed."

McElhone drew himself up in his chair which sent a jolt of pain through him from his leg, but he made a good effort at being the decisive commander: "What got the lieutenant killed was disobeying orders. He was where he wasn't supposed to be. If he'd obeyed orders —"

Pat was having none of it: "My people. You picked expendables. Screw-ups, no families. What were we supposed to be? Target practice for the doctor's 'weapon system'?"

"No! No! Nothing like that, Pat. The selection criteria … it was just … a contingency."

"All respect, Colonel," Jinski said, "you say 'contingency' one more time 'n' your head 'n' Mr. Ax here are gonna have a come-to-Jesus meeting."

"It was in case things went wrong," Pat said.

"Yes."

"Expendable by any other name."

"Pat, we never thought this could happen."

"*Bullshit!* You knew the possibility was always there! That's the definition of a contingency. You had a contingency with that hatch, why you picked my men – why you picked *me* – because it would be no great loss to the Army and nobody to ask questions if you all fucked up and made a mess."

"I was given orders," McElhone said, "and I did my best with them." It was clear that sounded lame even to McElhone. "Just as I gave you orders. Just as you gave orders. That's what we do."

"That line didn't work at Nuremburg and it's not working with me now, Colonel." She turned to Cordell. "And you threw me to him."

Cordell could only turn away. "I wasn't thinking about … I just wanted to see you again."

"Fucking child," Pat said, exasperated at that thinking.

"Now can we kill 'em?" Jinski asked.

"He's not joking, is he?" Cordell asked.

"Not even close," Pat said. She went over to Ostrow, set her boot on the edge of his chair seat between his legs and gave it a sharp shove, sending it rolling and crashing against one of the control consoles. "What happened, Doctor?"

Ostrow seemed puzzled by his own miscalculations. "We —"

"By which you mean *you.*"

"I'd been making notes when you arrived, for corrections —"

"Corrections?"

"Hm, yes, probably not the right word. Adjustments."

"Adjustments. Jesus, you people…"

"It was thought an instinct for self-preservation would be necessary for effective decision-making in the field. But we —" Ostrow stopped, seemed to think it best to back away from any attribution of blame. "The strength of that survival drive was underestimated, these systems were able to operate more independently than conceived, and perhaps the obedience centers weren't developed to a level —"

That bitter laugh from Pat, again. "Don't you get it, Jinks? These things figured out what they were being bred for, and they didn't want to be cannon fodder any more than any other soldier! You wanted a new kind of soldier, Doctor? You got 'em and you got a mutiny along with them. Ya gotta love the irony! Get the joke, Jinks? *They made these things too well!*" She looked at her watch again. She looked over at Jinski who looked up from his own watch. She knew they were both thinking about Cho and the men getting caught out in the open.

"I cannot tell you how much this all pains me, Major," Ostrow said. "All I ever wanted from this was to save lives."

"Well, I feel bad for your pain, Doc, but here's some you didn't save!" Pat pulled from her pocket the small loop of chain holding the dog tags of Pritchard, Sanborn, and Elmonte, and hurled it at Ostrow.

Ostrow grabbed it with fumbling hands, unsure of what it was, until he held it up to the light and saw the names of the men. He seemed to melt into himself, then.

"That's a little light because we never found two of my men," Pat said. "You can add them to the body count your weapon systems have run up in this tomb of yours!" And another issue answered itself for her: "You're the one who killed my man Delaney, aren't you? Last night, the man in the surveillance trailer; that was you, not one of your weapon systems!"

Ostrow couldn't take his eyes off the ID tags in his hands. "Your man…was already dead. One of them had … I was trying to protect the project."

Pat saw Ostrow's eyes widen at something behind her. She turned, saw Jinski, dead-eyed and stone-faced, ax in both hands, marching toward Ostrow. Pat stood in front of him. "When I know we don't need him."

As he usually did, Jinski saw the practicality and stepped back...reluctantly. "You're on borrowed time, Mr. Shoes," he said to Ostrow.

Pat went back to her seat by McElhone. "You were talking about contingencies. One of them had to be for a situation like this."

"We do have something. There's an emergency beacon. When it's activated, it sends a pre-coded flash alert to Nellis, and when they receive it, it initiates a heavily armed air evac protocol."

Pat quickly scanned the control consoles. "Where is it? I don't see anything lighting up. Everything here is dead."

"This complex is powered by a small atomic reactor on the lowest level: seven levels below us. The beacon is activated from the power exchange control room."

"What the hell's it doing down there?"

"Again: contingency."

"Man, I'm really gettin' to hate that word," Jinski said.

"The idea," McElhone went on, "was it couldn't possibly be cut off if it's close to the power source."

"Jesus, we've got to fight our way through seven levels of these things?"

"Maybe not," Jinski said. "The elevator shaft goes all the way down, right? That'd get us down there without these things seein' us. It might be a little tricky gettin' 'round where the car's stuck, but still, better than the stairs."

"That gets you to the right level, Pat," said Cordell. "That doesn't get you into the control room. There's an electronic lock."

"What is it? Keypad? Key card?"

"Voice print."

"Shit. Whose voice?"

Cordell pointed to McElhone.

"It's programmed for four," McElhone said. "The head engineer —"

"Who's no longer with us."

"The security chief —"

"Two for two."

"Me…and Dr. Ostrow. I'll go down with you," and he started trying to get out of his chair.

Cordell pushed him back down. "He won't make it, Pat. I'm no doctor, I did the best I could following the manual, but there was nothing in the kit to stitch the wound closed. All I had were safety pins."

"Ew," Jinski said.

"He walks on that leg, and I don't think they'll hold."

"That's kinda tough shit for him," Jinski said, turning his head to look directly at McElhone before continuing, "with all respect, Colonel"; the last delivered with a sneer.

"That's tough shit for all of us," Cordell said. "Pat, he'll bleed out. If that happens before you get to the power exchange room, then what?"

"I'll go, Pat," McElhone insisted.

"I don't know what I hate more," Pat said, "that you're right, David, or that it's *you* who's right." She stepped over to Ostrow.

He looked up at her from his chair, as if he'd just worked out the answer to a simple equation. "Of course." Then his mind seemed to go elsewhere, his face softened into something more thoughtful. "'I heard the voice of the Lord saying, 'Whom shall I send? Who will go for us?' And I said, 'Here am I'." He nodded, agreeing with the thought. "Here am I."

"You're quite the paradox, Doctor. You like your prayers and at the same time, you build these perfect killers."

"I told you, Major," Ostrow said, rising to his feet, "I was trying to save lives. You'll want these back, yes?" He held out the chain of dog tags.

Pat took them and dropped them back in her breast pocket.

She tried to reach Cho on her walkie-talkie but as she'd feared, the signal couldn't get through the thick complex walls. She saw Jinski looking at her with a *Well?* question on his face to which she grimly answered with a *No dice* shake of her head.

"Pat." It was McElhone. He took his own dog tag chain from his neck and tossed it to Pat. There was a key on the chain along with the colonel's tags. "That locker." McElhone pointed to a wide, double-doored locker of heavy steel standing against one wall.

Pat used the key to unlock the doors. Inside was a rifle rack of a dozen M4s along with four M203s which were M4 carbines with a grenade launcher attached under the foregrip.

Jinski beamed. "Now that's gonna make it a real party!"

Pat and Jinski each took an M203, stuffed extra magazines and rifle grenades in the deep pockets of their utilities. There was also a case of hand grenades and Pat dropped a few in her bag with her Willis-made Molotovs.

"Do you want to carry something, Doctor?" Pat asked Ostrow.

Ostrow shook his head. "I wouldn't know how to use it."

"Yet another irony," Pat said.

Ostrow shrugged; even he could see it.

Pat went back to McElhone to hand him back his tags.

"Maybe you better hang on to those," McElhone said.

Something about that set off an alarm in Cordell. "Pat, if you make it down there, how're you going to get back?"

"David, dear, for your sake, you better hope I don't." Pat handed one of the Molotovs to McElhone. "Despite the bang-up job the good doctor did on his 'weapon system', they don't seem to do well with fire. If they try coming up the elevator shaft…"

McElhone nodded.

"Jinks, my man; ready?"

"Hooah!"

"I'll lead off, you help Science Guy get across to the ladder and follow up."

"Pat!" It was Mariska Woltz this time. She beckoned Pat over. "Pat —"

"You've got nothing to say to me, Mariska."

"I know, I know, it's not that." She beckoned Pat to come close, so she could whisper. "Pat, I've been with Dr. Ostrow since the project began. I've seen how he is about it. You have to understand what it is that's driving him."

"Yeah, I get it," Pat said dismissively. "He was trying to save lives, blah blah blah. Well, he dropped the ball on that. Big time."

"That's not what I'm saying. This was about his son."

"I got that. He's still not getting a pass from me —"

"You're still not understanding me. You need to watch him. He killed your man last night, didn't he? He's going to be protective."

"What do you mean protective?"

"I know this will sound insane to you, and it is, but these…things…in his mind, they're like his stepchildren."

225

ENDGAME

The ironies of Aaron Ostrow were adding up. For someone with no trepidation about constructing the perfect biological killing machine, it was ironic he was balky about firearms, ironic that he seemed sincerely spiritual, and now Pat could add that the fearless killer-maker was afraid of heights.

Pat was hanging on the elevator shaft maintenance ladder by one hand, only one foot on a rung, while she leaned out over the shaft trying to grab Ostrow's blindly flailing arm, the doctor's eyes fixed on the shaft below which no doubt looked even deeper since the bottom was lost in darkness.

"For Christ's sakes, don't look down!" Pat hissed, trying to restrain herself from exasperatingly shouting and having it echo down the shaft. But Ostrow was frozen at the sight of the apparently bottomless shaft.

Ostrow's feet remained anchored to the edge of the floor, his other hand had an iron grip on Jinski's arm, the big man standing behind him inside the partly open elevator doors. Jinski looked mightily annoyed. "I got half a mind to shove this fucker down the hole."

Pat gave him a that's-not-helping-glare. She finally got hold of Ostrow's arm and tugged but the doctor couldn't get his feet to move or let go of Jinski. "Doctor, just step over! I've got you!"

All she got from Ostrow was a strained groan.

"Fuck this," Jinski grumbled, and then, "Catch!" And with that, he pulled Ostrow's grip free and shoved him through the elevator doorway.

Ostrow made some sort of strangled cry as Pat pulled him toward the ladder, sweeping one of his legs close with her free leg, finally wrestling him against the ladder where Ostrow hugged it tightly, gasping, murmuring something Pat suspected was a Hebrew prayer.

Pat snaked down the ladder and got below Ostrow. "Just keep your eyes forward, Doctor. Better, don't even open them. I'll help you step down," and she did, guiding his one tentative foot to the next rung, and then the next, and so on. When he was down far enough, Jinski easily made the step over to the ladder and followed.

Because of Ostrow, it took the trio longer to get down the ladder to the roof of the stuck elevator car than it had taken Pat and Jinski to make the climb up.

Pat gave Ostrow a minute to gather himself, catch his breath. Then, "Ready?"

Ostrow glumly nodded.

"Ok, from now on, no talking. Hand signals only. Doctor, you take your cues from the sergeant. You two wait here until I call for you."

Jinski popped the inspection hatch in the roof of the elevator car, then easily lowered Pat inside, setting her lightly down inside.

She stayed close to the wall, moving slowly and as quietly as possible until she could peep through the partly open doors.

From there, she could see down the lab suite corridor. The doors at the near end had been torn off their hinges and cast aside. The fire alarm and sprinklers had stopped, the fires at the far end having been extinguished. The heavy detention area door had been bent and twisted open.

She waited, she listened. Nothing. She looked back to the hatch where Jinski was waiting. She signaled him to hold.

The elevator car was stuck about three feet above the floor. Pat sat at the edge of the car floor and slid silently off onto the hub floor. She quickly glanced down the other corridors leading off from the hub. She was about to turn and signal Jinski to follow…

Footsteps. Distant, heavy but dull – bare paws. Echoing down one of the corridors. And along with it, another sound: a shuffling, sliding noise, something being dragged along the floor.

She signaled Jinski to pull back, he dropped the hatch back into place.

Pat slithered through the space under the elevator car, feet first, on her back. With her weapon, utility belt, and her bag, it was a tight and clumsy fit. She had to reach out blindly with one foot, hoping to snag the ladder as the footsteps, with a steady thumping, drew closer.

She was dangerously extended over the shaft, barely holding onto the elevator car floor until she finally got one foot around the near rail of the ladder, used that to pull her further into the shaft. She groped around inside the shaft with one hand, trying to find something — anything — to grab hold of, couldn't do better than wedging herself between the ladder rail and the front wall of the shaft, trying to suspend her own weight and the weight of her gear with nothing more than the pressure of pushing her back against the shaft wall, her feet against the ladder rail.

And then to do it without breathing heavily because the thing coming down the corridor was now in the hub.

She heard it freeze.

She held her breath.

Please move on, pleasepleaseplease…

The muscles in her leg were burning from the strain.

Footsteps, again, but moving toward the elevator.

Fuck…

She couldn't even reach for her weapon. If it stuck its head through the gap, she was done; there was enough spill from the emergency lights in the hub that she knew, with its night-vision ability, it would find her.

For some reason, whatever had drawn the creature no longer held its interest, and she could hear it and its dragged load moving off down the lab suite corridor.

When she thought it was a good distance down the corridor, Pat pushed herself off the shaft wall, reached for the ladder and managed to get one hand on it as her feet slipped free and she found herself hanging by that one hand, dangling in the shaft. She managed to swing her feet over onto the rungs, hung there trying to catch her breath, let the burn in her legs subside. She wiped at the sweat now burning her eyes, then she leaned over to where she could see out through the elevator doors.

The creature was far down the corridor now, heading toward the detention area, dragging what she thought was another mutilated corpse after it.

She remembered Ostrow's words, and a sick feeling ran through her: *They would live off the combat environment.*

Pat waited until the creature disappeared inside the detention area. She couldn't see trying to climb back out onto the hub, wrapped the barrel of her weapon on the ladder rail twice, hoping Jinski would understand the signal.

She was relieved to hear him land on the elevator floor above her, then a few seconds later he was on his knees at the elevator doors staring in at her. She signaled for him to follow.

Jinski reached up into the elevator car and helped Ostrow down.

Pat steeled herself; getting him across the shaft to the ladder at the top of the shaft was hard enough. This was going to be brutal.

Pat pantomimed that Jinski should send Ostrow through on his belly, headfirst. Jinski looked down the shaft, looked at Ostrow, made a quick judgment, drew out his Army issue handkerchief, motioned to Ostrow to remove his eyeglasses, and tied the handkerchief around the scientist's eyes.

God, this guy's good!

Jinski fed Ostrow through, the doctor reaching out with his arms. Again, Pat had to lean out until she could grab one of the doctor's hands, then Jinski pushed him completely through.

Ostrow made one of his panicked noises as he swung free, and Pat pulled him onto the ladder. "Grab hold, dumbass!" she hissed.

Ostrow's hands flailed about until they finally found the rungs of the ladder.

Following the same process as the first part of the climb, Pat led the way down, helping Ostrow find the rungs for his feet. Jinski, as usual, despite the tighter fit for him getting in under the elevator car, handled the move to the ladder better than either of them.

The shaft bottomed a few feet below the level of the last floor in something like a waist-high well.

As Pat gave them a few minutes to recover their breath, she listened at the closed elevator doors.

Nothing.

She knew small or soft noises wouldn't make it through the doors. Still, prying them open was going to be a gamble.

"You better be worth the trouble," she heard Jinski whisper to Ostrow, "'cause I'm already not a fan."

Pat signaled Jinski over to open the doors but only a few inches. Pat winced at the groaning noise of the doors being levered open by Jinski's ax, brought her weapon up and ready just in case.

Jinski stepped back, Pat waited to see if anything poked a curious face in the gap.

Nothing.

She put her own face to the gap. Another hub lit only by the glaring emergency lights.

Nothing.

She nodded at Jinski to grab one door while she grabbed the other and they pulled them open enough to fit through. Jinski boosted her up, she signaled to wait until she got a good look down the spoke corridors, then signaled her OK. Jinski boosted Ostrow up then followed.

One of the corridors was sealed with another naval-type door, large enough to fit heavy equipment through, locked with dog latches. Above the door:

> ENGINEERING CREW AND
> ALPHA PERSONNEL ONLY
> ALL OTHERS REQUIRE COMMAND SIGNATURE
> AUTHORIZATION

Another sign with a radiation symbol:

> OBSERVE CONTAMINATION ALERTS

Ostrow pointed to that door. While Jinski covered their rear, Pat undid the latches and swung the door open.

It was a long, blank-faced corridor. There was one door halfway down the corridor, and another naval door at the end:

> MAINTENANCE CREWS ONLY

ENTER ONLY WITH COMMAND SIGNATURE
AUTHORIZATION

Jinski latched the door closed behind them as Ostrow led them to that single door down the corridor. It was featureless metal, not even a handle or knob. Alongside was an electronic pad with a small screen, a microphone grill, two lights: one green, one red. Only the red was lit.

Ostrow looked to Pat, a *Now?* on his face.

"How come this door still has juice?" Pat asked.

"Dedicated circuit," Ostrow said. "The control room is isolated from the rest of the complex."

Pat and Jinski looked at each other: "Contingency," they said almost at the same time.

Pat nodded at Ostrow to go ahead.

Ostrow leaned into the mic grill. "Vocal identification," he said, and the screen lit up.

PROCEED WITH VOCAL IDENTIFICATION

"Ostrow, Aaron, Alpha classification. Recognize and confirm identification."

There was a pause, long enough that Pat and Jinski began exchanging worried looks, but then appearing on the screen:

OSTROW AARON

IDENTIFICATION RECOGNIZED

AND CONFIRMED

The red light went off, the green one lit up, there were little metallic *thunks* of bolts being withdrawn and a quiet hiss as the airtight door swung open.

As Ostrow had said, the electrical connections to the power exchange control room had been uninterrupted and the room, unlike the rest of the complex, was brightly lit. Along one side of the room was a bank of control stations quite alive with glowing and blinking lights, dials, twitching gauges, monitor screens, and reactor annunciators. Behind the walls they could hear the hum of the turbines, the throbbing pulse of the coolant pumps.

Pat had picked up a noticeable change in Ostrow's carriage in the passage from the elevator shaft to the power exchange room. The doctor had left the shaft still shaking from the climb, visibly cowed, but walking along the corridor, his steps had become sure and confident, his bearing more erect. In front of the entry door, he had seemed less in tow and more in command. Now standing in front of the reactor control consoles, for the first time since they'd left the command cupola, Pat felt Ostrow was where he wanted to be instead of where he'd been forced to be.

And that, she felt in her gut, might not be a good thing.

Ostrow stood in front of the central console — which had a slight curved recess where the operator could stand — looking like he was almost being hugged by the enwrapping control panels.

The central console reminded Pat of a church altar – and she did think it a strange connotation. On either side of Ostrow were glowing perpendicular indicators showing the position of the reactor's control rods, tall, like altar candles. In the middle of the console, in front of Ostrow, was a stainless-steel box-like affair; a tabernacle. Next to it, another electronic pad like the one by the entry door.

Ostrow looked over at Pat, a strange, discomforting look of confidence, of *watch-this* on his face, and stepped into the console's recess where the indicator lights around him filled his eyeglass lenses with reflected glows. He went through the same protocol he'd used to get through the door, speaking into the little microphone grill: "Ostrow, Aaron, Alpha classification. Recognize and confirm identification."

And received the same response on the screen:

OSTROW AARON

IDENTIFICATION RECOGNIZED AND CONFIRMED

The face of the box slid open revealing a keyboard and computer screen. Pat signaled to Jinski to watch the door while she stepped up to look over Ostrow's shoulder.

Ostrow powered up the system. On the screen, typing the expected responses to the usual prompts:

USER: AOstrow

PASSWORD: fatherson

And then:

WHICH PROGRAM DO YOU WISH TO ATTACH

"I'm responsible for these creatures," Ostrow said as he typed:

0001alpha

"I'm responsible for what they've done…and what will be done to them." Ostrow hit "Execute" and the screen then displayed:

CONFIRM PROGRAM 0001 ALPHA

PROGRAM NAME: MEGIDDO

REQUEST VOICE CONFIRMATION

Megiddo. It tugged at Pat.

"They'll be blamed but they shouldn't be," Ostrow said. "They only did what they were designed to do. The flaw was in the design. That could've been corrected. In time. But circumstances…" He sighed, then leaned into the mic on the electronic pad. "Ostrow, Aaron, confirming program Megiddo. Initiate."

PROGRAM INITIATED

Ostrow stepped back, the door of the box rapidly slid closed. Red warning lights across all the consoles began to light up, the control rod indicators began to move.

Then Pat remembered an old history class reference: *Megiddo. The Holy Land site of Armageddon.*

Nausea. *I'm too fucking late!*

An alarm buzzer began issuing regular blasts, and from a speaker overhead, an AI-generated voice:

"Destruct sequence has been engaged. All personnel are advised to initiate rapid evacuation protocols. Destruct sequence has been engaged. All personnel are advised to initiate rapid evacuation protocols. Destruct sequence has been engaged…"

Jinski came running over from where he'd been watching the entry door. "What did this crazy fucker do?"

Pat pushed Ostrow out of the way, tried to pry open the tabernacle. "Open it!" she told Ostrow.

"I can't. Wouldn't matter. Once this program is engaged…" He shrugged.

Pat looked at the control rod indicators all moving in the same direction. "I think he's pulled the control rods. But that would just mean a meltdown. Something else is going on."

"Destruct sequence has been engaged…"

"I couldn't just abandon them," Ostrow said. "The reactor is small, and this building should contain most of the blast. It will register as no more than a moderate seismic event. They won't even feel it in Vegas."

"I can hear the pumps slowing down!" Jinski said.

Ostrow slowly lowered himself to his knees. It came out in a sing-songy voice: "Blessed be the One who spoke the world into being." He looked up at Pat with sad eyes. "I'm sorry for your people who were hurt. And for your people who are going to be hurt."

The burst from Jinski's weapon pulled Ostrow off his knees and sent him flying backward in a spray of blood until he fell splayed on the floor, blood spreading out from under his body in dark wings.

Jinski stepped to the body, looked down and spat. "'Sorry' just wasn't gonna cut it, motherfucker." Then, to Pat: "What do we do?"

For a moment, Pat froze, wondering if there was anything to do except stand there and wait for the self-destruct mechanism to vaporize them. But then the entry door crashed inward, revealing a creature wedged in the narrow doorway, and there wasn't any thinking left to do.

Jinski wheeled toward the creature immediately and let a rifle grenade go. The explosion nearly blasted the creature in half, but in the space of the power exchange room, the backblast threw Pat and Jinski off their feet, and set their ears ringing.

Pat tried to shake off the daze as she stumbled to her feet. Sure that Jinski couldn't hear even a shouted order over the whine the blast had put in their ears, she waved at him to follow. They stepped over the shredded creature torso outside the entry door. In one direction, the door to the hub was open and Pat could see the shadows of other creatures moving around in the dimly lit space beyond.

She pushed Jinski in the other direction, toward the door marked for maintenance crews. "Get it open!" she shouted, still not sure if he could hear, but he understood and ran for the door while she stayed in the shelter of the entry door to cover him. Some of the creatures began to gather around the open corridor door. Pat fired a rifle grenade into the hub and ducked into the doorway, hands over ears, mouth open against the backpressure of the blast.

She stuck her head out after the detonation, saw only smoke at the end of the corridor, and looked down toward the maintenance door. Jinski had the door open, was screaming at her. She still couldn't hear but his frantic waving was message enough and she ran toward the maintenance door, gesturing at Jinski to go on through, not to wait.

At the door, she looked back, again saw figures moving around in the hub, then starting to move down the corridor. She slipped her bag off her shoulder, pulled the pin on one of the grenades in the bag, then sent the bag and its contents of grenades and Molotovs sliding down the corridor before ducking through the maintenance door and slamming it shut. She and Jinski were still turning the dog latches when they heard the muffled explosion — actually, a rapid-fire series of explosions as the other grenades in the bag went off. The gasoline of the Molotovs must've lit off as well; she could detect the now familiar sound of the complex's fire alarm.

Pat recognized where they were; under the vent grill she'd seen beside the lab blockhouse when she'd first flown into the valley. She guessed it was some sort of ventilation shaft; the air was warm and moist, almost unbearably so, laced with tendrils of steam. Pat's hearing was coming back and she almost wished it hadn't. The self-destruct alarm and AI warning were amplified as they echoed off the metal walls. There were ladder rungs running up the side of the shaft past maintenance doors on each level, all the way to the surface.

"How much time do we have?" Jinski had to shout to be heard over the reverberating alarm and AI voice.

"I don't know." She pointed at the ladder and started scrambling up as fast as she could, Jinski following.

Pat had just passed the fourth level maintenance door when she heard what had become the gut-twistingly familiar sound of the door below her being forced out of its setting to crash at the bottom of the ventilation shaft. Knowing what was coming, she tried moving faster, got only another rung before something clamped around her ankle as tight and firm as a steel vise. She knew what it was, screamed with the effort to hold on to the ladder rungs as she was pulled down.

Then…the grip loosened.

She looked down. Jinski was hanging on to the ladder below the doorway, one-handed, swinging his ax with his other hand. He didn't have the leverage to completely sever the creature's arm but, with a second blow, cut deep enough for the creature to draw back inside the maintenance door. Jinski screamed at Pat to *"GOGOGO!"*

Her one leg was sore from the strain of being pulled, her ankle in pain, but she pulled herself from rung to rung as best she could. Hearing and feeling an explosion below, she knew Jinski must've tossed a grenade into the open doorway. It almost shook her loose from the ladder, but she felt Jinski's massive, steadying hand reach up, lay against her back, and keep her from falling.

C'mon, Sister, gotta move! Gotta move!

With that, the pain in her leg and ankle didn't matter, even as she pounded up the ladder and the effort sent white-hot flashes through her, she rocketed up the remaining levels.

The ladder ended at a hatch held closed by nothing more than a padlock. She put the muzzle of her carbine near the lock, turned away to protect her eyes and fired.

Battered, the lock still held.

Jinski climbed up alongside her. "Do this with me!"

They both put their backs against the hatch and shoved, pushing until the muscles in their backs screamed…

The lock finally gave.

Exhausted, they crawled out of the hatch and collapsed on the sand beside the ventilation grill. After the steamy shaft, even the desert air seemed a relief.

"What now?" Jinski asked.

What now?

Pat had been moving on instinct, reflexive training, a primal desire not to let one of these things tear her apart. But what now? When the reactor blew…

This is it, Sister. There's no place to run.

"Hey!" Jinski sat up. "Hear that?"

At first, Pat thought it was just the pounding of blood in her ears from fighting her way up the ventilation shaft…but this was something *outside* her head; the heavy *whumpwhumpwhump* of helicopter blades.

The two of them got to their feet, listening to the sound grow closer — almost thundering. Then a Black Hawk came soaring over the rim of the valley, dipped down, hovered over the lab compound, and began to set down. Pat squinted against the dust thrown up by the down blast, but she could see this chopper – unlike the bird which had first brought her to Lab 7 – had a machine gunner in each door. And there were her men – Cho, Pritchard, Willis, all the rest – crowded on the canvas seats in the cargo compartment.

Pat pointed Jinski to the open hatch. "Hold them until you can't!"

He nodded, taking a position over the hatchway.

Pat limped/ran to the Black Hawk.

It was Pritchard who knew the question in Pat's mind, shouted the answer over the sound of the helicopter's blades: "It was those radio check-ins you had us make! When Nellis stopped getting them last night and they couldn't raise us, that sent up red flags!"

In the pilot's seat, a familiar face: Warrant Officer Noonan. "Major, what the hell's going on?" Noonan shouted. "I get told to shoot up here battle ready."

Pat pulled Cho close, pointed to the pilot: "Make sure she stays."

Cho nodded.

Pat turned to run as best she could toward the blockhouse, looking over her shoulder to see what the situation was with Jinski. The sergeant had unslung his ax, held it over the hatchway, seemed to be taking careful aim, then let it go. Given the way he beamed a second later, Pat assumed the ax had found its target.

She ran, her sore leg dragging at her, around to the side of the blockhouse where ladder rungs led up to the command cupola. As she passed around the front, she waved toward the cupola window, hoping someone was watching, indicating they should move back. She took aim at the door to the cupola with her grenade launcher and fired.

The blast didn't completely take the heavy steel door off its hinges but knocked it loose enough that when she climbed the ladder to the blockhouse roof, she could slip past it.

The blast had filled the cupola with smoke. David Cordell, coughing and gasping, came staggering up to her.

"Pat —"

She shoved him toward the doorway. "There's a helicopter outside. Go!"

Even as a part of her was thinking, *Why am I bothering with this sonofabitch?*

But it was an automatic reflex. She'd been trained for combat. Not for murder. And an army of murderers were what they'd been "building" at Lab 7.

McElhone was where she'd left him, still positioned in the open elevator doors, spare carbine magazines, hand grenades and the Molotov she'd left with him by his side. But now he was firing his carbine down into the shaft. The things had found a way past the stuck elevator car.

"Colonel, let's go!"

He shook his head. "I'll cover."

"Colonel —"

"Go!" He gave Pat a look and she saw he'd made his decision. Guilt, duty, shame — whatever it was — Colonel Ian McElhone, 103rd in a West Point graduating class of 892, veteran of tours in Afghanistan and Iraq, with a wife and three grown children waiting for him in his native Indiana, had made his decision to stay.

Pat turned to Mariska Woltz where she still knelt by the unmoving body of her husband.

"He's gone," Mariska said.

"Then there's no reason to stay." Pat grabbed Mariska by the arm, but the woman shrugged her off.

"I have no reason to go."

Pat saw it; everything Mariska Woltz could possibly to have lived for was lying dead by her side.

Pat scooped up one of McElhone's hand grenades, handed it to Mariska. "In case they get up here. You know how this works? Just pull this ring and hold it close."

More firing from McElhone, then an explosion down below as he dropped a grenade down the shaft. "Pat, for Christ's sakes, get the hell out of here!"

Outside and down, in a limping run, she crossed to Jinski who was dropping grenades down the ventilation shaft. "Go!" and she pointed him to the Black Hawk. "I'll hold them until you make the bird, then you cover me!"

"You go! I'll follow!"

"Jinks, this is an order! You've been covering me all day! My turn!"

She could tell Jinski could see there was no arguing. With an obvious reluctance, he turned and ran for the helicopter.

Pat couldn't see much down the shaft. Jinski's gunfire and grenades had left holes in the steam lines, and jets of steam clouds, along with smoke from the grenade explosions, swirled throughout the shaft.

Shouts behind her, from the Black Hawk. She turned, saw a creature on the blockhouse roof.

McElhone was no longer an obstacle.

Pat slammed a fresh rifle grenade into her launcher, aimed and let go, hitting the creature square in the chest.

The thing's appearance had answered Noonan's question of what the hell was going on and it was answer enough for the pilot to take the Black Hawk up. A body leaped from the helicopter before it had gotten ten feet off the ground, which was clearance enough for Noonan to send it roaring for the valley rim.

Pat ran to the man writhing on the ground. It was Cho. He was clutching his ankle. "I think it's broken."

"What the hell were you thinking?"

"I'm not sure I was."

Cho looked past her. Pat didn't bother to turn; she could hear the groan and squeak of twisting metal as a creature forced itself through the ventilation shaft hatchway. Cho was carrying an M4 in one hand, so she grabbed his free arm and pulled it around her neck. Getting him o his feet, the two of them limped toward the blockhouse ladder.

"The pilot saw that thing —" Cho began to explain.

"Yeah, I know. Can't say I blame her."

At the ladder, Pat pushed Cho ahead of her, each of them hopping up one rung at a time. From the blockhouse roof, they hurried over to the ladder running up the side of the command cupola.

Through the blasted door of the cupola, she could hear the self-destruct alarm and warning.

What am I doing? What am I buying us? A few minutes? Pick your poison, Sister: those things or getting vaporized in an atomic blast.

And maybe that's all it came down to; why she and Cho were now at the top of the command cupola, back-to-back, weapons ready as creatures started crawling out of the ventilation shaft grill, another one showing up on the blockhouse roof just below them.

"Major..."

"I see them."

"I don't think we can hold them off very long."

Listening to the self-destruct warnings, Pat said, "We may not have to."

She loaded another rifle grenade, pointed the muzzle at the roof of the cupola between them. The blast would make it instantaneous for them both. She closed her eyes and put her finger around the grenade launcher trigger. This would be better than —

"Major!"

The Black Hawk was back, every man with a weapon joining the door gunner in raining fire down on the creature on the blockhouse roof until it staggered backward, falling over the roof edge to the ground.

The helicopter came to a careful hover just a few feet above the command cupola. Pat boosted Cho up until Jinski, standing in the Black Hawk's door, yanked him inside, then reached down to do the same for Pat. As Pat climbed in, she saw that Noonan's return had not been much of a heroic act; Pritchard was holding the muzzle of his pistol against Noonan's helmet.

"I'm in!" Pat yelled. "Let's go!"

Noonan wasted no time in whipping the Black Hawk away from the compound and out of the valley. Pat got a quick glimpse behind them: creatures were bubbling up out of the ventilation grill and out the cupola door like ants from a kicked-over hill.

Pat yelled at her men to buckle in as she pulled herself into the cockpit, yelling at Noonan to be heard over the engine noise roaring through the open cargo doors: "You remember that nuke crater you showed me the day you brought me in? You have to get in there!"

Noonan yelled something back, Pat couldn't quite hear it, but it was probably something along the lines of what-the-hell-for?

"You don't get us in there, you're going to be part of a brand-new nuke crater! Redline this sonofabitch!"

But the Black Hawk was wavering, Noonan was struggling to hold it steady. Warning lights were going off on the control panel. "We're overweight!" the pilot yelled.

What to do? What to do?

"Everybody! Dump your weapons! The door guns, too!"

Noonan tapped Pat on the back, pointed forward. The test blast crater was in view.

God, let there be enough time!

"Everybody hold tight!" Pat was the only one without a seat; she grabbed hold of the co-pilot's seat, the co-pilot holding on to her arms. The Black Hawk's nose dipped sharply, Pat got a quick glimpse of the rim of the crater passing by the cockpit windows, the sharp angle cutting through all the fear and adrenaline that had been carrying her since she'd been pulled onto the helicopter and bringing back the old fear of flying hitting her deep in her stomach.

The crater lit up with a blinding flash –

Then a roar such as Pat had never heard before, never in combat, never in a nightmare, as if the sky itself was being torn apart.

The shock wave of the detonation may have passed over them across the top of the crater, but it compressed the air below, a wave slamming into the Black Hawk from above.

The helicopter dropped, whirled, as Noonan fought to keep it from being thrown into the walls or the bottom of the crater.

"Help me with this fucking thing!" Noonan yelled to her co-pilot and the two of them grappled with their control sticks.

Then the Black Hawk seemed to stop its careening, but it was still unsteady, still wavering, warning lights on the control panel were still glowing.

"What's the problem?" Pat yelled.

Noonan looked puzzled. "We're still overweight!"

The Black Hawk was carrying more troops than it was designed for, but weight shouldn't have been a problem: *These things can carry a Humvee! What the hell could possibly –*

Shouts came from the cargo compartment. Pat turned, saw the ugly scaly arm of a creature reaching from outside the helicopter, its long fingers clamped around a screaming David Cordell's ankle. Cho and Willis were holding onto him, desperately trying to keep him from being dragged out. Pat could see the creature hanging on to one of the Black Hawk's skids with its other hand.

There was only one weapon left in the Black Hawk: Pat's .45.

"Count to ten, then bank hard to port!" she yelled at Noonan and made her way back into the cargo compartment, waving at Jinski to follow. "Hold on to my belt!"

Jinski grabbed hold of one of the seat frames with one hand and shoved the thick fingers of his other through the back of Pat's utility belt as she leaned out the door.

Noonan put the helicopter into a sharp banking turn which swung the creature more clearly into sight.

The crater swirled below, sending Pat's head and stomach spinning. She fought the urge to close her eyes — to vomit.

Her father's voice: *"Focus on the target, Sweets. That's all you need to see."*

She locked her eyes on the creature's massive head, ignored the gaping mouth lined with razor teeth, and the waiting maw of the crater beyond it. She raised her pistol. It wouldn't be easy; the creature was swaying as the helicopter held its tight turn.

She sensed Cho and Willis were losing the tug of war, out of the corner of her eye — she saw more of Cordell slipping out the door.

Only the target…only the target…Grandpa, Dad, if there's any of you left in this pistol…HELP ME!

The creature's swaying was regular, she could time it – *and fire!*

She emptied the magazine, and one of the bullets – she didn't know which – found its mark. The creature's left eye burst, erupting in a geyser of viscous fluid. The creature let go of Cordell as both its hands went to its exploded eye, its mouth opened in a silent scream as it fell backward, tumbling until it disappeared into the shadows at the bottom of the crater.

EPILOGUE

Pat made sure Noonan could see her sliding a fresh magazine into her .45. "Do you have enough fuel to reach Vegas?"

Noonan looked puzzled. "Why, do you want to fly into Harry Reid?"

"I don't. Downtown. Where all the casinos are. What do they call it? The Strip? Find a rooftop, an empty parking lot, set it down there."

Noonan was now more than puzzled. "Major, pardon my saying, but are you nuts?"

"The boys have had a rough time. They deserve some R&R, don't you think? Do it."

"My orders —"

"Are coming from me." Pat leaned further into the cockpit, holding her .45 with a casualness that looked anything but sincerely casual. "And if you try notifying Nellis, or accept any transmissions from them, your co-pilot is going to get an instant promotion to pilot. You read me?"

Noonan's eyes went from the .45 to Pat's eyes which looked just as threatening as the pistol's muzzle. "I read you five-by-five, Ma'am."

Pat made her way back into the cargo compartment, beckoned Willis to move so she could sit next to Cordell who was massaging the bruises left by the creature's grip on his leg.

"You should know, David; we're not going to Nellis. Downtown Vegas. That should get some attention, raise some questions. Maybe even get us on the evening news. I'm not going to let them bury this thing."

Cordell shook his head, as if maybe the roar of the rotors had produced something unclear but vaguely threatening. But like a fog burning off, what Pat had said seemed to clear for him, and his face went from puzzlement to disbelief to…collapse. He sank into his seat, the pain in his leg forgotten…or perhaps just secondary to a bigger concern.

In response, he could only muster a feeble, "You can't mean this."

Pat didn't have to answer. The look on her face was confirmation enough.

"Nobody'll believe you!" A desperate attempt at dissuasion.

Pat shrugged nonchalantly. "Oh, I'll leave out the more incredible parts. I was there and I'm still having trouble believing them. But you know something, David? There's a brand new big-ass hole out in that desert that's going to be hard for somebody to explain and will make me look like I'm not totally insane."

"Your career'll be over, you know that don't you? You could even wind up in Leavenworth!"

"Possible."

She could see him struggling to process it. "Look, Pat, I understand why you'd —"

"No, you don't." *Because, David, your head simply doesn't work in a way that would. That's not who you are.*

He sat there for a moment, shaking his head; it still wouldn't process. "Why, Pat?"

"I've got five good reasons, David. Want to hear their names?"

He turned away.

"I didn't think so."

"What do you expect me to do? You expect me to back you up?"

She almost laughed at that. "Actually, David, I don't expect a goddamn thing from you. I'm not even sure why I pulled your ass out of that place. You do what you want. But I can't do anything else."

They were both quiet for a bit, then, Cordell's eyes aimed out the open cargo door, watching the desert slide by several hundred feet beneath them. He began shaking his head again.

"Pat...I don't know that I can face — The questions I'm going to get asked. Maybe you should've left me back there."

"Maybe."

David Cordell stood, turned to her as he held himself in the open doorway, the slipstream rippling through his hair, fluffing the back of his shirt. He said something she couldn't make out. She held a hand to her ear, signifying she hadn't caught it.

He felt self-conscious, even embarrassed to have to repeat it so loudly: "I said I really did care about you."

"Not enough."

Then he stepped out and was gone.

Jinski took Cordell's seat, leaving Pat sitting between the big sergeant and Cho.

"You alright, Major?" Jinski asked.

Again, Pat almost laughed. Why was everything so goddamned funny? Was she that burned out? "You're kidding, right?" She fished her father's cigarette lighter out of her pocket. "Anybody here have a cigarette?"

A pack of something was passed along the seats to Cho who shook one out for Pat. Cho helped her shield the lighter's flame from the wind streaming through the cargo compartment until Pat got the cigarette lit. She took a deep drag, then coughed hard enough to hurt her chest.

"I've been cogitating on a certain salient fact," Cho said, accessing his crossword vocabulary.

"Is that so? And?"

"It was designated Lab 7."

"So?"

Jinski's face lit up with understanding. "So, what are they doing at the other six labs?"

Pat thought about it, but just for a moment. Her leg hurt, she was exhausted physically and mentally, and she was trying hard as hell to ignore the fact that she was flying. She flicked the cigarette out the cargo door where it was immediately whipped away by the slipstream, leaned back, and closed her eyes.

"One nightmare at a time, gentleman," she said. "For now, I'm tired. Don't wake me." She said it again, then drifted off to sleep.

> *A government report in the mid-1970s indicated toxic chemicals were present in the Nevada test site.*
>
> *According to the report, it was the government's position that halting work at the site ran "against the national interest,"*
> *and the "costs... are small and reasonable for the benefits received."*

The costs are small and reasonable for the benefits received.